Shalamov
    Graphite

Also by Varlam Shalamov · KOLYMA TALES · Translated by John Glad

GRAPHITE

Nadezhda Mandelstam and Varlam Shalamov

GRAPHITE

BY Varlam Tikhonovich Shalamov

TRANSLATED FROM THE RUSSIAN
BY JOHN GLAD

>>>
>>>

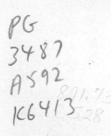
W·W·NORTON & COMPANY · NEW YORK · LONDON

FIRST EDITION

Library of Congress Cataloging in Publication Data
Shalamov, Varlam Tikhonovich.
  Graphite.
  Translation of: Kolymskie rasskazy.
  I. John Glad. II. Title.
PG3487.A592K6413   891.73'42   81-3918   AACR2
ISBN 0-393-01476-2

W. W. Norton & Company, Inc. 500 Fifth Avenue, New York, N.Y. 10110
W. W. Norton & Company Ltd. 25 New Street Square, London EC4A 3NT

1 2 3 4 5 6 7 8 9 0

4/82 — Norton — #18625

Contents

>>>

Foreword

>>>

THIS SECOND VOLUME OF STORIES by Varlam Shalamov, Russia's greatest living writer, again deals with life in the Soviet forced labor camps in Kolyma, the northeastern area of Siberia, which is separated by the Bering Strait from Alaska.

Kolyma had been used as a place of exile and a source of gold even under the czars. The czarist official Muraviov-Amurski, for example, was able to send three tons of gold to Saint Petersburg in 1853, using convict labor.

The Soviets, who are the world's second largest gold producer, have used Kolyma as an enormous forced-labor camp, where the principal occupation is gold mining. In 1949 the Pole Kazimierz Zamorski estimated that 3 million people had been exiled to Kolyma, and not more than one-half million had survived.* In 1978, the well-known historian Robert Conquest estimated that roughly 3 million people met their death in Kolyma—but certainly not fewer than 2 million.†

It is difficult to grasp such large figures. By way of illustration, if 3 million people were to lie down head to foot, they would form a chain that would extend from Miami to Sitka, Alaska.

The years 1937–39 were the years of the great purges. Millions of people were arrested, held for months in appalling prison conditions, tried under ridiculous charges, and either executed or sent in cattle cars to Siberia. Emaciated from a hopelessly inadequate diet, denied even sufficient drinking water and toilet facilities, freezing from the cold, they would

---

* Silvester Mora (pseudonym of Kazimierz Zamorski), *Kolyma: God and Forced Labor in the USSR* (Foundation for Foreign Affairs, Washington, D.C. 1949), p. 17.
† Robert Conquest, *Kolyma* (New York: Viking, 1978).

arrive at the Siberian ports of Vladivostok, Vanino, or Nak-
hodka after a trip that lasted anywhere from thirty to forty
days. There, they were held in transit camps for varying
periods of time and then were sent from the "mainland" by
ship to Kolyma.

The transit camps served as slave markets for the various
mining operations in Kolyma. Some of the mines sent representatives to examine the prisoners to ensure that they were
capable of work. Other mines, evidently, simply had standing
orders for a fixed number of new prisoners each year. Because
of the incredible mortality rates in Kolyma, there was a constant shortage of manpower.

The transit camps were terribly overcrowded, and the
prisoners who had survived the long journey were totally
exhausted. Typhus epidemics killed enormous numbers of
people.

The ships used to transport prisoners to Kolyma were pur-
chased in England, Holland, and Sweden and formerly bore
names such as *The Puget Sound* and *The Commercial Quaker*.
Their builders had never intended them to carry passengers,
but their Soviet purchasers found their capacious holds ideally
suited for human cargo. In the freezing weather, prisoners
could be easily controlled by use of the fire pumps. (See the
story "The Procurator of Judea.")

In 1931, a Soviet trust bearing the name "Far Northern
Construction" was founded to take charge of all forced-labor
projects in northeastern Siberia. With headquarters in the city
of Magadan, Far Northern Construction controlled all of
Kolyma, an enormous natural prison bounded by the Pacific
on the East, the Arctic Circle on the North, and impassable
mountains on the third side of the triangle. Far Northern Construction steadily increased its jurisdiction westward toward
the Lena River and southward to the Aldan—a territory four
times the size of France. Its territory may even have extended
as far west as the Yenisey River. If this is true, Far Northern's
authority would have extended over a territory as large as all
of Western Europe.

Reingold Berzin, a Latvian communist, was in charge of Far Northern Construction from 1932 to 1937. His chief deputy, I.G. Filippov, was in charge of USVITL (the Administration of Northeastern Corrective Labor Camps). During this period, conditions are reported to have been relatively tolerable: prisoners received adequate food and clothing, were given manageable work assignments, and could shorten their sentences by hard work. In 1937 Berzin, Filippov, and a number of others were arrested and shot as Japanese spies. Management of Far Northern Construction was handed over to K.A. Pavlov and a pathological murderer, Major Garanin. (Garanin was himself executed in 1939.) The changes in leadership were signaled by Stalin in a 1937 speech in which he criticized the "coddling" of prisoners.

Under Pavlov and Garanin, food rations were reduced to a point where most prisoners could not hope to survive: clothing rations were insufficient for the harsh climate, and prisoners were sent to work in temperatures as cold as minus 60°. Prisoners too enfeebled to fulfill their work quotas were executed *en masse*.

The camps were arranged in a hierarchy that provided virtually unlimited power and privilege to the senior bureaucrats. At the bottom of the nonconvict pecking order were soldiers and former convicts who had been released but were not allowed to return to the "mainland." Their living conditions were only slightly better than those of the prisoners. Among the prisoners, common criminals received trustee positions, whenever possible. Having become accustomed to violence, they easily controlled the political prisoners, though the latter outnumbered them. In general, one of the worst features of the camps was that political prisoners were constantly brutalized and murdered by professional criminals.

In 1941 the official workday was extended from ten to twelve hours (although unofficially it was often sixteen), and the bread ration was cut from one kilo to one-half.

The postwar period was evidently not quite as grim as the 1938–45 period had been, and a general amnesty was declared immediately after Stalin's death for all prisoners with less than a five-year sentence. Unfortunately, only common criminals had such light sentences.

During the Khrushchev period, the politicals were released and declared to be "rehabilitated." In the unique doublespeak of the Soviet government, this meant that the government admitted that they had committed no crimes. When it became clear, however, that the government's admission of mass bloodletting could cause the overthrow of the regime, such admissions ceased to be made.

What is the true nature of the Soviet Union, our ally in World War II and our recent partner in détente? All the present Soviet leaders have come up through the ranks during the purges, and their careers were formed under the tutelage of Joseph Stalin. When we sell them the technology so necessary to their economy, will they use it to make war against us? We can only judge men by their past conduct, and Shalamov presents a vivid instance of that conduct in the story "Lend-Lease" (*Kolyma Tales*). It tells how an American bulldozer, presented to the Russians under the Lend-Lease program during World War II, was subsequently used:

A grave, a mass prisoner grave, a stone pit stuffed full with undecaying corpses of 1938 was sliding down the side of the hill, revealing the secret of Kolyma.

In Kolyma, bodies are not given over to earth, but to stone. Stone and the permafrost keep secrets and reveal them. All of our loved ones who died in Kolyma, all those who were shot, beaten to death, sucked dry by starvation, can still be recognized decades later. There were no gas furnaces in Kolyma. The corpses wait in stone, in the permafrost. . . .

These graves, enormous stone pits, were filled to the brim with corpses. The bodies had not decayed; they were just bare skeletons over which stretched dirty, scratched skin bitten all over by lice.

The North resisted with all its strength this work of man, not accepting the corpses into its bowels. Defeated, humbled, retreating, stone promised to forget nothing, to wait and preserve its secret. The severe winters, the hot summers, the winds, the six years of rain had not wrenched the dead men from the stone. The earth opened, baring its subterranean storerooms, for they contained not only gold and lead, tungsten and uranium, but also undecaying human bodies.

The bulldozer scraped up the frozen bodies, thousands of bodies of thousands of skeletonlike corpses. Nothing had decayed: The twisted fingers, the puss-filled bloody toes, and, eyes burning with a hungry gleam. . . .

One must remember that Kolyma is only one section of Siberia. Estimates as to the total number of people murdered by the Soviet government run as high as 20 million, but the KGB is silent and simply expresses regret over the "excesses of the cult of personality." One day the Nuremberg trials will be reconvened—not in Germany but in the Soviet Union. And the permafrost of Kolyma will yield up those same bodies described in "Lend-Lease." They will come out of the ground undecayed, with only the gold in their teeth missing, and there will be a plywood tag attached to the left shin of each corpse with an identification number.

I have chosen the title of the story "Graphite" as a title for this collection. In it Shalamov describes how these tags are filled out only in pencil, since graphite markings will last for eternity.

A number of Soviet books on Kolyma have appeared. Andrei Zimkin spent from 1933 to 1961 in Kolyma but makes no mention of convicts in this book, *At the Headwaters of the Kolyma River (U istokov Kolyma,* 1963). It is not clear whether he himself was a convict or a civilian employee of the camps.

An utterly fantastic Soviet book by Viktor Urin on Kolyma is *Along the Kolyma Highway to the Pole of Cold (Po kolymskoi trasse—k poliusu kholoda,* 1959). It is a sort of tourist's notebook of travel impressions. The book has a large number of pictures (even including women in bathing suits!), and the effect is somewhat similar to that of an early *National Geographic* in black and white. Urin intersperses his travel description with poems, the poetic quality of which corresponds roughly to his own moral integrity.

In reading Shalamov's stories, one is shocked by what is

traditionally called "man's inhumanity to man." In *Kolyma Tales* Shalamov writes: "Friendship is not born in conditions of need or trouble. Literary fairy tales tell of 'difficult' conditions that are an essential element in forming any friendship, but such conditions are simply not difficult enough. If tragedy and need brought people together and gave birth to their friendship, then the need was not extreme and the tragedy not great. Tragedy is not deep and sharp if it can be shared with friends."

Who were these people? Were they already morally deformed when they entered the prisons to begin the long trip to Kolyma? Or could their conduct be explained by the peculiarities of the "Russian personality"? On examination of the stories, another picture emerges. The story "Committees for the Poor" illustrates the moral qualities of prisoners who all chipped in ten percent of their meager cash accounts to aid their penniless cellmates. These same people, later in the camps, were to learn never—under any circumstances—to help their fellow man in time of need. In the story "Condensed Milk" (*Kolyma Tales*) Shalamov provides a revealing illustration of camp mores:

"Let's have a spoon," Shestakov said, turning to the laborers surrounding us. Licked clean, ten glistening spoons were stretched out over the table. Everyone stood and watched as I ate. No one was indelicate about it, nor was there the slightest expectation that they might be permitted to participate. None of them could even hope that I would share this milk with them. Such things were unheard of, and their interest was absolutely selfless. I also knew that it was impossible not to stare at food disappearing in another man's mouth. I sat down so as to be comfortable and drank the milk without any bread, taking a gulp of cold water from time to time. I finished both cans. The audience disappeared—the show was over.

The lesson these stories teach is not that these people are unusual in their brutality to each other but that they are ordinary people caught up in terrible circumstances.

Shalamov was evidently first arrested for some unknown
"crime" in 1929 while he was only twenty-two and a student
at the law school of Moscow University. He was sentenced to
five years in Solovki, a former monastery that had been confiscated from the church and converted into a concentration
camp. In 1937 he was arrested again and sentenced to five
years in Kolyma. In 1942 his sentence was extended "till the
end of the war"; in 1943 he received an additional ten-year
sentence for having described Ivan Bunin, the Nobel laureate,
as a "classic author of Russian literature." He appears to have
spent a total of seventeen years in Kolyma. Shalamov was
forced to sign a statement disavowing his prose work. He now
lives in Moscow; only his poetry is published in the USSR.

Obviously, comparisons between the art of Shalamov and
Solzhenitsyn are bound to occur, both among critics and general readers. Geoffrey Hosking has summed up the matter
well:

> Like *Gulag Archipelago* . . . this volume . . . constitutes a chron-
> icle and indictment of labour camp life. Yet anyone who comes to it
> with *Gulag Archipelago* in mind is likely to be very surprised. Out-
> wardly at least. Shalamov's work is about as different from Solzheni-
> tsyn's as it is possible to imagine. Where Solzhenitsyn constructs a
> single vast panorama, loose and sprawling, Shalamov chooses the
> most concise of literary forms, the short story, and shapes it con-
> sciously and carefully, so that his overall structure is like a mosaic
> made of tiny pieces. Where Solzhenitsyn writes with anger, sarcasm
> and bitterness, Shalamov adopts a studiedly dry and neutral tone.
> Where Solzhenitsyn plunges into his characters' fates, telling their
> story from a variety of subjective viewpoints, Shalamov takes strict
> control of his discourse, usually conducting his narrative from an
> undivided viewpoint and aiming at complete objectivity. When Sol-
> zhenitsyn is fiercely moralistic and preaches redemption through
> suffering, Shalamov contents himself with cool aphorisms and asserts
> that real suffering, such as Kolyma imposed on its inmates, can only
> demoralize and break the human spirit.*

* "The Ultimate Circle of the Stalinist Inferno," *New Universities Quarterly*,
34 (spring 1980).

Although Shalamov's stories describe a far more savage era than that depicted by Chekhov, they are nevertheless in the Chekhovian tradition: a brief plot devoted to one incident (although the stories occasionally are more compact than Chekhov's), an objective, dispassionate narration intended to provide a contrast to the horror of the moment, and a *pointe* at the end. The Shalamov-Solzhenitsyn comparison is actually a repetition of the Chekhov-Tolstoy comparisons made earlier by a number of Russian and Western European critics. Chekhov, a writer who respected the rights of the reader in the artistic process, consciously avoided making conclusions for the reader. Tolstoy, on the other hand (like Solzhenitsyn later), constantly lectured the reader on what he should think.

In the preface to *Kolyma Tales* I predicted that Shalamov would be recognized as a major writer, and the gratifying reviews of the book certainly appear to have confirmed that prediction. Shalamov, not Solzhenitsyn, is the chronicler of Kolyma. By his own admission, Solzhenitsyn barely touches on this area in *The Gulag Archipelago*. He asked Shalamov to coauthor *The Gulag Archipelago* with him, but Shalamov— already an old, sick man—declined. Nevertheless, Solzhenitsyn writes: "Shalamov's experience in the camps was longer and more bitter than my own, and I respectfully confess that to him and not me was it given to touch those depths of bestiality and despair toward which life in the camps dragged us all."

Shalamov seems to some readers to describe exceptional situations, as opposed to Solzhenitsyn who, in *One Day in the life of Ivan Denisovich,* describes the absolutely typical. I personally do not agree that Shalamov describes the exceptional, but I do think it is fair to say that he picks the moments of greater intensity—partly because he is working with the genre of the short story. There are, after all, degrees of typicality. As for the overall picture, everything I have learned of life in the camps suggests that this is a scrupulously accurate presentation of life in that world separated from the United States by only fifty-five miles of water.

Perhaps central to any discussion of Shalamov's writing is the subject of genre. We have here a literary genre attempting to bridge the gap between fact and fiction. The closest parallel is the historical novel, but the historical novel remains fiction. Shalamov's stories represent a fusion of art and life in which both coexist as equal partners. Thus, it is not possible to separate aesthetic evaluation from historical appraisal. Any work constitutes a unique entity and thus must be judged by its own unique laws.

In addition, I feel that Shalamov's stories cannot be judged as single entities. Each constitutes a piece of the total puzzle, and they impart an understanding and achieve an emotional impact in their totality. I believe that Varlam Tikhonovich would agree with me on this point.

There is a pantheistic surrealism in Shalamov's work. In the story "Fire and Water," magical mushrooms with caps cold as snakeskins grow taller than the bushes, while people live in tents lower than the rocks. Water and fire become primordial forces, on the periphery of whose competition man barely survives. Fire scampers through the dry grass like a snake, runs up tree trunks, roars, and topples them. A growling river is as muscular as a wrestler, ripping up trees and flinging them into the current. The shore of the river is the shore of life, and the tiny boat is a metaphor for man's tremulous journey through that life. It is a vision that the primitivist Rousseau might have been able to reproduce—but without the serenity of Rousseau's work. The mood is more that of Edvard Munch's *The Scream*.

The general tone of *Graphite* is calmer than that of *Kolyma Tales*. In this sense, this volume presents a somewhat different view of the camps. If one disregards the more extreme horrors of such a macrocosm (difficult as that may be), one gets a picture of life in its less tense moments. *Graph-*

ite is more heavily documentary than *Kolyma Tales*, drier, contains less of the purely belletristic. But if the general tone is less shrill, the same musicians occupy the same chairs, and we are simply listening to movement two of the Kolyma symphony.

An interesting footnote in the history of Russian literature is provided by the Soviet establishment writer, Konstantin Simonov. As has been mentioned earlier, Shalamov received an additional sentence for stating that Bunin was a "classic author of Russian literature." Later, the climate changed, and Simonov was sent to Paris, where Bunin was living, to ingratiate himself with the Nobel laureate.

Simonov, whose 1943 pamphlet titled "Moscow" was published by the Soviet Kolyma Press in Magadan, wrote another pamphlet in 1944: "Camp of Death." The Red Army had just retaken Lublin, and they had discovered a death camp a few miles from the city. It is fitting, I believe, that the 1944 statement of this Soviet spokesman be quoted in pronouncing sentence on the perpetrators of Kolyma:

I am far from knowing all the facts and all the figures. I have spoken with, perhaps, one-hundredth of the witnesses and I may have seen a tenth of the material evidence of the crime. Nevertheless, a person who has seen all this cannot wait. I want to tell now— Today!—of the initial evidence of this crime, tell of what I have heard in these days, what I have seen with my own eyes. . . .

This is the end of a chain which includes all of Germany. At one end of this chain is the henchman . . . who pulled gold teeth and pushed people into death traps. At the other is (a woman) who merely received the belongings of the murdered people in exchange for her work. They are different ends of the chain, but it is a single chain. They will all have to pay—some more, some less. So let them not point accusing fingers at each other. They must realize once and forever: they will all have to pay.

———

I would like to express my deep gratitude to Diana Glad, Deborah Colman Johnson, Robert Ledbetter, Leonard Meyers,

Larisa Romanov, Cynthia Rosenberger, and Emily Tall for their help in preparing this volume.

I owe a special debt to Susan Ashe for her numerous suggestions on style.

I also wish to thank Carol Houck Smith, my editor for both *Graphite* and *Kolyma Tales*, for her support, numerous insights, and sensible advice. I approached eight publishers with a proposal to publish *Kolyma Tales*, and Ms. Smith recognized Varlam Shalamov's genius and had the courage to accept the manuscript.

John Glad

College Park, Maryland
January 1981

PART ONE

LIVING

The Businessman

>>>

HIS NAME WAS "RUCHKIN"; there were a lot of Ruchkins in camp. "Ruchka" means hand in Russian, and so "Ruchkin" became a common nickname. If they called you Ruchkin, that meant your hand was injured, not that your teeth were knocked out. But which Ruchkin? The Greek? Or the tall one from the seventh ward? This was Kolya Ruchkin, the businessman.

Kolya's right hand had been torn off at the wrist by an explosion. It was a case of self-mutilation. In the camp records such incidents were all lumped together in the same column, whether it was a case of a person maiming himself with a gun, explosives, or a sharp tool. It was against the rules to put such persons in the hospital if they didn't have a high, "septic" temperature. Kolya Ruchkin had just that kind of temperature. For two months Kolya had sprinkled dirt on his wound to keep it infected. In the end, however, his youth had won out, and his days in the hospital were coming to an end. It was time to return to the mine. Kolya, however, was not afraid. What threat could the gold mines hold for him, a one-handed man?

Camp authorities struggled with the problem as best they could. One-armed men were forced to spend the entire working day in deep, loose, crystal snow, tramping down a path for people and tractors at the timber-clearing sites. Then convicts began to blow off their feet by placing a nitroglycerin capsule in the boot and lighting a Bickford fuse protruding from their boot at the knee. So they stopped sending one-armed men to tramp down snow. As for panning for gold, how could a one-armed man even attempt it? At best, in the summer, they could be sent for a day or two. If it wasn't raining.

Kolya's mouth spread wide in a toothy grin; scurvy had not yet taken his teeth. Kolya Ruchkin had already learned to roll a cigarette with one hand. Well-rested from the hospital and only slightly hungry, Kolya smiled and smiled. He was a businessman, this Kolya Ruchkin. Incessantly bartering and trading, he smuggled forbidden herring to the diarrhea patients in exchange for bread. They too needed to extend their stay in the hospital. Kolya would trade soup for porridge or porridge for two portions of soup. He knew how to "divvy up" a ration of bread entrusted to him to exchange for tobacco. He got the bread from the patients who were too ill to get out of their beds—people swollen with scurvy, people with serious fractures from the Traumatic Illnesses Ward. (Or, as Pavel Pavlovich, the orderly, used to say, never suspecting the irony of his error: "The Dramatic Illnesses Ward.")

Kolya's happiness began the day his hand was blown off. He was almost full, almost warm. As for the curses of the camp authorities and the threats of the doctors, Kolya considered them all trivial. And they were.

On several occasions during this blissful stay in the hospital, strange and frightening things had happened. Kolya's nonexistent hand ached just as before. He could feel every bit of it. His fingers were bent in the position they had acquired from grasping the handle of a pick and shovel—no more and no less. It was difficult to grasp a spoon with such a hand, but there was no need for a spoon back at the mine. Everything edible was slurped directly from the bowl: soup and porridge and the thin cranberry pudding and tea. It was possible to hold a ration of bread in those eternally clenched fingers. But Ruchkin had blown them off altogether. Why then did he still feel those fingers, clenched just as they had been back at the mine? After all, the fingers on his left hand had begun to unflex, to bend like rusty hinges that had received a drop of oil, and Ruchkin cried from joy. Already, if he lay face down with his left hand pressed under his stomach, he could unbend the hand—easily.

The pain in his missing hand usually came at night. Cold from fear, Ruchkin would wake up and cry, afraid to ask his neighbors for advice. Maybe this meant something? Maybe he was going mad?

The missing hand had begun to hurt less and less frequently, the world was returning to its normal state, and Ruchkin rejoiced in his happiness. And he smiled and smiled, thinking how well he'd pulled the whole thing off.

The orderly, Pavel Pavlovich, came out of the toilet stall holding an unlit homemade cigarette in his hand and sat down next to Ruchkin.

"Can I get you a light, Pavel Pavlovich?" Ruchkin groveled before the orderly. "Just one second!"

Ruchkin rushed to the stove, opened the door, and with his left hand scattered a few burning coals on the floor. Tossing up the smoldering coal with agility, Ruchkin rolled it back and forth in his palm. The coal blackened but kept on flaming, and Ruchkin blew on it to support the flame, holding it directly up to the face of the orderly who was bending forward slightly. Holding the cigarette in his mouth, the orderly sucked in as much air as he could through the cigarette and finally managed to light up. Shreds of blue smoke rose above the orderly's head, and Ruchkin's nostrils flared. In the wards, patients were awakened by that smell, and they tried vainly to inhale the smoke which was no smoke at all but a shade fleeing from smoke. . . .

It was clear that Ruchkin would get the butt. He thought how he would take two drags himself and then take the butt to Surgical Ward to the "political" with the broken back. That would get him a whole ration, which was no joke. And if Pavel Pavlovich left a bit more, that would produce a new cigarette that would be worth more than just a ration.

"You'll be checking out of here soon, Ruchkin," Pavel Pavlovich allowed in an unhurried fashion. "You really dragged it out, fattened yourself up. But that's water under the bridge. . . . Tell me, how'd you get your nerve up to do it? I want to tell my children. If I ever see them."

"Well, I don't hide it, Pavel Pavlovich," Ruchkin said, hurriedly sizing up the situation. Evidently Pavel Pavlovich had not rolled the cigarette very tightly. You could just see the flame move along the paper when he inhaled. The orderly's cigarette didn't glow; it burned like a Bickford fuse. Just like a Bickford fuse. That meant he had to make it a short story.

"Well?"

"I wake up in the morning, get my ration, and stick it inside my shirt. We get two rations per day. I go to Mishka, the powderman. 'How's about it?' I say.

" 'All right,' he says.

"I give him the whole eight-hundred gram ration for a capsule and a section of fuse. Then I go back to my 'countrymen' in my barracks. We weren't really from the same area, we just called each other that. One's name was Fedya, and the other was Petro, I think.

" 'Ready?' I ask.

" 'Ready,' they say. 'Let's have it,' I say. They give me their two rations; I put them under my shirt, and we push off for work. When we get there, while the work gang is being issued tools, we take a burning log from the fire and go behind a heap of mined rock. We stand shoulder to shoulder, and all three of us hold the capsule—each with his right hand. We light the fuse and—Zap!—fingers fly everywhere. Our gang leader starts shouting: 'What the hell are you doing?' The senior guard marches us off to camp, to the first-aid station.

"They bandaged us up there. Later my countrymen got sent away somewhere, but I had a temperature and ended up in the hospital."

Pavel Pavlovich had almost finished his cigarette, but Ruchkin was so engrossed in telling his story that he nearly forgot about the butt.

"But what about the rations? You had two left. Did you eat them?"

"Damn right! I ate them right after I got bandaged up. The other two wanted me to break a piece off for them. I told them to go to hell. Business is business."

The Apostle Paul

≫≫≫

WHEN I SLIPPED OFF the slick pole ladder in the test pit and sprained my ankle, the director realized I would be limping for quite a while. Since the rules wouldn't allow me just to sit around, I was sent as an assistant to Adam Frisorger, our carpenter. We were both quite pleased.

In his "first life" Frisorger had been a pastor in some German village near Marxstadt on the Volga.* We had met in one of the enormous transit prisons during the typhoid quarantine and had arrived together at this coal prospecting area. Like me, Frisorger had spent time in the taiga, had been on the brink of death, and had been sent half insane from a mine to the transit prison. We were sent to the coal-prospecting group as invalids, as "help." All the working members of the prospecting group were civilians working on contract. True, they were yesterday's convicts, but they had served their sentences. In camp the attitude toward them was condescending, even contemptuous. On one occasion, while we were still on the road, the forty of them hardly managed to scrape up two rubles to buy some homegrown tobacco. Even so, they were already different from us. We all understood that in two or three months they would be able to buy clothing, get something to drink, be issued internal travel passports. Perhaps they would even go home in a year. These hopes gleamed all the brighter when Paramonov, the man in charge of the

* There are approximately 2 million Germans in the USSR.—TRANS.

group, promised them enormous salaries and polar rations. "You'll all go home in top hats," he kept saying. As for us convicts, there were no promises of top hats and polar rations.

On the other hand, Paramonov was not rude to us. No one would give him any convicts to work as prospectors, so all he managed to wheedle out of the higher-ups was the five of us as helpers.

None of us knew one another, but when we were presented to Paramonov's bright, piercing gaze, he had reason to be pleased with his crew. One of us, the gray-mustached Izgibin, was a stove builder. He was the joker in the crowd, and his wit had not abandoned him even in camp. Thanks to his skill, he was not as emaciated as the rest of us. The second was a one-eyed giant from Kamenets-Podolsk. He presented himself to Paramonov as a "steamboat stoker."

"So, you must be something of a mechanic," Paramonov said.

"That's right, I am," the "stoker" responded eagerly.

He had quickly calculated the advantages of working in a civilian prospecting group.

The third was the agronomist, Riazanov. Paramonov was ecstatic over this find. As for the agronomist's appearance, no importance was attached to the torn rags in which he was clothed. In camp, a man's worth was never appraised according to his clothing, and Paramonov knew the camp well enough.

I was the fourth. I was neither stove builder nor handyman nor agronomist, but Paramonov found my great height reassuring, and he decided not to make a fuss by altering the list over one man. He nodded.

The fifth man, however, was acting very strangely. He muttered prayers, covered his face with his hands, and couldn't hear Paramonov. But this was nothing new for our boss, and he turned to the detail assignment officer standing next to him with a stack of yellow folders containing our "cases."

"He's a carpenter," the detail assignment officer said, guessing at Paramonov's question. The reception was over, and we were led away to prospect.

Later Frisorger told me that he had been terrified by his case inspector back at the mine, because when they called for him, he thought he was going to be shot. We lived nearly a year in the same barracks, and we never quarreled—something unusual among convicts both in camp and in prison. Quarrels arise over trivia, and verbal abuse becomes so heated that the only possible sequel appears to be a knife—or at best a poker. But I quickly learned not to pay any attention to these elaborate oaths. Intense feelings would simmer down, and those involved would continue lazily to curse each other, but this was done for appearances—to save face.

Frisorger and I, however, never once quarreled. I think this was his achievement, for there was no one more gentle than he. He offended no one and spoke little. He had a creaky old man's voice—the kind of voice that a young actor assumes when playing the role of an old man. In the camps, many attempt (often quite successfully) to appear older and physically weaker than they actually are. This is not the result of a conscious effort on their part but somehow occurs instinctively. It was one of life's ironies that the majority of those attempting to add on years and subtract strength were actually in worse shape than they tried to depict. But there was nothing false in Frisorger's voice.

Every morning and evening Frisorger would pray silently, turning away from the others and staring at the floor. He would take part in the conversation only if it had to do with religion, and that was very seldom, since convicts do not favor religious topics. With all his charm and obscene wit, Izgibin tried futilely to poke fun at Frisorger, who turned aside all Izgibin's witticisms with the most peaceful of smiles. The entire prospecting group liked Frisorger—even Paramonov, for whom Frisorger spent half a year making a writing desk.

Our cots were next to each other, and we frequently

engaged in conversations. Frisorger would wave his arms in childlike amazement whenever he encountered in me a familiarity with any of the popular Gospel tales that he, in his simplicity, thought were known only to a narrow circle of religious believers. Giggling delightedly whenever I revealed any such knowledge, he would grow excited and begin to tell me Gospel stories that I either vaguely remembered or had never known at all. He very much enjoyed these discussions.

Once, while reciting the names of the twelve apostles, Frisorger made a mistake. He called the Apostle Paul the true founder of the Christian religion, its most important theoretician. I knew a little of the biography of this apostle and could not pass up the opportunity to correct Frisorger.

"No, no," Frisorger said laughing. "You just don't know." And he began to count on his fingers: "Petrus, Paulus, Markus . . ."

I told him everything I knew about the Apostle Paul. He listened to me closely without speaking. It was already late and time to sleep. I woke up that night in the flickering smoky light of the kerosene lantern and saw that Frisorger's eyes were open. He was whispering: "God, help me! Petrus, Paulus, Markus . . ." He did not sleep until dawn. He left early that morning for work and returned late, when I was already asleep. I was awakened by quiet sobbing—like that of an old man. Frisorger was praying on his knees.

"Is something the matter?" I asked when he had finished praying.

Frisorger found my hand and squeezed it.

"You're right," he said. "Paul wasn't one of the twelve apostles. I forgot about Bartholomew." I said nothing.

"Do my tears suprise you?" he asked. "Those are tears of shame. How could I forget such things? I, Adam Frisorger, need a stranger to point out my unforgivable mistake. No, no, you're not to blame. It's my sin, mine. But it's good that you corrected me. Everything will be all right."

I barely managed to calm him down, and after that (just before I sprained my ankle) we became even closer friends.

Once when there was no one in the workshop, Frisorger took a soiled cloth wallet from his pocket and gestured to me to come over to the window.

"Here," he said, handing me a tiny, rumpled photograph of a young woman with the inconsequential expression that one often sees in snapshots. The yellow, cracked photograph was lovingly framed with a piece of colored paper.

"That's my daughter," Frisorger said proudly. "My only daughter. My wife died a long time ago. My daughter doesn't write to me; I guess she doesn't know my address. I write to her a lot. Only to her. I never show this photograph to anyone. I took it from home. I took it from the chest of drawers six years ago."

Paramonov had walked silently into the workshop.

"Your daughter?" he asked, glancing at the photograph.

"Yes, sir, it's my daughter," Frisorger answered with a smile.

"Does she write?"

"No."

"How could she forget her old man? Write up a request for an address search, and I'll forward it. How's your leg?"

"I'm still limping, sir," I answered.

"O.K. Keep at it." Paramonov left.

From then on, making no further attempt to conceal it from me, Frisorger would lie down on his cot after the evening prayer, take out his daughter's photograph, and stroke the colored border.

We had lived about a half-year together when one day the mail came. Paramonov was off on a trip, and the mail was being handled by his secretary, the convict Riazanov. Riazanov had turned out to be not an agronomist but an Esperantist, but that didn't hinder him from expertly skinning dead horses, bending thick iron pipes and filling them with hot sand heated in the campfire, and carrying on the bookkeeping duties of the supervisor's office.

"Look at this," he said. "Look what came for Frisorger."

In the package was an official document with a request to show convict Frisorger (crime, sentence) his daughter's declaration. A copy of the declaration was enclosed. In it she wrote briefly and simply that she was convinced her father was an enemy of the people and that she renounced him and requested that her relationship to him be regarded as non-existent.

Riazanov twirled the paper in his hands. "Disgusting," he said. "Why did she have to go and do a thing like that? Maybe she wants to become a party member?"

I was occupied with something else. Why would anyone forward this sort of declaration to a convict father? Was it some unusual variety of sadism as when relatives were informed of nonexistent deaths? Or was it the simple desire to do everything "according to the law"? Or perhaps something else?

"Listen, Ivan," I said to Riazanov. "Did you register the mail?"

"No, it just came."

"Give me the package." I explained the matter to Riazanov.

"But how about the letter?" he said hesitatingly. "She's sure to write a letter."

"You can detain the letter as well."

"O.K., take it."

I crumpled the declaration in my hand and tossed it into the open door of the heated stove.

A month later the letter came—just as short as the declaration—and we burned it in the same stove.

Not long after that I was taken away, and Frisorger stayed behind. I don't know what happened to him. I often thought of him while I still had the strength to remember. I could hear his creaky, excited whisper: "Petrus, Paulus, Markus . . ."

Committees for the Poor

>>>

THE PAGES OF RUSSIAN HISTORY written in '37 and '38 contain
lyrical as well as tragic lines, and the handwriting of those
lines is rather unusual. Butyr Prison is an enormous edifice
whose numerous "basements," "towers," and "wings" are
filled to overflowing with prisoners under investigation. It is a
devil's dance of arrests, shipments of prisoners who know neither what they are accused of nor the length of their sentences, of cells packed with prisoners who have not yet
perished. In this complicated life a curious tradition has grown
up, a tradition that has survived for decades.

The disease of "vigilance," whose seeds were widely
sown, had grown into a spy mania and laid hold of the entire
country. In the investigators' offices a sinister, secret meaning
was attached to every trifling remark, every slip of the tongue.

The prison authorities' contribution consisted of forbid-
ding prisoners under investigation to receive any clothing or
food packages. Sages of jurisprudence maintained that two
French rolls, five apples, and a pair of old pants were enough
to transmit any text into the prison—even a fragment of *Anna
Karenina*.

Such "messages from the free world"—an invention of
the inflamed minds of diligent bureaucrats—were effectively
prevented. A regulation was issued that only money could be
sent, and it had to be in round figures of ten, twenty, thirty,
forty, or fifty rubles; thus, numbers could not be used to work
out a new "alphabet" of messages.

It would have been simpler and more reliable to forbid
anything at all to be sent into the prisons, but this measure
was reserved for the investigators. They could, "in the interest
of the investigation," forbid anything to be sent to a particular

prisoner. There was also a commercial side to the question: Butyr Prison's commissary or "shop" increased its sales many times over after clothing and food packages were forbidden.

For some reason, the administration could not make up its mind to reject all assistance from relatives and acquaintances, even though they were certain that such an action would cause no protest either within the prison or without.

Russians do not like to bear witness in court about infringements of the ephemeral rights of prisoners under investigation. The witness in a Russian trial is, by tradition, only barely distinguishable from the defendant, and his "involvement" in the matter may serve as a black mark against him in the future. The situation of prisoners under investigation is still worse. They will all eventually serve sentences, for "Caesar's wife is perfect," and the Ministry of Internal Affairs does not make mistakes. No one is arrested without due cause, and sentencing is an inevitable sequel to arrest. Whether the prisoner under investigation receives a heavy or a light sentence depends partly on "luck" and partly on a tangled web of factors which include the bedbugs that tormented the investigator on the night before the trial and the voting in the American Congress.

In essence, there is only one way out of those prisons where preliminary investigations are conducted—via the "black raven," the prison bus that takes convicted prisoners to the train station. At the station, prisoners are loaded into freight cars that have been adapted to carry people. From there the innumerable prison cars begin their slow journey, en route to the thousands of "labor" camps.

This doom-laden atmosphere puts its stamp on the conduct of prisoners under investigation. Cheerfulness and bravado are replaced by gloomy pessimism and a weakening of morale. At the interrogations the prisoner struggles with a ghost, a ghost possessing the strength of a giant. The prisoner is accustomed to dealing with reality, but now he must battle with a shadow. But this shadow is a "fire that burns, a spear that draws blood." Everything is terrifyingly real, except the "case" itself. His nerves strained to the breaking point, the prisoner is crushed in his struggle with fantastic phantoms of incredible stature, and he loses the will to resist. He "signs" everything the investigator has invented and from that moment himself becomes a figure in the unreal world with which he earlier struggled. He is transformed into a pawn in a terrible, dark, bloody game played out in the investigators' offices.

"Where did they take him?"

"To Lefortovo Prison. To sign."

Prisoners under investigation know they are doomed. The camps always had more than their share of prisoners under investigation; sentencing in no way exempted the prisoner from all the other articles of the criminal code. They remained "in effect," just as they had outside the prison walls—except that here all the accusations, punishments, and interrogations were still more brazen, still more fantastic in their crudeness.

When clothing and food packages were forbidden in the capital, the "outlying districts"—the camps—introduced a special ration for prisoners under investigation: a mug of water and 300 grams of bread (two-thirds of a pound). These were punishment–cell conditions, and they quickly edged prisoners under investigation closer to their graves. This "investigatory ration" was used to obtain the "best evidence of all"—the accused's personal confession.

In 1957, Butyr Prison permitted prisoners to receive up to fifty old-style rubles (about five dollars) a month. Anyone with money credited to his account could use it to buy food at the prison "shop." "Shop days" were held once a week, and up to thirteen rubles could be spent on each occasion. If the prisoner possessed more money on his person when he was arrested, it was credited to his account, but he could not spend more than fifty rubles a month. Of course, receipts were issued instead of cash, and the amount remaining was noted by the shop assistant on the back of these receipts in red ink.

Contact with prison authorities and comradely discipline had been maintained from time immemorial by a system of cell leaders elected by the prisoners themselves. Before each "shop day" the prison administration would issue the cell leader a slate tablet and a piece of chalk. The cell leader used the tablet to list all purchases which the inmates of the cell wished to make. Usually the front of the tablet listed all the separate items and the quantity desired by each individual. The total quantities ordered were indicated on the reverse side.

This activity usually took a whole day, since prison life is filled to overflowing with all sorts of events, and in the eyes of the prisoners, the scale by which these events are evaluated is one of high seriousness. On the following morning the cell leader would take one or two inmates with him and go to the commissary to collect the purchases. The remainder of the day would pass in sorting out the different food items, weighing and dividing them according to "individual orders."

The prison store boasted a large selection of food: butter, sausage, cheeses, white rolls, cigarettes, cheap tobacco . . .

Once established, the prison rations never changed. If a prisoner forgot the day of the week, he could recognize it by the smell of the lunchtime soup or the taste of the only dish served for supper. Pea soup was always served for lunch on Mondays, and supper was wheat kasha. On Tuesdays it was millet soup for lunch and pearl-barley kasha for supper. In six months each prison dish was served exactly twenty-five times. The food of Butyr Prison was famed for its variety.

Anyone who had money could spend at least thirteen rubles four times a month to supplement the watery prison soup and pearl barley (referred to as "shrapnel") with something more tasty, more nutritious, more useful.

Prisoners who didn't have money could not, of course, make any purchases at all. There were always people in the cell—and not just one or two—who did not have a single kopeck. There might be someone from another city who had been arrested on the street and whose arrest was classified as "top secret." His wife would rush from one prison to another, from one police station to another in a vain attempt to learn her husband's address. She would take a package from one prison to another; if they accepted it, that meant her husband was alive. If they did not accept it, anxious nights awaited her.

Or the man arrested without money might be the head of a family. Immediately after the arrest they would force his wife, children, and relatives to denounce him. By tormenting him with constant interrogations from the moment of arrest, the investigator would attempt to force a "confession" of an act that the man had never committed. As an additional means of intimidation, aside from threats and beatings, the prisoner might be denied money.

Relatives and acquaintances were justifiably afraid to go to the prison with packages. Anyone who insisted on having his package accepted or on a search for the missing person would raise suspicion. Undesirable consequences at work or even arrest could result. Such things happened.

There was yet another type of convict without money. Lyonka was in cell 68. He was seventeen years old and came from the Tumsk area of the Moscow Oblast—in the thirties a very rural area. Lyonka was chubby, had a white face and unhealthy skin that had not known fresh air for a long time. Lyonka felt great in prison. He was fed there as he had never been fed in his entire life. Almost everyone treated him to something from the prison store. Instead of homegrown tobacco, he learned to smoke *papirosy*—cigarettes attached to a short cardboard mouthpiece. He was delighted by everything—at how interesting it was here and how nice the people were! This illiterate teenager from the Tumsk Region had discovered an entire world. He considered his case to be some sort of game, a kind of craziness, and he couldn't have cared less about it. His only worry was how to extend forever his investigation and his life in this prison where there was so much food and everything was so clean and warm.

His case was an amazing one. It was an exact repetition of a Chekhov story titled "Evil-Doers." Lyonka had been unscrewing nuts from railroad ties, had been caught on the spot, and was arrested as a spy under Point Seven of Article Fifty-Eight. Lyonka had never heard of Chekhov's story but tried to prove to the investigator, just as Chekhov's protagonist had done, that he didn't unscrew two nuts in a row, that he "understood . . ."

The investigator was using the Tumsk lad's testimony to build a case involving some unusual "concepts," the most innocent of which carried the death penalty. But the investigator hadn't managed to link Lyonka with anyone else, and Lyonka was now spending a second year waiting for the investigator to establish such a link.

Persons who had no money in their personal account at the prison were supposed to be limited to the official ration without any supplementary nourishment. Prison rations are far from stimulating. Even a small amount of variety in the food brightens the prisoner's life and somehow raises his spirits.

In all probability the proteins, fats, and carbohydrates of the prison ration (as opposed to the ration in camp) were arrived at on the basis of certain theoretical calculations and experimental data. These calculations were probably derived from some "scientific" studies; scientists like to be involved in that sort of work. It is just as probable that in the Moscow Investigatory Prison the quality of food preparation guarantees the living consumer a sufficient number of calories. It is also quite likely that the official sampling of the food by a doctor is not a complete mockery or a formality as it is in the camps. Some old prison doctor might even ask the cook for a second helping of lentils, the dish highest in calories, before searching out the line in the official form where he is to place his signature to approve the menu. The doctor might even joke that the prisoners have no reason to complain about the food

—on the grounds that he himself had just finished a bowl with relish. But then, the doctors are given plates of *today's* lentils.

No one ever complained about the food in Butyr Prison. It wasn't that it was particularly good, but that the prisoners had other things to worry about. The most disliked prison dish was boiled beans. Somehow it was prepared in such a singularly unappetizing fashion that it was termed "a dish to choke on." Nevertheless, no one complained even about the beans.

Sausage, butter, sugar, cheese, and fresh rolls from the commissary were sheer delight. Everyone enjoyed eating them with tea—not the raspberry-flavored boiling water issued by the prison, but real tea steeped in a mug and poured from an enormous bucket-sized teapot of red copper, a teapot left over from czarist days, a teapot from which Russian revolutionaries of the nineteenth century might have drunk.

Naturally, "shop day" was a joyous event in the life of the cell. Denial of "shop privileges" was a severe punishment that always led to quarrels; prisoners feel such deprivations very keenly. Any accidental noise heard by the guard in the corridor or a disagreement with the commandant on duty was looked on as an act of insubordination, the punishment for which was denial of shop privileges. The dreams of eighty persons quartered in twenty different places went up in smoke. It was a severe punishment.

One might think that those prisoners who had no money would be indifferent to the withdrawal of shop privileges, but that was not the case.

Once the food was brought in, evening tea would commence. Everyone bought whatever it was he wanted. Those who had no money felt out of place at the general holiday. They were the only ones not to experience the nervous energy characteristic of "shop day."

Of course, everyone would treat them. A prisoner could drink a mug of tea with someone else's sugar and eat a white roll; he could smoke someone else's cigarette—even two—but he didn't feel "comfortable," and it was not the same as if he had bought it with his own money. The prisoner who had no money was so sensitive that he was afraid to eat an extra piece.

The adroit collective brain of the prison found a way out, a way of ending the discomfiture of those who had no money, a way of protecting their self-respect and providing even the most impoverished prisoners with the official right to make use of the commissary. They could spend their own money independently and buy whatever they chose.

Where did this money come from?

A famous phrase from the days of military communism, from the first years of the revolution, was reborn: "Committees for the Poor." Some unknown person mentioned it in one of the prison cells, and the phrase caught on in an uncanny fashion and migrated from cell to cell—by tapping on the walls, by notes hidden under a bench in the bathhouse, and, easiest of all, by transfers from one prison to another.

Butyr Prison is famed for its smooth functioning. The twelve thousand convicts in this enormous prison are in constant round-the-clock movement; every day, regularly scheduled buses take prisoners to Lubyanka Prison, bring prisoners from Lubyanka Prison for interrogation, for meetings with witnesses, for trial. Other buses transfer prisoners to other prisons . . .

In instances of cell-rule violations, the internal prison administration transfers prisoners under investigation to the Police Tower, Pugachev's Tower, North Tower, or South Tower, all of which have special "punishment" cells. There is even a wing with cells so small that one cannot lie down but must sleep sitting up.

One-fifth of the population of the cells is moved every day—either to "photography," where profile and full-face pictures are taken and a number is attached to a curtain next to which the prisoner sits, or to "piano lessons"—that is, finger printing (a process that for some reason was never considered offensive). Or they might be taken along the endless corridors of the gigantic prison to the interrogation wing. As they walk down the corridor, the guard taps the key against his own brass belt buckle to warn of the approach of a "secret prisoner." And until the guard hears hands clap in response, he will not let the prisoner proceed. (At the Lubyanka Prison the snapping of fingers is used instead of the jingling of keys. As in Butyr, the response is a hand clap.)

Movement is perpetual, and the entrance gates never close for long. Nevertheless, there has never been an instance when codefendants ended up in the same cell.

If a prisoner's trip is canceled and he has crossed the threshold of the prison even for a second, he cannot return without having all his things disinfected. That's the way things are done; it is known as the Sanitation Code. The clothes of those who are frequently taken to Lubyanka Prison for interrogation are quickly reduced to rags. Even without these special trips, clothing wears out much more quickly in prison than in civilian life. Prisoners sleep in their clothes, tossing on the boards that cover the berths. This and the frequent and energetic steam treatments intended to kill lice quickly destroy the clothing of every prisoner brought in for investigation.

No matter how strict the control, however, the words of the author of *The Charterhouse of Parma* ring true: "The jailor thinks less of his keys than the prisoner does of escape."

"Committees for the Poor" came into being spontaneously, as a comradely form of mutual aid. Someone happened to remember the original Committees for the Poor. Who can say, perhaps the author who injected new meaning into the old term had himself once participated in real committees for the poor in the Russian countryside just after the revolution?

These committees were set up in a very simple way so that any prisoner could give aid to his fellows. When sending his order to the "shop," each prisoner donated 10 percent to the committee. The total sum received in this fashion was divided among all those in the cell who were "moneyless." Each of them had the right independently to order food from the "shop."

In a cell with seventy or eighty persons, there were always seven or eight who had no money. More often than not, money eventually arrived, and the "debtor" attempted to pay back his cellmates, but he was not obliged to. In turn, he simply deducted his own 10 percent whenever he could.

Each "beneficiary" received ten or twelve rubles per "shop day" and was able to spend a sum roughly equal to what the others spent. No thanks were expressed for such help, since the custom was so rigidly observed that it was considered the prisoner's inalienable right.

For a long time, perhaps even for years, the prison administration had no inkling of this "organization." Or perhaps they ignored the information of loyal cell informers and secret agents. It is hard to believe the authorities were not aware of these committees. Probably the administration of Butyr Prison had no desire to repeat its sad experience in unsuccessfully attempting to put an end to the notorious game of "matches."

All games are forbidden in prison. Chess pieces molded from bread chewed up by the "entire cell" were confiscated and destroyed as soon as they were noticed by the watchful eye of the guard peering through the peephole in the door. The very expression, "watchful eye," acquired in prison a literal rather than figurative meaning: the attentive eye of the guard framed by the peephole.

Dominoes and checkers were strictly forbidden in the investigatory prison. Books were not forbidden, and the prison library was a rich one, but the prisoner under investigation derived no benefit from reading other than that of taking his mind off his own important and tormenting thoughts. It is impossible to concentrate on a book in a common cell. Books serve as amusement and distraction, taking the place of dominoes and checkers.

Cards are customary in cells that contain criminals, but there are no cards in Butyr Prison. Indeed, there are no games there other than "matches."

Matches is a game for two. There are fifty matches to a box. Thirty are left in the lid, which is placed on end. The lid is then shaken and raised, and the matches fall out onto the floor.

Players use one match as a lever to pick from the pile any matches that can be removed without disturbing the remainder. When one player commits an error, the other takes his turn.

Matches is the well-known child's game of pick-up sticks, adapted by the agile prison mind for the prison cell.

The entire prison played matches from breakfast to dinner, and from dinner to supper. People became very wrapped up in the game. Match champions appeared, and there were matches of a special quality—those that had grown shiny from constant use. Such matches were never used to light a cigarette.

This game soothed the prisoners' nerves and introduced a certain calm into their troubled souls.

The administration was powerless to destroy or forbid this game. After all, matches were permitted. They were issued (individually) and were sold in the commissary.

Wing commandants tried destroying the boxes, but the game could go on without them.

The administration was rendered helpless in this struggle against pick-up sticks; none of its efforts made any difference. The entire prison continued to play matches.

For this same reason—out of fear of being shamed—the administration ignored the Committees for the Poor. They were loath to become involved in this far-from-glorious struggle.

But rumors of the committees spread to higher and higher levels and ultimately reached a certain Institution which issued a stern order to liquidate the committees. Their very name seemed to indicate a challenge, an appeal to the conscience of the revolution.

How many cells were checked and admonished! How many criminal slips of paper with encoded calculation of orders and expenditures were seized in the cells during sudden searches! How many cell leaders spent time in the punishment cells of the Police Tower or Pugachev's Tower! It was all in vain; the committees continued to exist in spite of all the warnings and sanctions.

It was indeed extremely difficult to control the situation. The wing commandant and the overseer who worked for years in the prison had, moreover, a somewhat different view of the prisoner than did their high-placed superiors. On occasion they might even take the prisoner's side against the superior. It wasn't that they abetted the prisoner, but when it was possible they simply ignored violations and did not go out of their way to find fault. This was particularly the case if the guard was not a young man. From the point of view of the prisoner, the best superior is an older man of low rank. A combination of these two conditions more or less guarantees an almost decent person. It's even better if he drinks. Such a person is not trying to build a career. The career of a prison guard—and especially of a camp guard—must be lubricated with the blood of the prisoners.

But the Institution demanded that the committees be eliminated, and the prison administration vainly attempted to achieve that result.

An attempt was made to blow up the committees from within. This, was, of course, the most clever of solutions. The committees were illegal organizations, and any prisoner could refuse to make contributions that were forced on him. Anyone not desiring to pay these taxes and support the committees could protest, and his refusal would be supported wholeheartedly by the prison administration. It would have been ludicrous to think otherwise, for the prisoners' organization was not a state that could levy taxes. That meant that the committees were extortion, a "racket," robbery . . .

Of course, any prisoner could refuse to make contributions simply by claiming he didn't want to, and that would have been that. It was his money, and no one had any right to make any claims, etc., etc. Once such a statement was made, nothing would be deducted and everything ordered would be delivered.

But who would risk making such a statement? Who would risk placing himself in opposition to the entire group, to people who are with you twenty-four hours a day, where only sleep can save you from the hostile glare of your fellow inmates? In prison everyone involuntarily turns to his neighbor for spiritual support, and it is unthinkable to subject oneself to ostracism. Even though no attempts are made to exert any "physical" influence, rejection by one's fellows is more terrible than the threats of the investigator.

Prison ostracism is a weapon in the war of nerves. And God help the man who has had to endure the demonstrated contempt of his fellow inmates.

But if some antisocial citizen is too thick-skinned and stubborn, the cell leader has another, still more humiliating and effective weapon at his disposal.

No one can deprive a prisoner of his ration (except the investigator, when this is necessary for "the case"), and the stubborn one will receive his bowl of soup, his portion of kasha, his bread. Food is distributed by a person appointed by the cell leader; this is one of his prerogatives.

Bunks line the walls of the cell and are separated into two rows by the passageway leading from the door to the window. The cell has four corners, and food is served from each of them in turn. One day it is served from one corner, and the next day from another. This alternation is necessary to avoid upsetting the already hypernervous prisoners with some trifle, such as which part of the thin prison soup they will receive, and to guarantee that each has an equal chance at getting thicker soup, at the right temperature. . . . Nothing is trivial in prison.

The cell leader declares that the soup can be served and adds: "And serve the one who doesn't care about the committees last."

This humiliating, unbearable insult can be repeated four times a Butyr day, since there is tea for morning and evening, soup for dinner, and kasha for supper.

A fifth opportunity presents itself when bread is distributed.

It is risky to appeal to the wing commandant in such matters, since the entire cell will testify against the stubborn one. Everyone lies—to a man—and the commandant will never learn the truth.

But the selfish person is no weakling. Moreover, he believes that he alone had been unjustly arrested and that all his cellmates are criminals. His skin is thick enough, and he doesn't lack stubbornness. He easily bears the brunt of his cellmates' ostracism; those eggheads and their trick will never make him cave in. He might have been swayed by the ancient device of physical threat of violence, but there are no physical crimes in Butyr Prison. Thus, the selfish one is about to celebrate his victory—the sanction has proved futile.

The inmates of the cell and their leader, however, have at their disposal one more weapon. The cells are checked each evening when the guard is changed. The new guard is required to ask if they wish to make any "statements."

The cell leader steps forward and demands that the ostracized man be transferred to a different cell. It is not necessary to explain the request; it simply has to be stated. No later than the next day, and perhaps even earlier, the transfer is sure to be carried out, since the public statement relieves the cell leader of any responsibility for discipline in the cell.

If he were not transferred, the recalcitrant man might be

beaten or killed, and such events involve repeated explanations by the guard to the commandant and to still higher
prison officials.

If an investigation of a prison murder is conducted, the
fact that the guard was warned is discovered immediately.
Thus, it is judged best to accede to the demand and not resist
making the transfer.

To be transferred to another cell, not brought in from the
"free world," is not a very pleasant experience. This always
puts one's new cellmates on their guard and causes them to
suspect that the transferred person is an informer. "I hope he's
been transferred to our cell only for refusing to participate in
the committee," is the first thought of the cell leader. "What if
it's something worse?" The cell leader will attempt to learn the
reason for the transfer—perhaps through a note left in the bottom of the wastebasket in the toilet or by tapping on the wall,
using the system worked out by the Decembrist, Bestuzhev,
or by Morse Code.

The "newcomer" will receive no sympathy or confidence
from his new comrades until an answer is received. Many days
pass, the reason for the transfer is clarified, passions have quieted down, but the new cell has its own committee and its own
deductions.

Everything begins again—if it begins at all, since the
newcomer had learned a bitter lesson in his former cell. His
resistance is crushed.

There were no Committees for the Poor in Butyr Prison
until clothing and food packages were forbidden and commissary privileges became practically unlimited.

The committees came into being in the second half of the
thirties as a curious expression of the "personal life" of prisoners under investigation, a way for those who had been
deprived of all rights to make a statement as to their own con-
tinuing humanity. Unlike the "free" world "outside" or the
camps, society in prison is always united. In the committees

this society found a way to make a positive statement as to the right of every man to live his own life. Such spiritual forces run contrary to all prison regulations and investigatory rules, but they always win out in the end.

Dominoes

≫≫

THE ORDERLIES lifted me off the scales, but their cold, powerful hands would not let me touch the ground.

"How much?" the doctor shouted, dipping his pen into the inkwell with a click.

"One hundred and six pounds."

They put me on the stretcher. My height was six feet, and my normal weight was 177 pounds. Bones constitute 42 percent of a man's total weight, seventy-four pounds in my case. On that icy evening I had only thirty-two pounds of skin, organs, and brain. I was unable to make this calculation at the time, but I vaguely realized that the doctor peering at me from under his eyebrows was doing precisely that.

He unlocked the desk drawer, carefully pulled out a thermometer, leaned over me, and gently placed it under my left armpit. Immediately one of the orderlies pressed my arm to my chest, and the other grasped my left wrist with both hands. Later I came to understand these carefully planned movements; there was only one thermometer in the hospital of a hundred beds. The value of this piece of glass was measured on a totally new scale; it was treasured as if it were a rare jewel. Only the very seriously ill and new patients could have their temperature taken with this instrument. The temperature of recovering patients was recorded "according to their pulse," and only in instances of doubt was the desk drawer unlocked.

The windup clock on the wall chimed ten o'clock, and the doctor carefully extracted the thermometer. The orderlies' hands relaxed.

"93.7 degrees," the doctor said. "Can you answer?"

I indicated with my eyes that I could. I was saving my strength. I could only pronounce words slowly and with difficulty, as if translating from a foreign language. I had forgotten everything. I didn't even remember what it was like to remember. They finished recording the history of my disease, and the orderlies easily lifted the stretchers on which I lay face-up.

"Take him to the sixth ward," the doctor said. "Close to the stove."

They put me next to the stove, on a wooden cot supported by sawhorses. The mattresses were stuffed with branches of dwarf cedar, the needles had fallen off, dried up, and the naked branches protruded menacingly from under the dirty, striped material. Straw dust seeped from the grimy, tightly packed pillow. A thin, washed-out cotton blanket with the word "feet" sewn in gray letters covered me from the entire world. The twinelike muscles of my arms and legs ached, and my frost-bitten fingers and toes itched. But fatigue was stronger than pain. I curled up on my side, seized my legs with my hands, leaned my chin against the coarse, crocodile-like skin of my knees, and fell asleep.

I awoke many hours later. My breakfasts, dinners, and suppers were on the floor next to the cot. Stretching out my hand, I grabbed the nearest tin bowl and began to eat everything in the order in which the bowls lay. From time to time I would nibble some of the bread ration. Other patients on similar wooden cots supported by sawhorses watched me swallow the food. They did not ask who I was or where I came from; my crocodile skin spoke for itself. They didn't want to stare at me, but they couldn't help it. I knew myself how impossible it was to tear your eyes from the sight of a man eating.

I ate all the food that had been left for me. Then there came warmth, an ecstatic weight in my belly, and again sleep, but not for long this time, since an orderly had come for me. I threw over my shoulders the only gown in the ward. Filthy, burned by cigarette butts, and heavy with the absorbed sweat of hundreds of people, it was also used as a coat. I stuck my feet into enormous slippers and shuffled behind the orderly to the treatment room. I had to go slowly, since I was afraid of falling. The same young doctor stood by the window and stared out at the street through frosty panes shaggy from the ice that had formed on them. A rag hung from the corner of the sill, and water dripped from it, drop by drop, into a tin dinner bowl. The cast-iron stove hummed. I stopped, clinging with both hands to the orderly.

"Let's continue," the doctor said.

"It's cold," I answered quietly. The food I had eaten had ceased to warm me.

"Sit down next to the stove. Where did you work before prison?"

I spread my lips and moved my jaw—my intention was to produce a smile. The doctor understood and smiled in reply.

"My name is Andrei Mihailovich," he said. "You don't need any treatment."

I felt a sucking sensation in the pit of my stomach.

"That's right," he repeated in a loud voice. "You don't need any treatment. You need to be fed and washed. You have to lie still and eat. I know our mattresses aren't featherbeds, but they're better than nothing. Just don't lie in one position for too long, and you won't get bedsores. You'll be in the hospital about two months. And then spring will be here."

The doctor smiled. I was, of course, elated. An entire two months! But I was too weak to express this joy. I gripped the stool with both hands and said nothing. The doctor wrote something into my case history.

"You can go now."

I returned to the ward, slept, and ate. In a week I was already walking shakily around the ward, the corridor, and the other wards. I looked for people who were chewing, swallowing. I stared at their mouths, for the more I rested, the more I wanted to eat.

In the hospital, as in camp, no spoons were issued. We had learned to get along without knives and forks while we were still in prison under investigation, and we had long since learned to slurp up our food without a spoon; neither the soup nor the porridge was ever thick enough to require a spoon. A finger, a crust of bread, and one's own tongue were enough to clean the bottom of a pot or bowl.

I searched out mouths in the process of chewing. It was an insistant demand of my body, and Andrei Mihailovich was familiar with the feeling.

One night the orderly woke me up. The ward was filled with the usual nocturnal hospital sounds: snoring, wheezing, groans, someone talking in his sleep, coughing. It all blended into a single peculiar symphony of sound—if a symphony can be composed of such sounds. Take me to such a place, blind-folded, and I will always recognize a camp hospital.

On the windowsill was a lamp—a tin saucer with some sort of oil (but not fish oil this time!) and a smoking wick twisted from cotton wool. It couldn't have been very late. Lights went out at 9:00, and somehow we would fall asleep right away—just as soon as our hands and feet warmed up.

"Andrei Mihailovich wants you," the orderly said. "Kozlik will show you the way."

The patient called Kozlik was standing in front of me.

I walked up to the tin basin, washed my hands and face, and returned to the ward to dry them on the pillowcase. There was a single towel for the entire ward, an enormous thing made from an old striped mattress, and it was available only in the mornings. Andrei Mihailovich lived in the hospital, in one of the small far rooms normally reserved for postoperative patients. I knocked at the door and went in.

A heap of books was pushed to the side on the table. The books were alien, hostile, superfluous. Next to the books stood a teapot, two tin mugs, a bowl full of some sort of kasha . . .

"Feel like playing dominoes?" Andrei Mihailovich asked, peering at me in a friendly fashion. "If you have the time . . ."

I hate dominoes. Of all games, it is the most stupid, senseless, and boring. Even a card game like lotto is more interesting. For that matter, any card game is better. Best of all would have been checkers or chess. I squinted at the cupboard to see if there wasn't a chess board there, but there wasn't. I just couldn't offend Andrei Mihailovich with a refusal. I had to amuse him, to pay back good with good. I had never played dominoes in my life, but I was convinced that no great wisdom was required to learn this art.

"Let's have some tea," Andrei Mihailovich said. "Here's the sugar. Don't be embarrassed; take as much as you like. Help yourself to the kasha and tell me about anything you like. But then I guess you can't do both things at the same time."

I ate the kasha and the bread and drank three mugs of tea with sugar. I had not seen sugar for several years. I felt warm.

Andrei Mihailovich mixed the dominoes. I knew that the one who had the double six began the game. Andrei Mihailovich had it. Then, in turns, the players had to attach pieces with the matching number of dots. That was all there was to it, and I began to play without hesitation, sweating and constantly hiccuping from fullness.

We played on Andrei Mihailovich's bed, and I got pleasure from looking at the blindingly white pillowcase on the down pillow. It was a physical pleasure to look at the clean pillow, to see another man rumple it with his hand.

"Our game," I said, "is lacking its main appeal. Domino players are supposed to smack their pieces down on the table when they play." I was not joking. It was this particular aspect of the game that struck me as the most crucial.

"Let's switch to the table," Andrei Mihailovich said affably.

"No, that's all right. I'm just recalling all the various pleasures of the game."

The game continued slowly. We were more concerned

with telling each other our life histories. As a doctor, Andrei Mihailovich had never been in the general work gang at the mines and had only seen the mines as they were reflected in their human waste, cast out from the hospital or the morgue. I too was a by-product of the mine.

"So you won," Andrei Mihailovich said. "Congratulations! For a prize I present you with—this." He took from the night table a plastic cigarette case. "You probably haven't smoked for a long time?"

He tore off a piece of newspaper and rolled a cigarette. There's nothing better than newspaper for homegrown tobacco. The traces of typographic ink not only don't spoil the bouquet of the homegrown tobacco but even heighten it in the best fashion. I touched a piece of paper to the glowing coals in the stove and lit up, greedily inhaling the nauseatingly sweet smoke.

It was really tough to lay your hands on tobacco, and I should have quit smoking long ago. But even though conditions were what might be called "appropriate," I never did quit. It was terrible even to imagine that I could lose this single great convict joy.

"Good night," Andrei Mihailovich said, smiling. "I was going to go to bed, but I so wanted to play a game. I really appreciate it."

I walked out of his room into the dark corridor and found someone standing in my path near the wall. I recognized Kozlik's silhouette.

"It's you. What are you doing here?"

"I wanted a smoke. Did he give you any?"

I was ashamed of my greed, ashamed that I had not thought of Kozlik or anyone else in the ward, that I had not brought them a butt, or a crust of bread, a little kasha.

Kozlik had waited several hours in the dark corridor.

The Letter

>>

THE HALF-DRUNK RADIO OPERATOR yanked open my door. "There's a message for you from headquarters; come over and pick it up." He disappeared into the snow and the darkness. I'd brought some frozen rabbits home from my last trip, and I was thawing them out in front of the stove. They had been given to me as a present, but ten carcasses were nothing unusual. It was a good season for rabbits, and a man barely had time to set his traps before they were full. They had to be thawed before they could be eaten, but I immediately lost all interest in rabbits.

A message from headquarters: a telegram, a radiogram, a phone call for me. It was my first telegram in fifteen years. I was startled, anxious. Here, as in any village, a telegram means a tragedy; it deals with death. It couldn't be an announcement of my release, because I had long since been released. I set off for the radio operator's fortified castle with its loopholes and three high fences. Each fence had a gate fitted with a latch that had to be opened for me by the radio operator's wife. I squeezed through all the doors on my way to the landlord's abode. When the last door had shut behind me, I strode into a bedlam of wings, into the stench of poultry droppings and made my way through a flock of fluttering chickens and crowing cocks. Guarding my face, I crossed over one more threshold, but the radio operator wasn't there either. There were only pigs: three clean, well cared-for smallish boars and a somewhat larger sow. This was the last barrier.

The radio operator sat surrounded by crates of pickle brine and green onions. He truly intended to become a millionaire. There are different roads to wealth in Kolyma. One is hardship pay and special rations. The sale of cheap tobacco and tea is another. Raising chickens and hogs is a third.

Crowded to the very edge of the table by all his flora and fauna, the radio operator handed me a sheaf of telegrams. They all looked the same, and I felt like a parrot picking a card at random.

I sorted through the cables, but couldn't make head or tail of them. Condescendingly, the radio operator picked out my telegram with the tips of his fingers.

It read: "Come letter," that is "Come for your letter." The postal service economized on content, but the receiver, of course, understood what was meant.

I went to the area chief and showed him the telegram.

"How far is it?" he asked.

"Five hundred kilometers."

"Well, I guess so . . ."

"I'll be back in five days."

"Good. But don't drag things out. No sense waiting to hitch a ride. The local Yakut tribesman will take you by dog sled to Baragon. From there you'll have to go by reindeer. If you're not stingy, the postal service will take you. The main thing is to get to the highway."

When I walked out of the area chief's office, I realized I'd never make it to the damn highway. I wouldn't even make it to Baragon, because I didn't have a coat. I, a resident of Kolyma, didn't have a coat! Sergey Korotkov had given me an almost new white sheepskin coat. He gave me a big pillow too, but when I wanted to quit my job at the prison hospital and leave for the mainland, I sold the coat and the pillow. I didn't want to have any superfluous belongings that would just be stolen or taken away outright by the criminal element. I sold my coat and pillow, but the personnel office and the Magadan Ministry of Internal Affairs refused me permission to leave. So when my money ran out, I had to go back again for a job in Far Northern Construction. And I went to a place where there were flying chickens and a radio operator, but I didn't manage to buy a coat. You couldn't ask someone to loan you one for five days; that kind of request would simply be laughed at in Kolyma. So somehow I had to buy a coat in the village.

I found both a coat and someone willing to sell it. It was black with a luxurious sheepskin collar, but it was more like a jacket than a coat. It had no pockets and the bottom half was cut away. Only the collar and the broad sleeves remained.

"You mean you cut the bottom off?" I asked Ivanov, the camp overseer who sold me the coat. Ivanov lived alone; he was a gloomy type. He'd cut off the bottom half of the coat to make mittens. They were in great demand, and he made five pairs, each worth the price of a complete sheepskin coat. The pitiful part that was left could hardly be called a coat.

"What difference does it make? I'm selling a coat. For 500 rubles. You're buying it. Whether or not I cut off the bottom half has nothing to do with our deal."

He was right. It was an irrelevant question, and I paid him quickly and took the coat home, where I tried it on and began to wait for night.

I remember the sharp, black eyes of the Yakut who drove the dog sled, my own numb fingers gripping the sled, a river, ice, bushes painfully lashing my face. But I had tied everything on firmly. At a postal station an old friend of mine got me a ride on a reindeer sleigh. I would run beside it, but mainly I tried to ride. I would hold on tight, fall off, and run alongside again. By evening we reached the lights of the highway and could hear the roar of the trucks hurtling through the darkness.

I paid the Yakut and walked up to the dispatcher's warming shed. But it wasn't heated; there wasn't any firewood. Still it was a roof and walls. A line had already formed of people headed for town, for Magadan. It was a small line—one man. A truck honked and the man ran out into the darkness. The truck honked again and the man was gone. Now it was my turn to run out into the frost.

The five-ton truck shuddered and barely stopped for me. There was a lot of room in the cab, which was a good thing, because it would have been impossible to travel so far in the back, given such bitter cold.

"Where to?"

"To the Left Bank."

"Can't take you. I'm taking coal to Magadan, and it isn't worth taking you if you're headed for the Left Bank."

"I'll pay you all the way to Magadan."

"That changes things. Get in. You know the rate?"

"Right. A ruble a kilometer."

"Money in advance."

I took the money out of my pocket and paid him. The truck dove into the white darkness and slowed down. The fog made it impossible to go any farther.

"Let's sleep on it." We curled up in the cab and left the motor running. When dawn came, the white winter fog didn't seem as terrible as it had the night before.

"We'll make some strong tea and get moving."

The driver boiled a whole package of tea in a tin can, cooled it in the snow, and drank it. He boiled a second canful of tea, drank it, and put the can away.

"Let's get on the road."

"Where are you from?"

I told him.

"I was in those parts. I even worked there as a driver. You've got a real bastard there. His name is Ivanov, he's a supervisor. He stole my sheepskin coat. Said he needed it to get home. It was really cold last year. I never saw it again. Not a trace. He wouldn't give it back. I had some friends ask him for it, but he claimed he never took it. I intend to make a trip out there and get it back. It was a black coat, really nice. What does he need a sheepskin coat for? Maybe he cut it up for mittens and sold them. Everybody wants them nowadays. I could have cut it up myself for mittens. Now there's no coat, no mittens, no Ivanov."

I turned away, hunching beneath the collar of my coat.

"It was a black one, just like yours. The bastard. Well, we've had our sleep, we've got to get moving."

The truck lurched forward with a roar. Wide-awake from the incredibly strong tea, the driver honked on the bends.

The distance fell away behind us, bridge followed bridge, gold mine followed gold mine. Trucks met and passed each other in the morning light. All of a sudden everything collapsed with a loud clang, and our truck nosedived into a ditch.

"Everything's shot!" The driver was livid with rage. "The coal's scattered, the cab and the side of the truck are shot! Five ton of coal—gone!"

He was not even scratched, and at first I didn't understand what had happened.

Our truck had been knocked from the road by a Czechoslovak *Tatra*. There wasn't even a scratch on its iron side. The driver stopped the *Tatra* and climbed out.

"Figure up quick what your loss is, including fixing the side and the coal," the driver of the *Tatra* shouted. "We'll pay. But no report. You understand?"

"All right," said my driver. "That'll be . . ."

"We'll pay it."

"How about me?" I asked.

"I'll get you on another truck going the same way. It's only about forty kilometers. They'll get you there. Be a friend."

"Forty kilometers is an hour's ride," I protested, but finally agreed. I got into the cab of another truck and waved to Inspector Ivanov's friend.

By the time our truck began to brake, I had virtually turned to ice. We had reached the Left Bank, and I got out, hoping to find a place to spend the night. They didn't give out lodging along with letters.

I went to the hospital where I had once worked. It was against the rules to enter a camp hospital, but I went in for a minute to get warm. A civilian orderly whom I knew happened to be coming down the corridor, and I asked him to put me up for the night.

The next day I knocked and entered the office where the letter awaited me. I knew the handwriting well—swift, soaring, but at the same time precise and lucid.

It was a letter from Pasternak.

The Golden Taiga

>>>

THE TRANSIT PRISON is known as the "minor zone," and the "major zone" is the Office of Mines, with its endless stockily built barracks, prison streets, triple strands of barbed wire, and guard towers that look like starling roosts in the winter. The "minor zone" has even more towers, more barbed wire, more locks, and latches, for this is where transit prisoners are kept, and anything can be expected of them.

The architecture of the "minor zone" is ideal: one enormous square building intended for 500 prisoners and with bunks stacked four-high. That means that, if necessary, thousands of convicts can be squeezed in. But it is winter now, and only a few prisoner consignments are being prepared so that the "zone" seems almost empty inside. The barracks have not yet dried up; a white fog hovers in the room, and ice forms on the insides of the pine-log walls. Over the entrance hangs an enormous, thousand-watt bulb. Owing to the uneven current, the bulb alternates between a dull yellow and a blinding white light.

The zone sleeps during the day. At night the doors open, and people appear under the lamp, holding matches in their hands and calling out names in hoarse voices. Those whose names are called button up their pea jackets, step over the threshold—and disappear forever. Out there the guards are waiting and the truck motors are coughing. Prisoners are hauled away to mines, collective farms, and road gangs.

I am there too—on a lower bunk near the door. It's cold down here, but I don't dare crawl higher, where it's warmer, since I would only be thrown down. The upper berths are for the strong and, mainly, for hardened criminals. I don't have the strength anyway to climb the steps which have been nailed to a post. I'm better off down below. If there should be a fight for the lower bunks, I can always crawl under them.

I cannot bite or fight, although I have learned well all the tricks of prison fighting. The limited amount of space—a prison cell, a convict train car, crowded barracks—have dictated the methods of grabbing, biting, breaking. But I just don't have the strength for such tactics. I can only growl and curse. I struggle for every day, every hour of rest. Every part of my body prompts me to act this way.

I am called up the very first night, but I don't tighten the rope that serves as my belt, nor do I button my coat.

The door closes behind me, and I enter the space between the inner and outer doors.

The work gang consists of twenty men—the usual quota for one truck. They are standing at the next door, from which billow clouds of thick, white smoke.

The assignment man and the senior guard look over the men and take a head count. There is another man standing off to the right. He is wearing a quilted coat, felt pants, a fur hat with ear flaps, and fur mittens, which he beats energetically against his body. He's the one I need. I've been hauled around enough to know the "law" perfectly.

The man with the mittens is the "representative" who can accept or reject prisoners.

"Don't take me, sir. I'm sick, and I won't work at the mine. I need to be sent to the hospital."

The "representative" hesitates. Back at the mine they told him to select only good workers; they didn't need any other kind. That is why he has come.

The "representative" looks me over—my torn pea jacket, a filthy buttonless military shirt which reveals a dirty body scratched bloody from louse bites, rags around my fingers, other rags tied with string around my feet (in an area where the temperature drops to seventy-five degrees below zero), inflamed hungry eyes, and an incredibly emaciated condition. He has seen this sort of thing before, and he knows what it means. He takes a red pencil and crosses out my name with a firm hand.

"Go on back, you son of a bitch," the assignment man says to me.

The door swings open, and I am again inside the minor zone. My place on the bunk has been taken, but I drag out the intruder. He growls from habit but soon calms down.

I fall asleep as if knocked unconscious but awake at the first rustle. I have learned to wake up like a wild man or a beast—without any intermediate drowsy stage.

When I open my eyes, I see a slippered foot hanging from the upper bunk. The slipper is totally worn out, but it is nevertheless a slipper, and not a regulation-issue shoe. A dirty boy, who has been consorting with the professional criminals in camp, appears before me and addresses someone above me in the effeminate voice cultivated by many of the homosexuals:

"Tell Valyusha," he says to some unseen person on the upper berth, "that they brought in some performers . . ."

After a pause, a hoarse voice responds from above:

"Valyusha wants to know who they are."

"They're performers from the Cultural Division. A magician and two singers. One of the singers is from Harbin."

The slipper stirs and disappears. The voice from above says:

"Bring them here."

From the edge of my bunk I see three men standing under the lamp—two in pea jackets and one in a fur-lined jacket. The faces of all three express reverence.

"Which one is from Harbin?" the voice asks.

"I am," the man in the fur-lined jacket answers.

"Valyusha says you should sing something."

"In Russian? French? Italian? English?" the singer asks, stretching his neck.

"Valyusha says it should be in Russian."

"What about the guards? Is it all right if I sing quietly?"

"Don't worry about them . . . Do it right—just like in Harbin."

The singer steps back a few paces and sings "The Toreador" couplets. His breath frosts each time he exhales.

The singing is followed by a deep growl, and the voice from above commands:

"Valyusha says to sing a song."

The singer grows pale and tries again:

> Whisper, my golden one,
> Whisper, beloved,
> Whisper, my golden taiga.
> Twist and turn, pathways,
> One after the other,
> Through our free and handsome taiga.

"Valyusha says that was good," the voice utters from above.

The singer sighs in relief. Wet from nervousness, his steaming forehead looks as if it were surrounded by a halo. The singer wipes his brow with his palm, and the halo disappears.

"Now take off your jacket," the voice says. "Here's a replacement." A padded coat is tossed down from above.

The singer silently takes off his jacket and puts on the padded coat.

"You can go now," the voice says from above. "Valyusha wants to sleep."

The Harbin singer and his companions disappear in the barracks' fog.

I move back from the edge of the bunk, curl up, and fall asleep with my hands pushed up in the sleeves of my padded coat. In what seems like no more than a moment, however, I am awakened by a loud, emotional whispering:

"My friend and I were walking down a street in Ulan-Bator. It was time to eat, and there was a Chinese cafeteria on the corner. We went in and saw they had Chinese meat pies on the menu. I'm from Siberia, and I know our Siberian meat pies—the kind they make in the Urals. But these were Chinese. We decided to order a hundred. The Chinese manager burst out laughing; said that would be a lot and grinned from ear to ear. Well, how about ten? He kept laughing; said that would be a lot. So we ordered two. He shrugged his shoulders, went off to the kitchen, and brought them out. Each one was the size of your hand and had hot grease poured all over it. The two of us ate half of one and left."

"Let me tell you what happened to me one time . . ."

It takes a considerable effort of the will to stop listening and fall asleep again.

The smell of smoke awakens me. Above me, in the criminal kingdom, they are smoking. Someone with a homemade cigar climbs down, and the pungent aroma wakes everyone below.

Again I hear a whispering: "You can't imagine how many cigarette butts there were back at the Party Regional Office in Severnoye. My God, oh, my God! Aunt Polly, our cleaning lady, was constantly complaining that she couldn't get everything swept up. And I didn't even understand what a butt was back then . . ."

I fall asleep again.

Someone jerks my foot. It is the assignment man. His inflamed eyes are furious. At his command, I come out into the yellow strip of light by the door.

"All right," he says, "so you don't want to go to the mine."

I am silent.

"How about a warm collective farm, damn you! I'd go myself."

"No."

"How about a road gang? To tie brooms. Think about it."

"I know your brooms," I say. "Today I tie brooms, and tomorrow they bring me a wheelbarrow."

"Just what do you want?"

"To go to the hospital. I'm sick."

The assignment man writes something in his notebook and goes away. Three days later a medic comes to the minor zone and calls for me. He measures my temperature, looks at the ulcers on my back, and rubs in some sort of ointment.

Typhoid Quarantine

>>>

THE MAN IN THE WHITE GOWN held out his rosy, washed hand, and Andreev put his sweaty, stiff military shirt into the outstretched fingers. The man jerked back his hand and shook it.

"I don't have any underwear," Andreev said indifferently.

The orderly then took Andreev's shirt in both hands, turned the sleeves inside out with an agile, practiced movement, and took one look . . .

"He's full of them, Lydia Ivanovna," he said and bellowed at Andreev: "How could you let yourself get so lousy?"

But the doctor, Lydia Ivanovna, interrupted him.

"It's not their fault," she said quietly in a tone of reproach, stressing the word "their," and took a stethoscope from the table.

Andreev remembered this red-haired woman for the rest

of his life, thanked her a thousand times, and thought about her with warmth and tenderness. Why? Because she had stressed the word *"their"* in this, the only sentence that Andreev had ever heard from her. He thanked her for a kind word said at the right time. Did she ever learn of his thanks?

The examination was brief and did not require a stethoscope. Lydia Ivanovna breathed on a violet rubber stamp and pressed it to a printed form, leaning on it heavily with both hands. She wrote a few words on it, and Andreev was taken away.

The guard, who had been waiting in the entrance hall, did not take Andreev back to prison but to one of the warehouses in the center of the settlement. The area around the warehouse had a barbed-wire fence with the prescribed ten strands and a gate, next to which stood a sentry wearing a leather coat and holding a rifle. They entered the yard and approached the warehouse. A bright light shone through the crack in the door. The door was made for trucks, not people, and the guard opened it with great difficulty. The smell of dirty bodies, sour human sweat, and old clothing struck Andreev's nostrils. A muffled hum of human voices filled the vast box. The walls were entirely covered with four-tiered bunks cut from whole larch trees. The bunks were built solidly, to last forever—like Caesar's bridges. More than a thousand people lay on the shelves of the huge warehouse. This was only one of twenty enormous warehouses packed with living goods. There was a typhoid quarantine in port, and there hadn't been any "outgoing shipments" for more than a month.

There had been a breakdown in the camp's blood circulation system, whose erythrocytes were living people. Trucks stood idle, and the mines lengthened the prisoners' workday. In the town itself the bakery was not able to keep up with orders. Every prisoner had to receive 500 grams (a little over a pound) of bread per day, and bread was even being baked in private apartments. The authorities were growing ever more bitter over the fact that the town was slowly filling up with convict "slag" that had been thrown out by the mines in the taiga.

There were more than a thousand human beings in the warehouse to which Andreev had been brought and which bore the then-fashionable title of "section." This multitude was not immediately noticeable. On the upper bunks people lay naked in the heat; the prisoners on and beneath the lower bunks wore padded coats, pea jackets and hats. No one will ever explain why a convict almost never sleeps on his side. Most of the men lay on their backs, and their bodies seemed like growths or bumps in the wood, like bent boards in the enormous shelves.

People were clustered in small groups either around storytellers—"novelists"—or around incidents, and given such a concentration of people, incidents occurred nearly every minute. These men were being kept in the transit camp and had not been sent to work for more than a month. They were sent out only to the bathhouse to disinfect their clothing. Every day the camps lost twenty thousand workdays, one hundred and sixty thousand hours, perhaps even three hundred and twenty thousand hours; workdays vary. Or a thousand days of life were saved. Twenty thousand days of life. Statistics is a wily science, and figures can be read in different ways.

Everyone was in his place when food was handed out, distributed to ten prisoners at a time. There were so many people that no sooner had breakfast been distributed than it was time for lunch. As soon as lunch had been served, it was time for supper. Only bread and "tea" (warm boiled water) and half a herring were distributed to each man in the morning. No more bread was issued for the rest of the day. Lunch consisted of soup, and only kasha was served for supper. Nevertheless, there was not sufficient time to serve even this quantity.

The assignment man showed Andreev his place and pointed to the second bunk. A grumble of protest came from the top bunk, but the assignment man cursed back at the grumblers. Andreev gripped the edge of the shelf with both hands and unsuccessfully attempted to bring up his right leg. The assignment man's strong arm tossed him upward, and Andreev plunked down among the naked bodies. No one paid him any attention. The "registration" and settlement proce- dure had been carried out.

Andreev slept. He awoke only when food was distributed, after which he would carefully and precisely lick his hands and fall asleep again. His sleep was not sound, however, since the lice refused to leave him in peace.

No one questioned him, even though there were many people here from the taiga, and the rest were destined to end up there. They all knew this, and for that very reason they wanted to know as little as possible about their inevitable fate. They were right, Andreev reasoned. They should not know everything that he had seen. Nothing could be avoided or fore- seen. What use were extra fears? These were living people, and Andreev was a representative of the dead. His knowledge, a dead man's knowledge, was of no use to them, the living.

Bathhouse time came two days later. Bathing and cloth- ing disinfection were nothing but an annoyance, and all the prisoners prepared themselves reluctantly. Andreev, however, wanted to rid himself of lice. He had all the time in the world, and he examined the seams of his faded military shirt several times a day. But only the disinfection chamber held the prom- ise of final victory. He went to the bathhouse willingly and, although they issued him no underwear and he had to pull his reddish military shirt over his naked body, he no longer felt the usual bites.

At the bathhouse, the usual portion of water was issued— one basin of hot water and one of cold—but Andreev managed to deceive the water man and get an extra basin. A tiny piece of soap was issued, but it was possible to gather discarded fragments from the floor and work up a good lather. This was his best bath in a year. So what if blood and pus seeped from the scurvy ulcers on his shins? So what if people in the bathhouse recoiled from him in horror? So what if they walked around him and his lousy clothing in disgust?

When clothing was returned from the disinfection chamber, the fur socks of Andreev's neighbor Ognyov had shrunk so much that they looked like toys. Ognyov burst into tears, for the socks were his salvation in the north. Andreev, however, stared at him without sympathy. He had seen too many men cry for too many reasons. Some pretended, others were mentally disturbed, and still others had lost hope and were desperately bitter. Some cried from the cold. Andreev had never seen anyone cry from hunger.

When they returned through the silent city, the aluminum-hued puddles had cooled, and the fresh air had a smell of spring. After the session in the bathhouse, Andreev slept soundly. Ognyov, who had forgotten the incident in the bathhouse, said Andreev had "gotten his fill of sleep."

No one was permitted to leave, but there was one job in the "section" for which a man could be allowed to cross through "the wire." True, this had nothing to do with leaving the camp settlement and crossing the "outer wire"—a series of three fences, each with ten strands of barbed wire and a forbidden area beyond them circumscribed by another low fence. No one even dreamt of that. They could only contemplate the possibility of leaving the immediate yard. Beyond the barbed wire of the yard was a cafeteria, a kitchen, storehouses, a hospital—in a word, a very different life, one forbidden to Andreev. Only one person could pass through the fence—the sewage disposal man. And when he suddenly died (life is full of fortunate coincidences!), Ognyov accomplished miracles of energy and intuition. For two days he ate no bread. Then he traded the bread for a pressed-fiber suitcase.

"I got it from Baron Mandel, Andreev!"

Baron Mandel! A descendant of Pushkin! Far below, Andreev could make out the long, narrow-shouldered figure of the Baron with his tiny bald skull, but he had never had an opportunity to make his acquaintance.

Since he had been in quarantine for only a few months, Ognynov still had a wool jacket left over from the "outside." He presented the assignment man with the jacket and the suitcase and in exchange received the sewage disposal job. Two weeks later, Ognyov was nearly strangled to death in the dark by criminals. They took three thousand rubles from him. The ability to leave and enter quarantine evidently provided a number of business opportunities.

Andreev scarcely saw Ognyov during the heyday of his commercial career. Beaten and tormented, Ognyov made a confession to Andreev one night as he returned to his old place:

"They cleaned me out today, but I'll beat them in the end. They think they know cards, but I'll get it all back!"

Ognyov never helped Andreev with bread or money, nor was this the custom in such instances. In terms of camp ethics, he was acting quite normally.

One day Andreev realized with amazement that he had survived. It was extremely difficult to get up from his bunk, but he was able to do it. The main thing was that he didn't have to work and could simply lie prone. Even a pound of bread, three spoons of kasha and a bowl of watery soup were enough to resurrect a person so long as he didn't have to work.

It was at this precise moment that he realized he felt no fear and placed no value on his life. He also knew that he had passed through a great test and had survived. He knew he would be able to use his terrible experience in the mine for his own benefit. The opportunity for a convict to exercise choice, free will, did, in fact, exist—however minutely. Such an opportunity was a reality that could save his life, given the right circumstances. Andreev was prepared for the great battle when he would fight a beast with the cunning of a beast. He had been deceived, and he would deceive. He would not die. He would not permit that to happen.

He would fulfill the desires and commands his body had imparted to him at the gold mine. He had lost the battle at the mine, but it would not be the last he fought. He was the slag rejected from the mine. He had been deceived by his family, deceived by his country. Everything—love, energy, ability— had been crushed and trampled. Any justification the mind might seek was false, a lie, and Andreev knew this. Only the instinct of a beast, roused by the mine, could and did suggest a way out.

Precisely here, on these Cyclopian shelves, Andreev realized that he was worth something, that he could respect himself. He was still alive, and he had neither betrayed nor sold out anyone during the investigation or in the camp. He had succeeded in speaking the truth for the most part, and in suppressing his own fear. It was not that he feared nothing. No, but moral barriers had now been more clearly and precisely defined; everything, in fact, had become clear and precise. It was clear, for example, that Andreev was guilty of nothing. His former health was lost without a trace, broken forever. But was it forever? When Andreev had been first brought to this town, he thought he might live for another two or three weeks. To regain his former strength he would have needed complete rest for many months in resort conditions, with milk and chocolate. Since it was clear, however, that Andreev would never see any such resort, he would have to die. But that was not terrible; many of his comrades had died. Something stronger than death would not permit him to die. Love? Bitterness? No, a person lives by virtue of the same reasons as a tree, a stone, a dog. It was this that Andreev had grasped, had sensed with every fiber of his being precisely here at the city transit prison camp during the typhoid quarantine.

The scratch marks on Andreev's hands and arms healed faster than did his other wounds. Little by little, the turtle-shell armor into which his skin had been transformed disappeared. The bright, rosy tips of his frost-bitten fingers began to darken; the microscopically thin skin, which had covered them after the frostbite blisters ruptured, thickened slightly.

And, above all, he could bend the fingers of his left hand. In a year and a half at the mines, both of Andreev's hands had molded themselves around the handles of a pick and shovel. He never expected to be able to straighten out his hands again. When he ate, he would grasp his spoon by pinching the handle with the tips of his fingers, and he even forgot that a spoon could be held in any other manner. His living hand was like a hook, an artificial limb. It fulfilled only the functions of an artificial hand. He could, if he wished, use it to cross himself when praying to God. But in his heart there was nothing but bitterness, and his spiritual wounds could not so easily be healed. They were never to heal.

At last, to his amazement, Andreev managed to straighten out his left hand one day in the bathhouse. Soon would come the turn of the right hand—still bent claw-fashion. At night Andreev would quietly touch his right hand, and it seemed to him that it was on the verge of opening. He bit his fingernails in the neatest fashion and then proceeded to chew his dirty, thick, slightly moistened skin—a section at a time. This hygenic operation was one of Andreev's few amusements when he was not eating or sleeping.

The bloody cracks on the soles of his feet no longer hurt as much as they used to. The scurvy ulcers on his legs had not yet healed and required bandaging, but his wounds grew fewer and fewer in number, and were replaced by blue-black spots that looked like the brand of some slaveowner. Only his big toes would not heal; the frostbite had reached the bone marrow, and pus slowly seeped from them. Of course, there was less pus than there had been back at the mine, where the rubber galoshes that served as summer footwear were so full of pus and blood that his feet sloshed at every step—as if through a puddle.

Many years would pass before Andreev's toes would heal. And for many years after healing, whenever it was cold or even slightly chilly at night, they would remind him of the northern mine. But Andreev thought of the future. He had learned at the mine not to plan his life further than a day in advance. He strove toward close goals, like any man who is only a short distance from death. Now he desired one thing alone—that the typhoid quarantine might last forever. This, however, could not be, and the day arrived when the quarantine was up.

That morning all the residents of the "section" were driven out into the yard. The prisoners milled around silently, shivering for hours behind the wire fence. The assignment man stood on a barrel and shouted out the names in a hoarse, desperate voice. Those whose names were called left through the gate—never to return. Out on the highway trucks roared— roared so loudly that it was difficult to hear the assignment man.

"Don't let them call me, don't let them call me," Andreev implored the fates in a childish invocation. No, he would not be lucky. If they didn't call for him today, they would call for him tomorrow. He would return to hunger, beatings, and death in the gold mines. His frost-bitten fingers and toes began to ache, as did his ears and cheeks. Andreev shifted his weight more and more frequently from one foot to the other. He raised his shoulders and breathed into his clasped hands, but it was no easy thing to warm his numb hands and sick feet. It all was of no use. He was helpless in the struggle with the monstrous machine whose teeth were grinding up his entire body.

"Voronov! Voronov!" the assignment man called out. "Voronov! The bastard has to be here. . . ." In a rage the assignment man threw the thin yellow folder onto a barrel and put his foot down on the papers.

Suddenly Andreev understood. As lightning shows the way in a storm, so his road to salvation was revealed. In his excitement he immediately grew bold and moved forward toward the assignment man, who was calling out one name after the other. People disappeared from the yard, one after the other. But the crowd was still enormous. Now, now . . .

"Andreev!" the assignment man shouted.

Andreev remained silent and examined the assignment man's shaven jowls. When he had finished his examination, Andreev's gaze shifted to the remaining folders. There were only a few left. "The last truck," Andreev thought.

"Sychov! Answer—first name and patronymic!"

"Vladimir Ivanovich," an elderly convict answered, according to the rules, and pushed the crowd aside.

"Crime? Sentence? Step out!"

A few more persons responded to the assignment officer's call. They left, and the assignment man left with them. The remaining prisoners were returned to the "section."

The coughing, stamping, and shouting quieted down and dissolved into the polyphonic speech of hundreds of men.

Andreev wanted to live. He had set himself two goals and was resolved to achieve them. He saw, with unusual clarity, that he had to lengthen his stay here as long as he could, if possible to the very last day. He had to control himself and not make any mistakes. . . . Gold was death. No one in this transit prison knew that better than Andreev. No matter what the cost, he had to avoid the taiga and the gold mines. How could he, a slave deprived of all rights, manage this?

He had come to the conclusion that the taiga had been depopulated during the quarantine; cold, hunger, exhausting workdays, and sleeplessness must have deprived the taiga of people. That meant that trucks with prisoners would be sent to the mines from quarantine. (Official telegrams read: "Send 200 trees.") Only when all the mines had been filled again would they begin sending people to other places—and not to dig gold in the taiga. Andreev did not care where he was sent. Just as long as it wasn't to mine gold.

Andreev did not say a word about this to anyone. He did not consult with Ognyov or Parfentyev, his comrade from the mines, or with any of the thousand people who lay with him on those warehouse shelves. He knew that, if he were to tell them of his plan, any one of them would rush to tell the camp

authorities—for praise, for a cigarette butt, for no reason at all.
. . . He knew what a heavy burden it was to keep a secret, but
he could do it. Only if he told no one would he be free of fear.
It was two, three, four times easier for him to slip alone
through the teeth of this machine. The game was his alone;
that was something he had learned at the mine.

Andreev "did not respond" for many days. As soon as the
quarantine was up, convicts were again used for work assignments, and the trick was not to be included in the large
groups, since they were usually sent to do earth-moving with
picks, axes, and shovels. In smaller groups of two or three persons it was easier to earn an extra piece of bread or even some
sugar; Andreev had not seen sugar for more than a year and a
half. His strategy was simple and accurate. All these jobs
were, of course, a violation of regulations in the transit prison,
but there were many people who wanted to take advantage of
free labor. People assigned to earth-moving details hoped to be
able to beg for some tobacco or bread. And they succeeded—
even from passers-by. Andreev would go to the vegetable storage areas, where he could eat his fill of beets and carrots and
bring "home" a few raw potatoes, which he would cook in the
ashes of the stove and eat half-raw. Conditions demanded that
all nutritional "functions" be performed quickly; there were
too many hungry people around.

Andreev's days were filled with activity and began to
acquire a certain meaning. He had to stand in the cold every
morning for two hours, listening to the scheduling officer call
out names. And when the daily sacrifice had been made to
Moloch, everyone would tramp back into the barracks, from
where they would be taken to work.

Andreev worked at the bakery, carried garbage at the
women's transit prison, and washed floors in the guards' quarters, where he would gather up the sticky, delicious meat left-
overs from the officers' tables. When work was over,
mountains of bread and large basins of starchy fruit pudding

would be brought to the kitchen, and everyone would sit down, eat, and stuff their pockets with bread.

Most of all Andreev preferred to be sent alone, but that happened rarely. His small-group strategy failed him only once. One day the assignment man, who remembered Andreev's face (but knew him as Muravyov), said to him:

"I found you a job you'll never forget—chopping wood for the camp director. There'll be two of you."

Joyously the two men ran ahead of the guard, who was wearing a cavalry overcoat. The guard slipped, stumbled, jumped over the bottom of his coat with both hands. They soon reached a small house with a locked gate and barbed wire strung along the top of the fence. The camp director's orderly opened the gate, took them without a word to the woodshed, closed the door, and loosed an enormous German shepherd into the yard. The dog kept them locked up until they had cut and split all the wood in the shed. Later that evening they were taken back to camp. They were to be sent back to do the same job the next day, but Andreev hid under his bunk and did no work at all that day.

The next morning, before bread was distributed, a simple idea occurred to Andreev, and he immediately acted upon it. He took off his boots and put them on the edge of the shelf, soles outward, so that it looked as though he himself was lying on the bunk with his boots on. Then he lay down next to them, propping his head on his forearms.

The man distributing bread quickly counted off ten persons and gave Andreev an extra portion of bread. Nevertheless, this method was not reliable, and Andreev again began to seek work outside the barracks.

Did he think of his family? No. Of Freedom? No. Did he recite poetry from memory? No. Did he recall the past? No. He lived in a distracted bitterness, and nothing more.

It was then that Andreev came upon Captain Schneider.

The professional criminals had occupied a place close to

the stove. Their bunks were spread with dirty quilts and pillows of various sizes. A quilt is the inevitable companion of any successful thief, the only object that he carries with him from prison to prison. If a thief does not own a quilt, he will steal one or take it away from another prisoner. As for the pillow, it is not only a rest for his head, but it can be quickly converted into a table for endless card battles. Such a table can be given any form. But it is still a pillow. Card players will lose their pants before they will part with their pillows.

The more prominent criminals, that is, those who were the most prominent at that moment, were sitting on the quilts and pillows. Higher up, on the third shelf, where it was dark, lay other pillows and quilts. It was there that the criminals maintained the young effeminate thieves and their various other companions. Almost all the thieves were homosexuals.

The hardened criminals were surrounded by a crowd of vassals and lackeys, for the criminals considered it fashionable to be interested in "novels" narrated orally by prisoners of literary inclination. And even in these conditions there were court barbers with bottles of perfume and a throng of sycophants eager to perform any service in exchange for a piece of bread or a bowl of soup.

"Shut up! Senechka is talking. Be quiet! Senechka wants to sleep . . ."

It had been a familiar scene back at the mine.

Suddenly, among the crowd of beggars and the retinue of criminals, Andreev saw a familiar face and recognized the man's voice. There was no doubt about it—it was Captain Schneider, Andreev's cellmate in Butyr Prison.

Captain Schneider was a German communist who had been active in the Comintern, spoke beautiful Russian, was an expert on Goethe and an educated Marxist theoretician. Andreev's memory had preserved conversations with Schneider, intense conversations that took place during the long prison nights. A naturally cheerful person, this former sea captain kept the entire cell in good spirits.

Andreev could not believe his eyes.

"Schneider!"

"What do you want?" the captain turned around. His dull blue eyes showed no recognition of Andreev.

"Schneider!"

"So what do you want? You'll wake up Senechka."

But already the edge of the blanket had been lifted, and the light revealed a pale, unhealthy face.

"Ah, captain," came Senechka's tenor voice with a languid tone. "I can't fall asleep without you . . ."

"Right away, I'm coming," Schneider said hurriedly.

He climbed up on the shelf, folded back the edge of the blanket, sat down, and put his hand under the blanket to scratch Senechka's heels.

Andreev walked slowly to his place. He had no desire to go on living. Even though this was a trivial event by comparison with that which he had seen and was still destined to witness, he never forgot Captain Schneider.

The number of people kept decreasing. The transit prison was being emptied. Andreev came face to face with the assignment man.

"What's your name?"

Andreev, however, had prepared himself for such an occurrence.

"Gurov," he replied meekly.

"Wait!"

The assignment man leafed through the onion-sheet lists.

"No, it's not here."

"Can I go?"

"Go ahead, you animal!" the scheduling officer roared.

Once he was assigned to wash dishes and clean up the cafeteria for people who had served their sentences and who were about to be released. His partner was one of those "goners" who were so emaciated they were known as "wicks." The man had just been released from prison, and it was difficult to determine his age. It was the first time this "goner" had worked. He kept asking what they should do, would they be fed, was it all right to ask for something to eat before they began work.

The man said he was a professor of neuropathology, and Andreev recognized his name.

Andreev knew from experience that camp cooks (and not only camp cooks) did not like these "Ivan Ivanoviches," as the intellectuals were contemptuously nicknamed. He advised the professor not to ask for anything in advance and gloomily thought that he himself would have to do most of the work, since the professor was too weak. This was only just, and there was no reason to be offended; Andreev himself had been a bad, weak "partner" any number of times, and no one had ever said a word to him. Where were they all now? Where were Scheinin, Riutin, Khvostov? They had all died, and he alone, Andreev, had been resurrected. Of course, his resurrection was yet to come, but he would return to life.

Andreev's suspicions were confirmed: the professor was a weak, albeit fussy partner.

When the work was finished, the cook sat them down and placed an enormous tub of thick fish soup and a large plate of kasha before them. The professor threw up his hands in delight, but Andreev had seen men at the mines eat twenty meals, each consisting of three dishes and bread. He cast a suspicious glance at the proffered refreshments.

"No bread?" Andreev asked gloomily.

"Of course there's bread—a little." And the cook took two pieces of bread from a cupboard.

They quickly polished off the food. On such "visits" the prudent Andreev always saved his bread in his pocket. The professor, on the contrary, gulped the soup, broke off pieces of bread, and chewed it while large drops of dirty sweat formed on his shaven gray head.

"Here's a ruble for each of you," the cook said. "I don't have any more bread today."

This was magnificent payment. There was a commissary at the transit prison, where the civilians could buy bread. Andreev told the professor about this.

"Yes, you're right," the professor said. "But I saw that they also sold sweet *kvas* there. Or was it lemonade? I really want some lemonade, anything sweet."

"It's up to you, professor, but if I were you, I'd buy bread."

"Yes, I know, you're right," the professor repeated, "but I really want some sweet lemonade. Why don't you get some too?"

Andreev rejected that suggestion out of hand.

Ultimately Andreev managed to get himself assigned to washing floors alone at the bookkeeping office. Every evening he would meet the orderly, whose duties included keeping the office clean. These were two tiny rooms crowded with desks, each of which occupied more than four square yards. The work took only about ten minutes, and at first Andreev could not understand why the orderly "hired" someone to do the job. The orderly had to carry water through the entire camp himself, and clean rags were always prepared in advance when Andreev came. The payment was generous—cheap tobacco, soup, kasha, bread, and sugar. The orderly even promised to give Andreev a light jacket, but Andreev's stay came to an end before he managed to do that.

Evidently the orderly viewed washing floors as shameful so long as he could hire some "hard worker" to do it for him—even if it required only five minutes a day. Andreev had observed this characteristic in Russian people at the mines. If the head of the camp gave an orderly a handful of tobacco to clean the barracks, the orderly would dump half the tobacco into his pouch, and with the other half would hire a "political" to do the job for him. The latter, in turn, would again divide up the tobacco and hire someone from his barracks for two hand-rolled cigarettes. This man, who had just finished a twelve- or fourteen-hour shift, would wash the floor at night for these two cigarettes and consider himself lucky; he could trade the cigarettes for bread.

Currency questions represent the most complex area of camp economy. Standards of measurement are amazing. Tea, tobacco, and bread are the exchangeable, "hard" currencies.

On occasion the orderly would pay Andreev with coupons redeemable in the kitchen. These were rubber-stamped pieces of cardboard that worked rather like tokens—ten dinners, five main courses, and so on. When the orderly gave Andreev a token worth twenty portions of kasha, the twenty portions did not cover the bottom of a tin basin.

Andreev watched the professional criminals shove bright yellow thirty-ruble notes through the window, folded to look like tokens. This tactic always produced results. A large bowl filled to the brim with kasha would inevitably emerge from the window in response to such a token.

There were fewer and fewer people left in the transit prison. Finally the day arrived when the last truck was dispatched from the yard, and only two or three dozen men remained in camp.

This time they were not dismissed to the barracks but were grouped in military formation and led through the entire camp.

"Whatever they intend to do, they can't be taking us to be shot," an enormous one-eyed man next to Andreev said.

This was precisely what Andreev had been thinking: They couldn't be taking them to be shot. All the remaining prisoners were brought to the assignment man in the bookkeeping office.

"We're going to take your fingerprints," the assignment man said as he came out onto the porch.

"Well, if it's come to that, you can have me without raising a finger," the one-eyed man said cheerfully. "My name is Filipovsky."

"How about you?"

"Pavel Andreev."

The assignment man found their files.

"We've been looking for you for a long time," he said without a trace of anger.

Andreev knew that he had won his battle for life. It was simply impossible for the taiga not to have sated its hunger for people. Even if they were to be shipped off, it would be to some nearby, local site. It might even be in the town itself. That would be even better. Andreev had been classified only for "light physical labor," but he knew how abruptly such a classification could be changed. It was not his classification that would save him, but the fact that the taiga's orders had already been filled. Only local sites, where life was easier, simpler, less hungry, were still waiting for their final deliveries. There were no gold mines in the area, and that meant there was hope for survival. This Andreev had learned during the two years he had spent at the mines and these three months in quarantine, spent under animal-like tension. Too much had been accomplished for his hopes not to be realized.

He had to wait only one night for an answer.

After breakfast, the assignment man rushed into the barracks with a list—a small list, Andreev immediately noted with satisfaction. Lists for the mines inevitably contained twenty-five men assigned to a truck, and there were always several of such sheets—not just one.

Andreev and Filipovsky were on the same list. There were other people as well—only a few, but more than just two or three.

Those whose names were on the list were taken to the familiar door of the bookkeeping department. There were three other men standing there: a gray-haired, sedate old man of imposing appearance wearing a good sheepskin coat and felt boots; a fidgety, dirty man dressed in a quilted jacket and quilted pants with footcloths instead of socks protruding from the edges of his rubber galoshes. The third was wearing a fur jacket and a fur hat.

"That's the lot of them," the assignment man said. "Will they do?"

The man in the fur jacket crooked his finger at the old man.

"Who are you?"

"Yury Izgibin. Convicted under Article Fifty-Eight of the criminal code. Sentence: twenty-five years," the old man reported vigorously.

"No, no," the fur jacket frowned. "What's your trade? I can learn your case history without your help . . ."

"Stove builder, sir."

"Anything else?"

"I'm a tinsmith as well."

"Very good."

"How about you?" the officer shifted his gaze to Filipovsky.

The one-eyed giant said that he had been a stoker on a steamboat based in Kamenets-Podolsk.

"And how about you?"

The dignified old man unexpectedly muttered a few words in German.

"What's that all about?" the fur jacket asked with an air of curiosity.

"That's our carpenter. His name is Frisorger, and he does good work. He sort of lost his bearings, but he'll be all right."

"Why does he speak German?"

"He's from the German Autonomous Republic of Saratov."

"Ah. . . . And how about you?" This last question was directed at Andreev.

"He needs tradesmen and working people in general," Andreev thought. "I'll be a leather dresser."

"Tanner, sir."

"Good. How old are you?"

"Thirty-one."

The officer shook his head. But since he was an experienced man and had seen people rise from the dead, he said nothing and shifted his gaze to the fifth man, who turned out to be a member of the Esperantist Society.

"You see, I'm an agronomist. I even lectured on agronomy. But I was arrested as an esperantist."

"What's that—spying?" the fur coat asked indifferently.

"Something like that," the fidgety man responded.

"What do you say?" the assignment asked.

"I'll take them," the officer said. "You can't find better ones anyway. They've all been picked over."

All five were taken to a separate room in the barracks. But there were still two or three names left in the list. Andreev was sure of that. The scheduling officer arrived.

"Where are we going?"

"To a local site, where do you think?" the assignment man said. "Here's your boss."

"We'll send you off in an hour. You've had three months to 'fatten up,' friends. It's time to get on the road."

They were all summoned in an hour—not to a truck, but to the storeroom. "They probably want to change clothes," Andreev thought. "April is here, and it'll soon be spring." They would issue summer clothing, and he would be able to turn in his hated winter mine clothing—just cast it aside and forget it. Instead of summer clothing, however, they were issued winter clothing. Could this be an error? No, "winter clothing" was marked in red pencil on the list.

Not understanding anything, they donned quilted vests, pea jackets, and old, patched felt boots. Jumping over the puddles, they returned to the barracks room, from which they had come to the storehouse.

Everyone was extremely nervous and silent. Only Frisorger kept muttering something in German.

"He's praying, damn him . . ." Filipovsky whispered to Andreev.

"Does anyone understand what's happening?" Andreev asked.

The gray-haired stove builder who looked like a professor was enumerating all the "near sites": the port, a mine four kilometers from Magadan, one seventeen kilometers from Magadan, another twenty-three kilometers from the city, and still another forty-seven kilometers away. . . . Then he started on road construction sites—places that were only slightly better than gold mines.

The assignment man came running.

"Come on out! March to the gate."

Everyone left the building and went to the gates of the transit prison. Beyond the gates stood a large truck, the bed of which was covered with a green tarpaulin.

"Guards, assume command and take your prisoners."

The guard did a head count. Andreev felt his legs and back grow cold. . . .

"Get in the truck!"

The guard threw back the edge of the large tarpaulin; the truck was filled with people dressed in winter clothing.

"Get in!"

All five climbed in together. All were silent. The guard got in the cab, the motor roared up, and the truck moved down the road leading to the main "highway."

"They're taking us to the mine four kilometers from Magadan," the stove builder said.

Posts marking kilometers floated past. All five put their heads together near a crack in the canvas. They could not believe their eyes. . . .

"Seventeen . . ."

"Twenty-three . . ." Filipovsky said.

"A local mine, the bastards!" the stove builder hissed in a rage.

For a long time the truck wound down the twisted highway between the crags. The mountains resembled barge haulers with bent backs.

"Forty-seven," the fidgety esperantist squealed in despair.

The truck rushed on.

"Where are we going?" Andreev asked, gripping some-one's shoulder.

"We'll spend the night at Atka, 208 kilometers from Magadan."

"And after that?"

"I don't know. . . . Give me a smoke."

Puffing heavily, the truck climbed a pass in the Yablonovy Range.

Handwriting

>>>

LATE ONE NIGHT, Chris was summoned to "headquarters." That was how people in camp referred to the small house at the foot of the hill on the edge of the settlement. In this house lived the investigator who handled "particularly important matters." The phrase was a joke, since there were no "matters" that were not particularly important. Any violation of the rules or even the appearance of such a violation was punishable by death. It was either death or a verdict of total innocence. But what man had lived to tell the tale of such a verdict?

Prepared for everything and indifferent to everything, Chris walked down the narrow path leading to headquarters. The path was beaten down thoroughly. A light was burning in the bakery—probably the bread slicer cutting up "rations" for tomorrow's breakfast. Would there be a breakfast or even a tomorrow for Chris? He did not know, and he drew pleasure from his ignorance. Chris came upon something that looked like a chunk of snow or a piece of ice. He bent down, picked up the frozen object, and realized it was a turnip skin. The skin thawed quickly in his hands, and Chris stuffed it into his mouth. There obviously was no sense in hurrying. Chris examined the whole length of the long, snowy path from the barracks, and he realized that he was the first to walk along it that day. The path led along the outskirts of the settlement to the investigator's house. All along the way were frozen pieces of turnip that looked as if they were wrapped in cellophane. Chris found ten chunks—some larger, some smaller. It had been a long time since he had seen people who could discard turnip skins in the snow. It had to be a civilian, and not a convict. Perhaps it was the investigator himself. Chris chewed and swallowed all the skins. There was a smell in his mouth that he had long since forgotten—the smell of his native earth, of fresh vegetables. In a joyous mood Chris knocked at the investigator's door.

The investigator was short, thin, and unshaven. The room contained only his desk and an iron cot with a military blanket and a wrinkled grimy pillow. . . . The desk was a homemade table with rough-hewn drawers crammed with papers. A box of filing cards stood on the windowsill. The bric-a-brac shelf was also heaped with thick folders. There was an ashtray made from a tin can. On the wall a windup clock showed 10:30. The investigator was heating up the cast-iron stove with papers. He was pale—like all investigators. There was no orderly, and no revolver.

"Sit down, Chris," the investigator said, using the polite form of address as he shoved a stool in Chris's direction. He himself sat on a homemade chair with a high back.

"I've examined your case," the investigator said, "and I want to make you an offer. I don't know if you'll find it appropriate."

Chris froze in expectation. The investigator was silent for a few moments.

"I have to know a little more about you."

Chris raised his head and could not restrain a belch—a pleasant belch with the taste of fresh turnip.

"Write an application."

"An application?"

"Yes, an application. Here's a piece of paper and a pen."

"What kind of application? About what? To whom?"

"Anyone you like! If you don't want to do an application, write out a poem by Blok. It doesn't make any difference. Do you understand? Write out Pushkin's 'Bird.' " He began to declaim:

> I smashed a dungeon yesterday
> And freed my captive to the park,
> Returned a singer to the May
> And gave back freedom to a lark.

"That's not Pushkin," Chris whispered, straining all the faculties of his withered brain.

"Whose is it then?"

"Tumansky."

"Tumansky? Never heard of him."

"I understand. You need evidence. To see if I killed someone. Or maybe I wrote a letter to the 'outside?' Or forged some chits for the camp thugs?"

"That's not it at all. We never have trouble gathering that sort of evidence." The investigator smiled, revealing his swollen, bleeding gums and small teeth. Brief as the flash of his smile was, it nevertheless brightened the room and Chris's soul as well. He couldn't help staring at the investigator's mouth.

"Yes," the investigator said, catching his gaze, "it's scurvy. The civilians get it too. There aren't any fresh vegetables."

Chris thought about the turnip. There are more vitamins in the skin than in the meat. Chris, and not the investigator, had gotten the vitamins. Chris wanted to hold up his end of the conversation and tell how he had sucked and chewed the turnip rind that the investigator had cast aside, but he was afraid of seeming overly casual.

"Do you understand me or not? I need to take a look at your handwriting."

Chris understood nothing.

"Write," the investigator commanded: " 'To the chief of the mine from Convict Chris. Year of birth, crime, sentence. Application. I request to be transferred to an easier job.' That's enough."

The investigator took Chris's unfinished application, tore it up, and threw it into the fire. . . . The light from the stove burned brighter for a moment.

"Sit down to the desk. At the corner."

Chris had the calligraphic handwriting of a professional scribe. He himself drew pleasure from his handwriting, but all his friends laughed at it, saying it was not the handwriting of a professor and doctor of science. It was the handwriting of a quartermaster, and not that of a scholar, a writer, a poet. His friends joked and said he could have made a career for himself as a scribe for the czar in the story by Kuprin.

These jokes did not bother Chris, however, and he continued to recopy his manuscripts before giving them to the typists. The typists were pleased, but they too secretly laughed at this aberration.

His fingers, which had become accustomed to the handles of a pick and shovel, struggled to pick up the pen.

"Everything is chaos and disorder here," the investigator said. "I understand that, but you'll help me straighten things out."

"Of course, of course," Chris said. The stove was already hot, and the room had warmed up.

"If I could only have a smoke . . ."

"I don't smoke," the investigator said rudely. "I don't have any bread either. You won't go to work tomorrow. I'll tell the assignment man."

In this way, for several months, Chris would come once a week to the unheated, inhospitable house of the camp investigator, recopy papers, and file them.

The snowless winter of 1937–38 had already entered the barracks in death-dealing winds. Each night assignment men would run to the barracks, search for people on their lists, and wake them up to be shipped off. Even before, no one had ever returned from these journeys, but now no one even gave a thought to these nocturnal affairs. If they were preparing a group, there was nothing to be done. The work was too hard to leave a thought for anything else.

Work hours increased and guards were added, but the week passed, and Chris could barely drag himself to the investigator's familiar office to continue the endless job of filing papers. Chris stopped washing himself and shaving, but the investigator didn't seem to notice his fleshless cheeks and inflamed eyes. In spite of his hunger, Chris continued to copy and file, but the quantity of papers and folders kept growing and growing to the point where it was impossible to get them in order. Chris copied out endless lists containing only surnames. The top edge of each list was folded over, but Chris never made any attempt to learn the secret of these operations, even though he had only to lift the bent-back edge. Sometimes the investigator would take a stack of "cases" of mysterious origin and hurriedly dictate them to Chris to copy down.

The dictation would end at midnight, and Chris would return to his barracks and sleep and sleep. The next day's work assignments did not concern him. Week followed week, and Chris continued to lose weight and to write for this investigator, who was young enough to be his son.

Once the investigator picked up the latest file to read the name of the latest victim and bit his lip. He looked at Chris and asked:

"What's your full name?"

When Chris told him, the investigator's face grew whiter than snow. His quick fingers leafed through the thin papers included in the file; there were no more and no less than in any of the other files lying on the floor. The investigator flung open the stove door, and the room became so bright that it seemed that a soul had been bared to reveal something very important and human at its core. The investigator ripped the folder into shreds, which he shoved into the stove. The room became even brighter. Chris understood nothing. Without looking at Chris, the investigator said: "You'd think they were using a stencil. They don't know what they're doing, and they don't care." And he stared at Chris with resolute eyes.

"Let's continue. Are you ready?"

"I'm ready," Chris said. Only many years later did he realize that the burned file had been his own.

Many of Chris's friends were shot. The investigator was also shot. But Chris was still alive, and at least once every few years he would remember the burning folder and the investigator's decisive fingers as he tore up his "case"—a present to the doomed from the giver of doom.

Chris had a life-saving, calligraphic handwriting.

PART TWO

EATING

Vaska Denisov, Kidnapper of Pigs

>>>

HE HAD TO BORROW a pea jacket from a friend for this evening's journey. Vaska's own pea jacket was too dirty and torn
for him to take two steps through the civilian village. Anyone
might stop him.

People like Vaska could pass through the village only two
by two, with a guard. Neither the local military types nor the
civilian nonconvicts liked to see his kind walk alone on the
village streets. His kind didn't cause suspicion only when carrying firewood.

A small log was buried in the snow near the garage—next
to the sixth telegraph pole from the corner, in the ditch. That
had been done yesterday after work.

The driver slowed the truck, and, leaning over the edge of
the bed, Vaska slid to the ground. He at once found the place
where he had buried the log. The bluish snow was darker
there and slightly packed down; you could see that in the early
twilight. Vaska jumped into the ditch and kicked the snow
aside. The log appeared—gray and flat like a large frozen fish.
Vaska dragged the log out onto the road, stood it upright,
tapped it to knock off the snow, and bent down to put his
shoulder under it as he lifted it with his hands. He strode off
to the village, changing shoulders from time to time. He was
weak and exhausted, and he warmed up from the exercise
right away, but the warmth didn't last long. In spite of the
weight of the log, Vaska could not stay warm. Twilight thickened into a white fog, and the village lit all its yellow electric
lights. Vaska smiled, pleased with his calculation; in the white
fog he would easily reach his goal unnoticed. There was the
enormous broken larch tree and the stump, silver in the fog.
That meant it was the next house.

Vaska threw the log down by the porch, brushed the snow from his felt boots with his mittens, and knocked at the door, which opened to admit him. An elderly bare-headed woman in an unbuttoned sheepskin coat stared at him anxiously as if awaiting an explanation.

"I brought you some wood," Vaska said, struggling to spread the frozen skin of his face into the creases of a smile. "Could I speak to Ivan Petrovich?"

But Ivan Petrovich was already on the way out, holding the curtain up with his hand.

"Good," he said. "Where is it?"

"Outside," Vaska said.

"Wait and we'll saw it up. Let me get dressed." Ivan Petrovich took a long time hunting for his mittens. The two men went out onto the porch and cut the log in half without any sawhorses, holding it between their legs and raising it with their hands when necessary. The saw was dull and badly set.

"You can come by some other time," Ivan Petrovich said, "and set the teeth. Here's a splitting ax. Bring it right into the apartment when you're done. Don't leave it in the corridor."

Vaska's head was spinning from hunger, but he split the log into smaller pieces and carried them all into the house.

"Well, that's all," the woman said, coming out from behind the curtain. "That's all."

Vaska would not leave but stood shifting from one foot to the other. Ivan Petrovich appeared again.

"Listen," he said. "I don't have any bread just now. We gave all the soup to the pigs, so I don't have anything to give you. You can drop by next week. . . ."

Vaska remained silent but would not leave.

Ivan Petrovich searched through his wallet.

"Here's three rubles for you. Just for you, for such good wood. As for tobacco, you know it's really expensive nowadays."

Vaska stuck the wrinkled three-ruble note inside his shirt and left. Three rubles wouldn't buy even a pinch of tobacco.

Nauseous from hunger, he remained standing on the porch. The pigs had eaten Vaska's bread and soup. Vaska took out the green three-ruble note and tore it into tiny shreds. For a long time shreds of paper, seized by the wind, blew along the shining, polished snow crust. And when the last fragments had disappeared in the white fog, Vaska stepped down from the porch. Swaying slightly from weakness, he walked—not home, but through the village. He kept walking and walking—past one-storied, two-storied, and three-storied palaces. . . .

He walked up to the first porch and jerked the door handle. The door squeaked and gave way. Vaska walked into a dark corridor dimly lit by a dull electric bulb. He walked past the apartment doors. At the end of the corridor was a storage room, and Vaska leaned against the door, opened it, and stepped over the threshold. In the storeroom stood some sacks of onion, and perhaps salt. Vaska ripped open one of the sacks—barley. Angry and excited, he sank his shoulder into the sack and pushed it aside. Under the sack lay frozen hog carcasses. Vaska yelped with joy, but he was too weak to tear even a hunk from one of the carcasses. Farther back, under the sacks, lay frozen suckling pigs, and Vaska could see nothing else. He ripped free one of the frozen suckling pigs and, holding it in his arms like a baby, moved toward the door. But people were already coming out of the rooms, and white fog was filling the corridor. Someone shouted "Stop!" and dived at his legs. Vaska jumped upward, clutching the piglet in his arms, and ran out into the street. The residents of the house ran after him. Someone shot at him, someone bellowed like a beast, but Vaska ran on, seeing nothing. In a few minutes he realized that his legs were taking him of their own accord to the only official building that he knew in the village—the headquarters for "vitamin" expeditions, where Vaska had himself once worked as a gatherer of dwarf cedar, the needles of which were boiled for vitamin C.

The chase was close. Leaping up onto the porch, Vaska pushed the man on duty aside, and rushed down the corridor, the crowd hot on his heels. He ran to the office of the recreation officer and from there fled through a different door—to the lounge. There was no place else to run. Only then did Vaska realize that he had lost his hat. The frozen piglet was still in his hands. Vaska put the pig down, overturned the massive benches, and propped the door shut with them. Then he dragged the podium up against the doors as well. Someone shook the door handle, and silence ensued.

There and then Vaska sat down on the floor, took the raw piglet in both hands and started to gnaw.

When the guards arrived, the doors were opened, and the barricade was removed. Vaska had eaten half of the pig.

Fire and Water

>>

I'VE BEEN TESTED by fire on more than one occasion. As a boy I once ran down the streets of a blazing wooden town, and the brilliantly illuminated streets etched themselves forever into my memory. It was as if the town were dissatisfied with the sun and had itself demanded fire. Power surged from the spreading conflagration. Although there was no wind, the houses growled and shook their bodies, flinging burning boards onto the roofs of buildings on the other side of the street.

Inside the town it was clear, dry, warm, and bright, and I easily and fearlessly walked down those blazing streets that let me, a boy, pass, although they were about to be totally destroyed. Only the river saved the main area of town; everything up to the bank burned to the ground.

Another time, as an adult, I experienced the same sensation of calm during a fire. Childhood had long since slipped away, and I was a convict finishing a sentence in a geological prospecting group in the Urals. The expedition's storehouse had caught fire, but there was no fire engine available, and no bucket brigade could have put out the growing conflagration, even though the river was near.

The storehouse contained a great deal of equipment, and the head of the expedition realized that punishment—probably with implications of sabotage—would be meted out for the fire. He begged people to help, but none of the convicts would go into the fire. He promised everything he could think of—freedom, a hundred working days taken off our sentence for every day, every hour of the fire. Even though I didn't believe those empty promises, I went into the fire, because I wasn't afraid of it. Some of the camp authorities, seeing that we weren't perishing, themselves crossed the threshold of the burning storehouse's open gates.

It was nighttime, and the storehouse was dark. We could never have reached the leveling instruments and theodolites, could never have unpacked the numerous sacks of powder if it hadn't been for the fire. The fire illuminated the walls of the storehouse like a stage. It became dry, warm, bright. We dragged almost everything to the river bank. Only a heap of clothing in the corner was destroyed—work clothes, sheepskin coats, felt boots.

The head of the expedition was more angry than pleased, since he was left with all the same problems: someone would have to pay for the destroyed clothing. I never received a single day's credit for my efforts. No one even thanked me for fighting the fire. But I felt again my childhood sensation of fearlessness near the fire.

I've seen a lot of fires in the taiga. I've walked across luxurious blue moss a yard thick with patterns etched into it as if it were a fabric. I've picked my way through larch forests felled by flame. The trees, roots and all, had been torn from the soil, not by the wind, but by fire. Fire was like a storm, creating its own wind, hurling trees onto their sides, and leaving a black path through the taiga forever. And then collapsing helplessly on a river bank. A bright yellow flame would scamper through the dry grass, which would shake and sway as if a snake were crawling through it. But there are no snakes in Kolyma.

A yellow flame would race up the trunk of a larch, gather strength, roar, and shake the trunk. The trees' convulsions, death convulsions, were always the same. I have often seen the hippocratic death mask of a tree.

It had been raining for three days at the hospital, and I couldn't help but remember the fire. Rain would have saved the town, the geologists' storehouse, the burning taiga. Water is stronger than fire.

All recuperating patients were sent out to gather mushrooms and berries across the river, where blueberries and cowberries grew in unbelievable quantities and where there were veritable thickets of colorful mushrooms with slippery cold caps. The mushrooms seemed cold—like live cold-blooded animals, like snakes. They seemed like anything but mushrooms.

Mushrooms appear late. Sometimes they come after the rains, but not every year. But when they do appear, they surround every tent, fill every forest, pack the underbrush.

We were to gather them in baskets, sort them for drying or marinating by Uncle Sasha, the camp cook who, on this occasion at least, recalled his glorious past as a cook in Moscow's fashionable Prague Restaurant and his culinary education in Geneva. Uncle Sasha had been a chef at government dinners, and had even once been entrusted with preparing a meal in honor of the arrival of William Bullitt, the first American ambassador to the Soviet Union. The dinner was in the Russian style, the Russian genre. There was borscht, Russian cabbage soup, suckling pig with kasha. Uncle Sasha's assistants brought five hundred miniature ceramic pots from Kostroma. Each held a single serving of kasha. The creation was a success.

Bullitt praised the kasha. But the suckling pig! Bullitt pushed the pig away, ate the kasha, and asked for a second portion. Uncle Sasha was awarded the Order of Lenin.

Soon after that, Uncle Sasha was arrested. It was recorded in his file that Filippov, the director of the Moscow restaurant, The Prague, had invited Uncle Sasha to become head chef, promised him an apartment, an enormous salary, and trips abroad. "Soon after I switched to The Prague, Filippov asked me to poison the government. And I agreed."

Uncle Sasha directed our labors. Gathering wild mushrooms and berries is one of the Kolyma psychoses. We did it every day.

Today it was cold. There was a chilling wind, but it had stopped raining, and the pale autumn sky could be seen through the torn clouds, clearly indicating that it wasn't going to rain.

We had to go. A patient in the convict hospital couldn't feel secure if he wasn't doing something for the doctor, for the hospital. The women would crochet, a carpenter would make a table, an engineer would use a ruler to make up a supply of blank forms, a laborer would bring a basket of mushrooms or a bucket of berries.

We didn't choose to go for mushrooms; we had to go. There was a rich harvest after the rain, and three of us set out across the river in a small boat—just as we did every morning. The water was rising slightly, the current was swifter than usual, and the waves were darker.

Safonov pointed his finger at the water and then upriver, and we all understood what he meant.

"We've got enough time. There are a lot of mushrooms," Verigin said.

"We can't go back," I said.

"Let's do it this way," Safonov said. "The sun will be right

opposite that mountain at four o'clock. Let's return to the
shore at four. We'll tie the boat upstream."

We split up in various directions—each of us had his
favorite spot.

But as soon as I had entered the forest, I realized there
was no need to hurry. A mushroom kingdom lay right here at
my feet. The mushroom caps were as big as a man's cap or the
palm of his hand. It didn't take long to fill two big baskets. I
carried the baskets out to the meadow, near the tractor road,
so I could find them right away and set off to at least take a
look at the spots that I had selected long before.

I entered the forest, and my mushroom-gatherer's soul
was shaken. Everywhere were enormous mushrooms standing separately—higher than the grass, higher than the cowberry bushes. The firm, resilient, fresh mushrooms were
incredible.

Beaten by the Kolyma rains, these mushrooms had grown
into monsters with caps a half-yard in diameter. They grew
everywhere the eye could see—so fresh, so firm, so healthy
that it was impossible to make any decision other than to go
back, throw away everything I had gathered earlier, and
return to the hospital with these magical mushrooms in my
hands.

And that was exactly what I did.

It was all a question of time, but I calculated I would need
half an hour to get back down the path.

I descended the hill and pulled the bushes aside. Cold
water covered the path for yards. The path had disappeared
under water while I had been gathering mushrooms.

The forest rustled, and the cold water rose higher. An
ever-increasing roar could be heard. I walked back up the hill
and around the mountain to the right, to the place where we
were to meet. I didn't abandon the mushrooms; the two heavy
baskets hung from my shoulders, tied together with a towel.

From higher up on the hillside, I approached the grove

where our boat was supposed to be. The water had already reached the spot and was rising.

I climbed a hill on the shore.

The river was roaring, ripping up trees and flinging them into the current. Not a single shrub remained of the grove where we had beached that morning. The soil holding the trees had been washed away and the trees had been ripped up and carried off. The terrible muscular strength of the water was like that of a wrestler. The far shore was rocky, and the river was forced to vent its rage upon the wooded bank where I stood. The stream that we had crossed in the morning had long since been transformed into a monster.

It was getting dark, and I realized I had to retreat to the mountain and wait there for dawn—as far as possible from the raging, icy waters. Soaked to the skin, constantly slipping in the water, jumping from one hummock to another, I dragged the baskets to the foot of the mountain. The autumn night was black, starless, and cold, and the dull growl of the river drowned out any voices that I might have been able to hear.

Suddenly a light gleamed from a narrow valley, and I didn't even realize at first that it was not an evening star, but a bonfire. Could it be escaped convicts? Geologists? Fishermen? Hay mowers? I set out in the direction of the fire, leaving two baskets near a large tree so I could pick them up at dawn. The small basket I took with me.

Distances in the taiga are deceptive. A hut, a boulder, a forest, a river, a sea can be much nearer or farther away than they seem. The decision "yes or no" was a simple one. There was a fire, and I had to go there; that was all there was to it. The fire was another important power in the night. A saving power. I was prepared to walk as long as might be necessary—even if I had to feel my way. After all, the nocturnal fire meant people, life, salvation.

I walked along the valley, careful not to lose sight of the fire. After a half hour I circled an enormous boulder and sud-

denly saw a campfire before me—higher up, on a stone out-
cropping. The fire was burning before a tent that was as low
as a rock. People were sitting round the fire. They paid no
attention to me. I didn't ask what they were doing here but
walked up to the fire to get warm. I wanted to eat, but it is not
the custom to ask strangers for bread in Kolyma. They were
convict hay mowers from the hospital—the same hospital for
which I had been gathering mushrooms.

I couldn't ask for bread, but I could ask for an empty tin
can. They gave me a smudged, dented pot in which I scooped
up some water and boiled one of the mushroom giants.

The head mower unwrapped a dirty rag and silently
handed me a piece of salt, and soon the water in the pot began
to leap and squeak as it whitened with foam and heat. I ate
the tasteless monster mushroom, washed it down with boiling
water, and warmed up a little.

As I drowsed by the fire, dawn came slowly and silently,
and I set off for the river bank without thanking the mowers
for their hospitality. I could see my two baskets a half-mile
away. The water level was already dropping. I made my way
through the forest, clutching at those trees that had survived.
Their branches were broken, and their bark was ripped off. I
picked my way along the stones, occasionally stepping on
heaps of mountain sand. I approached the shore; yes, it was a
shore—a new shore defined by the wavering line of the flood
waters. Still heavy from the rains, the river rushed past, but it
was obvious that the water level was dropping.

Far away, very far away—on the other shore, which
seemed like the other shore of life—I could see figures waving
their arms. I saw the boat and began to wave my arms as well.
They understood me. The boat was carried upstream on poles
about a mile from the spot where I was standing. Safonov and
Verigin brought it in much farther downstream than the spot
where I stood. Safonov handed me my bread ration of 600
grams—a little more than a pound—but I had no appetite.

I dragged out my baskets with the miracle mushrooms.

What with the rain and my having hauled them through the forest at night and bumping them against the trees in the dark, there were only pieces left in the basket—pieces of mushroom.

"Maybe we should throw them away?" Verigin said.

"No, what for . . ."

"We threw ours away yesterday. Barely managed to get the boat across. We thought of you," Safanov said firmly, "but we decided we'd really get it in the neck if we lost the boat. No one would give a damn about you."

"No one gives a damn about me," I said.

"That's right. Neither we, nor the chief would get in trouble over you, but the boat. . . . Did I do the right thing?"

"Yes, you did the right thing," I said.

"Get in," Safonov said, "and take those damn baskets."

We pushed off from shore and began our journey back— a tiny boat in the still-heaving and stormy river.

Back at the hospital we were met without cursing or joy. Safonov was right to give first priority to the boat.

I had dinner, supper, and breakfast. Then I had dinner and supper. When I had eaten my entire two-day ration, I began to feel sleepy. I got warm. But for perfect bliss I needed tea—just boiling water, of course. Only the camp administrators drank real tea.

I sat down next to the barracks stove and put a pot of water on the fire—tame water on a tame fire. Soon the water began to leap furiously in the pot. But I was already asleep.

The Theft

>>

A GRAY SNOW WAS FALLING, the sky was gray, the ground was gray, and climbing from one snowy hill to another, the chain of people stretched along the entire horizon. We had to wait for a long time while the work-gang leader got his group into formation—as if some general were hidden beyond the hill.

The work gang lined up in pairs, and turned off the path—the shortest way home to the barracks—onto another road that had not yet been beaten down by convict feet. A tractor had passed this way recently, and the snow had not yet covered its tracks, which looked like the spoor of some prehistoric beast. The going was harder here than on the path, and everyone was hurrying. Every so often someone would stumble, fall behind, pull his snow-filled felt boots out of a drift, and rush to catch up with his comrades. Suddenly, as we came around an enormous snowdrift, there appeared the dark figure of a man in an enormous white sheepskin coat. Only when we came closer did I realize that the snowdrift was a low stack of flour sacks. A truck must have gotten stuck here, unloaded, and been towed away empty by the tractor.

The work gang walked rapidly past the stack of flour sacks toward the guard. Then they slowed down and the men broke ranks. Retreating in darkness, the men finally reached the glare of a large electric light bulb hanging above the camp gates.

Complaining of cold and exhaustion, the work gang hurriedly got into an uneven formation before the gates. The overseer came out, unlocked the gates, and admitted the people to the camp "zone." Even after we had entered the camp, people remained in formation right up to the barracks. I still understood nothing.

Only toward morning, when they started to divide up the flour, using a pot to scoop it up instead of a measuring cup, did I realize that for the first time in my life I had participated in a theft.

I did not find this particularly upsetting. Indeed, there was not even time to think about what had happened. We each had to cook our share by any means available—either as pancakes or as dumplings.

Berries

>>

FADEEV SAID: "Wait, let me talk to him." He walked over to me and put his rifle butt up against my head. I lay in the snow, clutching the log that had fallen from my shoulder, for I could not pick it up again to join the column of people descending the mountain. Each man carried a log on his shoulder, some larger and some smaller, and all were in a hurry to get home. Both the guards and the prisoners wanted to eat and sleep; they were all tired of this long winter day. But I was lying in the snow.

Fadeev always used the formal form of address in speaking to the prisoners.

"Listen, old man," he said. "Anyone as big as you can carry a log like that. It's not even a log—just a stick. You're faking, you fascist. At a time like this, when our country is fighting the enemy, you're jamming sticks in her spokes."

"It's not me who's a fascist," I said. "It's you. You look in the papers and read how the fascists kill old men. How do you think you're going to tell your bride about what you did in Kolyma?"

I had reached the stage of absolute indifference. I could

not tolerate rosy-cheeked, healthy, well-dressed, full people. I curled up to protect my stomach, but even this was a primordial, instinctive movement; I was not at all afraid of blows to the stomach. Fadeev's booted foot kicked me in the back, but a sudden warm feeling came over me, and I experienced no pain at all. If I were to die, it would be all the better.

"Listen," Fadeev said when he had turned me face upward with the tips of his boots. "You're not the first one I've worked with, and I know your kind."

Seroshapka, another guard, walked up.

"Let me have a look at you, so I'll remember you. What a mean one you are. . . ."

The beating began. When it ended, Seroshapka said: "Now do you understand?"

"I understand," I said as I got up and spat out salty, bloody saliva. I dragged the log to the accompaniment of chortles, shouting, and swearing from my fellow prisoners. The cold had gotten to them while I was being beaten.

The next morning Seroshapka led us out to a site where the trees had been cut down the previous winter, to gather anything that could be burned in our cast-iron stoves. The stumps were tall, and we ripped them out of the earth, using long poles as levers. Then we sawed them into pieces and stacked them.

Seroshapka hung "markers" in the few branches still remaining in the area where we were working. Made from braided dry yellow and gray grass, the markers indicated the area beyond which we were not permitted to set foot.

Our foreman built a fire on the hill for Seroshapka and brought him an extra supply of wood. Only the guards could have fires.

The fallen snow had long since been carried away by the winds, and the cold, frosty grass was slippery in our hands and changed color when we touched it. Hummocks of low mountain sweetbrier grew around the tree stumps, and the aroma of the frozen dark-lilac berries was extraordinary. Even more delicious than the sweetbrier were the frozen, overripe blue cowberries. The blueberries hung on stubby straight branches, each berry bright blue and wrinkled like an empty leather purse, but containing a dark blue-black juice that was indescribably delicious. By that time of the year, the berries had been touched by frost, and they were not at all alike the ripe berries, which are full of juice. The later berries have a much more subtle taste.

I was working with Rybakov, who was gathering berries in a tin can during the rest periods and whenever Seroshapka looked the other way. If Rybakov could manage to fill the can, the guards' cook would give him some bread. Rybakov's undertaking began to assume major dimensions.

I had no such customers, so I ate the berries myself, carefully and greedily pressing each one against the roof of my mouth with my tongue. The sweet aromatic juice of the crushed berry had a fleeting narcotic effect.

I never even considered helping Rybakov in his gathering, and he himself would not have desired such aid, since he would have had to share the bread.

Rybakov's can was filling slowly, and we were finding fewer and fewer berries. While working and gathering berries, we had approached the border of the forbidden "zone," without even noticing it. The markers were hanging right over our heads.

"Look at that," I said to Rybakov. "Let's go back."

Ahead, however, were hummocks of sweetbrier, cowberry, and blueberry. . . . We had noticed them earlier. The marker should have been hanging from a tree which stood two yards farther away.

Rybakov pointed at his can, not yet full, and at the sun, slowly setting on the horizon. Slowly he crept toward the enchanted berries.

I heard the dry crack of a shot, and Rybakov fell face-down among the hummocks. Seroshapka waved his rifle and shouted:

"Leave him there, don't go near him."

Seroshapka cocked his rifle and shot in the air. We knew what this second shot meant. Seroshapka also knew. There were supposed to be two shots—the first one a warning.

Rybakov looked strangely small as he lay among the hummocks. The sky, mountains, and river were enormous, and God only knew how many people could be killed and buried among the hummocks along these mountain paths.

Rybakov's can had rolled far away, and I managed to pick it up and hide it in my pocket. Maybe they would give me some bread for these berries, since I knew for whom they were intended.

Seroshapka calmly ordered us to get in formation, counted us, and gave the command to set off home.

He touched my shoulder with his rifle barrel, and I turned around.

"I wanted to get you," he said, "but you wouldn't cross the line, you bastard!"

A Day Off

>>>

Two squirrels the color of the sky but with black faces and tails were totally absorbed by something going on beyond the silver larch trees. I walked nearly up to their tree before they noticed me. Their claws scratched at the bark, and their blue shadows scampered upward. Somewhere high above they fell silent, fragments of bark stopped falling on the snow, and I saw what they had been watching.

A man was praying in the forest clearing. His cloth hat lay at his feet, and the frost had already whitened his close-cropped head. There was an extraordinary expression on his face—the kind people have when they recollect something extremely precious, such as childhood. The man crossed himself with quick, broad gestures as if using his fingers to pull his head down. His expression so altered his features that I did not immediately recognize him. It was the convict Zamiatin, a priest who lived in the same barracks as I.

He had not yet seen me, and his lips, numb from the cold, were quietly and solemnly pronouncing the words that I had learned as a child. Zamiatin was saying mass in the silver forest.

Slowly he crossed himself, straightened up, and saw me. Solemnity and tranquility disappeared from his face, and the accustomed wrinkles returning to his forehead drew his eyebrows together. Zamiatin did not like mockery. He picked up his hat, shook it, and put it on.

"You were saying the liturgy," I said.

"No, no," Zamiatin said, smiling at my ignorance. "How could I say mass? I don't have bread and wine or my stole. This is just a regulation-issue towel."

He shifted the dirty "waffled" rag that hung around his neck and really did create the impression of a priest's stole. The cold had covered the towel with snowy crystals which glimmered joyously in the sun like the embroidery on a church vestment.

"Besides, I'm ashamed. I don't know which way is east. The sun rises for two hours and sets behind the same mountain where it rose in the morning. Where is the east?"

"Is it all that important to know where the east is?"

"No, of course not. Don't leave. I tell you, I'm not saying mass, and I can't say one. I'm simply repeating, remembering the Sunday service. I don't even know if today is Sunday."

"It's Thursday," I said. "The overseer said so this morning."

"There, you see? No, there is no way I can say mass. It's just that it's easier for me this way. And I forget I'm hungry." Zamiatin smiled.

I know that everyone has something that is most precious to him, *the last thing that he has left,* and it is that something which helps him to live, to hang onto the life of which we were being so insistently and stubbornly deprived. If for Zamiatin this was the liturgy of John the Baptist, than my *last thing* was verse—everything else had long since been forgotten, cast aside, driven from memory. Only poetry had not been crushed by exhaustion, frost, hunger, and endless humiliations.

The sun set and the sudden darkness of an early winter evening had already filled the space between the trees. I wandered off to our barracks—a long, low hut with small windows. It looked something like a miniature stable. I had already seized the heavy, icy door with both hands when I heard a rustle in the neighboring hut, which served as a toolshed with saws, shovels, axes, crowbars, and picks. It was supposed to be locked on days off, but on that day the lock was missing. I stepped over the threshold of the toolshed, and the heavy door almost crushed me. There were so many cracks in the walls that my eyes quickly became accustomed to the semidarkness.

Two professional criminals were scratching a four-month-old German shepherd pup. The puppy lay on its back, squealing and waving its four paws in the air. The older man was holding it by the collar. Since we were from the same work gang, my arrival caused no consternation.

"It's you. Is there anyone else out there?"

"No one," I answered.

"All right, let's get on with it," the older man said.

"Let me warm up a little first," the younger man answered.

"Look at him struggle." He felt the puppy's warm side near the heart and tickled him.

The puppy squealed confidently and licked his hand.

"So you like to lick. . . . Well, you won't be doing much of that anymore. Semyon . . ."

Holding the pup by the collar with his left hand, Semyon

pulled a hatchet from behind his back and struck the puppy on the head with a short quick swing. The puppy jerked, and blood spilled out onto the icy floor of the shed.

"Hold him tight," Semyon shouted, raising the hatchet again.

"What for? He's not a rooster," the young man said.

"Skin him while he's still warm," Semyon said in the tone of a mentor. "And bury the hide in the snow."

That evening no one in the barracks could sleep because of the smell of meat soup. The criminals would have eaten it all, but there weren't enough of them in our barracks to eat an entire pup. There was still meat left in the pot.

Semyon crooked his finger in my direction.

"Take it."

"I don't want to," I said.

"All right," Semyon said, and his eyes ran quickly over the rows of bunks. "In that case, we'll give it to the preacher. Hey, Father! Have some mutton. Just wash out the pot when you're done. . . ."

Zamiatin came out of the darkness into the yellow light of the smoking kerosene lantern, took the pot, and disappeared. Five minutes later he returned with a washed pot.

"So quick?" Semyon asked with interest. "You gobbled things down quick as a seagull. That wasn't mutton, preacher, but dog meat. Remember the dog 'North' that used to visit you all the time?"

Zamiatin stared wordlessly at Seymon, turned around, and walked out. I followed him. Zamiatin was standing in the snow, just beyond the doors. He was vomiting. In the light of the moon his face seemed leaden. Sticky spittle was hanging from his blue lips. Zamiatin wiped his mouth with his sleeve and glared at me angrily.

"They're rotten," I said.

"Of course," Zamiatin replied. "But the meat was delicious—no worse than mutton."

PART THREE

WORKING

Through the Snow

>>>

How IS A ROAD beaten down through the virgin snow? One person walks ahead, sweating, swearing, and barely moving his feet. He keeps getting stuck in the loose, deep snow. He goes far ahead, marking his path with uneven black pits. When he tires, he lies down on the snow, lights a homemade cigarette, and the tobacco smoke hangs suspended above the white, gleaming snow like a blue cloud. The man moves on, but the cloud remains hovering above the spot where he reszed, for the air is motionless. Roads are always beaten down on days like these—so that the wind won't sweep away this labor of man. The man himself selects points in the snow's infinity to orient himself—a cliff, a tall tree. He steers his body through the snow in the same fashion that a helmsman steers a riverboat from one cape to another.

Five or six persons follow shoulder-to-shoulder along the narrow, wavering track of the first man. They walk beside his path but not along it. When they reach a predetermined spot, they turn back and tramp down the cleaf virgin snow which has not yet felt the foot of man. The road is tramped down. It can be used by people, sleighs, tractors. If they were to walk directly behind the first man, the second group would make a clearly defined but barely passable narrow paeth, and not a road. The first man has the hardest task, and when he is exhausted, another man from the group of five takes his place. Each of them—even the smallest and weakest—must beat down a section of virgin snow, and not simply follow in another's footsteps. Later will come tractors and horses driven by readers, instead of authors and poets.

Grishka Logun's Thermometer

>>

WE WERE SO EXHAUSTED that we collapsed in the snow beside the road before going home.

Instead of yesterday's forty degrees below zero, today was only thirteen below and the day seemed summery.

Grishka Logun, the foreman of the work area next to ours, walked past in an unbuttoned sheepskin coat. He was carrying a pick handle in his hand. Grishka was young, hot-tempered, and had an amazingly red face. Very low on the camp's administrative ladder, he was often unable to resist the temptation to put his own shoulder to a snowbound truck, to help pick up a log, or to break loose a box of earth frozen into the snow. All these were acts clearly beneath the dignity of a foreman, but he kept forgetting the loftiness of his position.

Vinogradov's work gang was coming down the road toward us. They were no better a lot than we were: the same former mayors and party leaders, university professors, middle-rank military officers. . . .

People crowded timidly to the edge of the road; they were returning from work and were letting Grishka Logun pass. But he stopped too. The gang had been working in his sector. Vinogradov, a talkative maen who had been the director of a Mechanized Tractor Station in the Ukraine, stepped forward.

Logun and Vinogradov were too far from where we were sitting for us to be able to hear what they were saying, but we could understand everything without the words. Vinogradov, waving his hands, was explaining something to Logun. Then Logun poked the pick handle into Vinogradov's chest, and Vinogradeov fell backward. . . . Vinogradov didn't get up, and Logun jumped on him and began to kick him, brandishing his pick handle all the while. None of the twenty men in his work gang made the slightest move to defend their leader. Logun picked up his hat, which had fallen in the snow, and walked on. Vinogradov got up as if nothing had happened. The rest of the group (the work gang was passing us) didn't express the slightest sympathy or indignation. When he reached us, Vinogradov twisted his broken bleeding lips into a wry smile: "That Logun's got a real thermometer," he said. "The thieves call kicking a man that way 'dancing,' " Vavilov said. "It's a sort of Russian folk dance."

Vavilov was an acquaintance of mine. We had arrived together at the mine from the same Butyr Prison. "What do you think of that?" I said. "We have to make some decision. No one beat us yesterday, but they might tomorrow. What would you do if Logun did to you what he just did to Vinogradov?"

"I guess I'd take it," Vavilov answered quietly. And I understood that he had been contemplating the inevitability of a beating for a long time.

Later I realized that it was all a matter of physical superiority when gang leaders, overseers, orderlies, or any unarmed persons were concerned. As long as I was strong, no one struck me. As soon as I weakened, everyone would. I would be beaten by the orderly, the worker in the bathhouse, the barber, the cook, the foreman, the work-gang foreman, and even the weakest criminal. The guard's strength was in his rifle.

The strength of the superior beating me was in the law, in the court, the tribunal, the guards, the troops. It was not hard for him to be stronger than I. The strength of the criminal element was in their numbers, the fact that they stuck together, that they could cut a man's throat over a couple of words. (I saw that happen more than once.) But I was still strong. I could be beaten by the director, the guard, the thief, but the orderly, the foreman, and the barber still couldn't beat me.

Poliansky, an erstwhile physical education teacher who now received a lot of food packages and never shared any of

them with anyone, said to me in a tone of reproach that he
simply could not comprehend how people could allow themselves to be reduced to such a condition. He was even indig-
nant when I didn't agree with him. Before the year was up,
however, I again met Poliansky—already a real "goner" picking up cigarette butts and eager to scratch the heels of any
important thief in camp (a common ritual of servility that was
thought to encourage relaxation).

Poliansky was honest. His secret torments were strong
enough to break through ice, through death, through indifference and beatings, through hunger, sleeplessness, and fear.

Once we had a holiday; on holidays we were all placed
under lock and key, and this was called "holiday isolation."
And there were people who met old friends, made new
acquaintances, and confided in each other during this "isolation." No matter how terrible or how degrading isolation was,
it was, nevertheless, easier than work for political prisoners
convicted under Article 58 of the criminal code. Isolation was,
after all, an opportunity to relax—even for a minute, and who
could say how much time it would take for us to return to our
former bodies—a minute, a day, a year, or a century? No one
could hope to return to his former soul. And, of course, no one
did.

But to get back to Poliansky, my bunk neighbor on that
"isolation day," he was honest.

"I've wanted to ask you something for a long time."

"What about?"

"I used to watch you a few months ago—the way you
walk, how you can't step over a log any dog would jump over,
how you drag your feet on the stones, and how the slightest
bump on your path seems an impossible barrier and causes
palpitations, heavy breathing, and requires long rest. I
watched you and thought: what a bum, a loafer, an experienced bastard, an imposter."

"And now? Have you understood anything?"

"I understood later. I did—when I got weak myself. When

everyone began to push me and beat me. Man knows no sensation more pleasant than to realize that someone else is still weaker, still worse off than he."

"Why are 'heroes of communist labor' always invited to production meetings? Why is physical strength a moral measure? 'Physically stonger' means 'better than me, morally superior to me.' How could it be otherwise? One man picks up a 400-pound boulder, and I'm bent over with a twenty-pound stone."

"I've realized all that now—I wanted to tell you."

"Thanks even for that."

Not long after that Poliansky died. He fell in one of the test pits. The foreman struck him in the face with his fist. The foreman was not Grishka Logun, but one of us—Firsov, a military man convicted under Article 58.

I remember very well how I was struck the first time. It was the first of hundreds of blows that I experienced daily, nightly.

It's impossible to remember all the blows one experiences, but I remember the first very well. I was even prepared for it by Grishka Logun's behavior and Vavilov's meekness.

In the cold, in the hunger of the fourteen-hour work day, of the frosty white cloud, of the rocky gold mine, happiness abruptly flitted my way, and an act of charity was thrust into my hand by a passer-by. This charity did not take the form of bread or medicine; it was in the form of time, an unscheduled relaxation.

The overseer of the ten men working in our sector was Zuev, then a free man, but he had once been a convict and knew what it was like to be in a convict's hide.

There was something in Zuev's eyes—sympathy, perhaps, for the thorny fate of humanity.

Power corrupts. The beast hidden in the soul of man and released from its chain lusts to satisfy its age-old natural instinct—to beat, to murder. I don't know if it's possible to receive satisfaction from signing a death sentence, but in this, too, there is doubtless some dark pleasure, some fantasy which seeks no justification.

I have seen people—many people—who had ordered the shooting of others and who were now themselves being killed. There was nothing but cowardice in them as they shouted: "I'm not the one who should be killed for the good of the state. I too am able to kill."

I don't know people who gave orders to kill. I only saw them from a distance. But I think that the order to shoot another man derives from that same spiritual strength, that same psychological foundation as the actual shooting itself, as murdering with one's own hands.

Power is corruption. The intoxication of power over people, irresponsibility, the willingness to mock, to degrade, to encourage all these things when necessary—all these are the moral measure of a supervisor's career.

But Zuev beat us less than the others did; we were lucky.

We had just arrived for work and were crowded together in a small area protected from the sharp wind by a cliff. Covering his face with his mittens, our foreman, Zuev, walked up, and sent the men off to the various mine shafts to work. I was left behind with nothing to do.

"I want to ask a favor of you," Zuev said, choking with his own boldness. "A favor—not an order!

"I want you to write a letter for me to Kalinin. To wipe out my prison record. I'll explain it all to you."

We went to the foreman's small shed where a stove crackled and where we were not normally allowed to enter. Any convict who dared open the door to breathe the hot breath of life even for a minute would immediately be driven out by fists and knees.

Animal instinct led us to this cherished door. Requests would be invented—how much time? Or it might be a question—should the excavation go to the right or the left?

"Can you give me a light?"

"Is Zuev here? How about Dobriakov?"

But these requests deceived no one in the shed. People were literally kicked through the open doors into the frost. Even so, there had been a moment of warmth. . . .

But no one threw me out; I was sitting right next to the stove.

"Who's that, the lawyer?" someone hissed contemptuously.

"That's right, Pavel Ivanovich. He was recommended to me."

"All right." It was the senior foreman condescending to recognize the needs of his subordinate.

Zuev's case (he'd served out his sentence the previous year) was the most ordinary village affair. It all began with support payments for his parents who had him sent to prison. His sentence was almost up when the prison authorities managed to have him sent to Kolyma. Colonization of the area demanded a firm line in creating barriers to departure, government assistance, and unflagging attention to arrivals and human shipments to Kolyma. Transporting convicts there was the simplest way of rendering the difficult land livable.

Zuev wanted to quit Far Northern Construction, and he was asking to have his prison record wiped out or at least to be allowed to return to the mainland.

It was difficult for me to write, and not just because my hands were rough and my fingers so permanently bent around the handle of a pick and ax that unbending them was unbelievably difficult. I managed to wrap a thick rag around pen and pencil to give them the thickness of a pick or shovel handle.

When I realized I could do that, I was ready to form letters.

It was difficult to write because my brain had become as coarse as my hands; like my hands, it too was oozing blood. I had to call back to life—to resurrect—words that, as I then thought, had left my life forever.

I wrote the letter, sweating and rejoicing. It was hot in

the shed, and the lice immediately began to stir and crawl over my body. I couldn't scratch for fear of being driven out into the cold. I was afraid of inspiring revulsion in my savior.

By evening I had written the complaint to Kalinin. Zuev thanked me and thrust a ration of bread into my hand. I had to eat the ration immediately; everything had to be devoured immediately and not laid aside until the next day. I had learned that lesson already.

The day was coming to an end—according to the foreman's watches only, for the fog was identical in the morning, at midnight, and at noon. We were led home.

I slept and had my perpetual Kolyma dream—loaves of bread floating through the air, filling all the houses, all the streets, the entire planet.

In the morning I waited to meet Zuev; maybe he'd give me a smoke.

And Zuev came. Making no effort to conceal anything from the work gang or the guards, he dragged me out of the wind shelter and roared at me.

"You cheated me, you bastard!"

He had read the letter that night. He didn't like it. His neighbors, the other foremen, also read it and didn't approve of it either. Too dry. Too few tears. It was useless to send that kind of letter. You couldn't get any sympathy from Kalinin with that sort of rot.

The camp had dried up my brain, and I could not, I just could not squeeze another word from it. I was not up to the job—and not because the gap between my will and Kolyma was too great, not because my brain was weak and exhausted, but because in those folds of my brain where ecstatic adjectives were stored, there was nothing but hatred. Just think of poor Dostoevsky writing anguished, tearful, humiliating letters to his unmoved superiors throughout the ten years he spent as a soldier after leaving the House of the Dead. Dostoevsky even wrote poems to the czarina. There was no Kolyma in the House of the Dead.

The Life of Engineer Kipreev

>>

FOR MANY YEARS I thought that death was a form of life. Comforted by the vagueness of this notion, I attempted to work out a positive formula to preserve my own existence in this vale of tears.

I believed a person could consider himself a human being as long as he felt totally prepared to kill himself, to interfere in his own biography. It was this awareness that gave me the will to live. I checked myself—frequently—and felt I had the strength to die, and thus remained alive.

Much later I realized that I had simply built myself a refuge, avoided the problem, for when at the critical moment the decision between life and death became an exercise of the will, I would not be the same man as before. I would inevitably weaken, become a traitor, betray myself. Instead of thinking of death, I simply felt that my former decision needed some other answer, that my promises to myself, the oaths of youth, were naïve and very artificial. It was Engineer Kipreev's story that convinced me.

I never in my life betrayed or sold anyone down the river. But I don't know how I would have held out if they had beaten me. I passed through all stages of the investigation, by the greatest good luck, without beatings—"method number three." My investigators never laid a finger on me. This was chance, nothing more. It was simply that I was interrogated early—in the first half of 1937, before they resorted to torture.

Engineer Kipreev, however, was arrested in 1938, and he could vividly imagine the beatings. He survived the blows and even attacked his investigator. Beaten still more, he was thrown into a punishment cell. Nevertheless, the investigators obtained his signature easily: they threatened to arrest his wife, and Kipreev "signed."

Throughout his life Kipreev carried with him this terrible weight on his conscience. There are more than a few humiliations and degradations in the life of a prisoner. The diaries of members of Russia's liberation movement are marked by one traumatic act—the request for a pardon. Before the revolution this was considered a mark of eternal shame. Even after the revolution former political prisoners and exiles refused to receive anyone who had ever asked the czar for freedom or for a reduction of sentence.

In the thirties, not only were petitioners for pardons forgiven but also those who had signed confessions that incriminated both themselves and others, often with bloody consequences.

Representatives of the former unyielding view had long since grown old and perished in exile or in the camps. Those who had been imprisoned and had passed through the process of investigation were all "petitioners."

For this reason no one ever knew what moral torments Kipreev subjected himself to in his departure for the Sea of Okhotsk—to Vladivostok and Magadan.

Kipreev had been a physicist and engineer at the Kharkov Physical Institute, where the first Soviet experiments with nuclear reactions were conducted. The nuclear scientist Kurchatov worked there. The purges had not passed over the Kharkov Institute, and Kipreev became one of the first victims of our atomic science.

Kipreev knew his own true worth, but his superiors did not. Moreover, moral stamina has little connection with talent, with scientific experience, or even with the love of science. Aware of the beatings at the interrogations, Kipreev prepared to act in the simplest manner—to fight back like a beast, to answer blow with blow without caring whether his tormenter was simply carrying out, or had personally invented, "method

number three." Kipreev was beaten and thrown into a punishment cell. Everything began again. His physical strength
betrayed him, and then so did his moral stamina. Kipreev
"signed." They threatened to arrest his wife. Kipreev knew
endless shame became of this weakness, because he, an educated man, had collapsed when he encountered brute force.
Right there in the prison Kipreev swore an oath never again to
repeat his shameful act. But then, Kipreev was the only one
who perceived his act as shameful. On the neighboring bunks
lay other men who had also signed confessions and committed
slander. They lay there and did not die. Shame has no boundaries. Or, rather, the boundaries are always personal, and each
resident of an interrogation cell sets standards for himself.

Kipreev arrived in Kolyma with a five-year sentence, con-
fident that he would find the path to early release to the mainland. An engineer had to be of value. An engineer could
always earn credit for extra working days, be released, have
his sentence shortened. While Kipreev had nothing but contempt for physical labor in camp, he quickly realized that only
death waited at the end of that path. If he could just find a job
where he could apply even a tenth of his technical skills, he
would obtain his freedom. At the very least, he would retain
his skills.

Experience at the mine, fingers broken in the scraper,
physical exhaustion, and emaciation brought Kipreev to the
hospital and from there to the transit prison.

The engineer's problem was that he could not resist the
temptation to invent; he could not restrain himself from
searching for scientific and technical solutions to the chaos
that he saw all around him.

As for the camp and its directors, they looked upon
Kipreev as a slave, nothing more. Kipreev's energy, for which
he had cursed himself a thousand times, sought an outlet.

The stakes in this game had to be worthy of an engineer
and a scientist. The stakes were freedom.

There is a brief ironic verse about Kolyma that describes it as a strange or wonderful planet; nine months is winter and the rest is summer:

Kolyma, Kolyma—chudnaya planeta,
Deviat' mesiatsev zima,
Ostal'noe - leto.

This is not the only strange thing about Kolyma. During the war, people paid a hundred rubles for an apple, and an error in the distribution of fresh tomatoes from the mainland led to bloody dramas. All this—the apples and the tomatoes— was for the civilian world, to which Kipreev did not belong. It was a strange planet not only because the taiga was the law, nor because it was a Stalinist death camp. And it wasn't strange just because there was a shortage there of cheap tobacco and the special tea leaves used to make *chifir,* a powerful, almost narcotic drink. *Chifir* leaves and cheap tobacco were the currency of Kolyma, its true gold, and they were used to acquire everything else.

The biggest shortage, however, was of glass—glass objects, laboratory glassware, instruments. The cold increased the fragility of glass, but the permitted "breakage" was not increased. A simple medical thermometer cost 300 rubles, but there were no underground bazaars that sold thermometers. The doctor had to present a formal request to the head of medical services for the entire region, since a medical thermometer was harder to hide than the Mona Lisa. But the doctor never presented any such request. He simply paid 300 rubles out of his own pocket and brought the thermometer with him from home to take the temperature of the critically ill.

In Kolyma a tin can is a poem. It is a convenient measuring cup that is always at hand. Water, various grains, flour, pudding, soup, tea can be stored in it. It is a mug from which to drink *chifir.* It is also a good vessel in which to brew *chifir.* The mug is sterile, since it has been purified by fire. Soup and tea can be heated in a tin can—either on a stove or over a campfire.

A three-liter tin can fastened to the belt with a wire handle is the classic cooking pot of every "goner." And who in Kolyma has not been or will not eventually become a "goner"?

In a wooden window frame, tiny pieces of broken glass, like cells, are arranged to serve as panes to let in light. A transparent jar can conveniently be used to store medication in the outpatient clinic. In the camp cafeteria, a pint jar is a serving dish for fruit compote.

But neither thermometers, nor laboratory glassware, nor simple jars make up the principal shortage of glass in Kolyma—electric lightbulbs.

In Kolyma there are hundreds of mines, thousands of sites, sections, shafts, tens of thousands of mine faces with gold, uranium, lead, and tungsten, thousands of work groups dispatched from the camps, civilian villages, camp zones, guard barracks, and everywhere there is one crying need— light, light, light. Kolyma has no sun, no light for nine months. The raging, never-setting summer sun provides no salvation, for in winter nothing is left of it. Light and energy come from pairs of tractors, or from a locomotive.

Industrial tools, gold washers, mine faces all demand light. Mine faces lit up by floodlights lengthen the night shift and make labor more productive. Electric lights are needed everywhere. Three-hundred, five-hundred, one-thousand-watt bulbs are shipped in from the mainland to provide light for the barracks and the mines, but the uneven supply of electricity from the portable generator motors guarantees that these bulbs will burn out earlier than they should.

The electric-lightbulb shortage in Kolyma is a national problem. It is not only the mine face that must be lit up but also the camp grounds, the barbed wire and the guard towers, which are built in greater and not lesser quantities in the Far North.

The guards on duty must have light. In the mines insufficient light is simply noted in the log, but in camp it might lead to escape attempts. Obviously there is nowhere to escape to from Kolyma, and no one has ever attempted to escape, but the law is the law, and if there isn't sufficient lighting or enough bulbs, burning torches are carried to the outer perimeters of the camp and left there in the snow until morning. A torch is made from a rag soaked in oil or gasoline.

Electric bulbs burn out quickly and cannot be repaired.

Kipreev wrote a note that amazed the chief of Far Eastern Construction. The chief could already feel the medal he would add to his other military decorations (military, not civilian).

It seemed the bulbs could be repaired if the glass was in one piece.

All over Kolyma stern instructions were hurriedly circulated to the effect that burned-out bulbs must be delivered carefully to Magadan. At the industrial complex forty-seven miles from Magadan, a factory for the repair of electric lightbulbs was built. Engineer Kipreev was appointed director of the factory.

All other personnel was civilian. This happy invention was entrusted to the hands of dependable civilians working on contract. Kipreev, however, paid no attention to this circumstance, believing that the creators of the factory could not help but take notice of him.

The result was stupendous. Of course, the bulbs didn't have a long life after being repaired, but Kipreev saved Kolyma a definite quantity of hours and days. There were many of these days, and the state reaped an enormous profit, a military profit, a golden profit.

The chief of Far Eastern Construction was awarded the Order of Lenin. All supervisors who had anything to do with repairing the bulbs received medals also.

Neither Moscow nor Magadan, however, ever considered rewarding the convict Kipreev. For them Kipreev was a slave, an intelligent slave, but nothing more. Nevertheless, the chief of Far Eastern Construction did not consider it possible to forget all about his pen-pal in the taiga.

A celebration of great pomp took place in Kolyma, a celebration so great that a small group of people in Moscow took note of it. It was held in honor of the chief of Far Eastern Construction, of all those who had received medals and official expressions of gratitude for work well done. Aside from the official expressions of gratitude for work well done, aside from the official governmental decree, the chief of Far Eastern Construction had also issued bonuses, awards, and official expressions of gratitude. All those who participated in bulb repair, all the foremen of the factory with the bulb-repair shop were presented with American packages, in addition to the medals and certificates. These packages, which had been received during the war under Lend-Lease, contained suits, neckties, and shoes. One of the suits had evidently disappeared during delivery, but the shoes were of red American leather and had thick soles—the dream of every foreman.

The chief of Far Eastern Construction consulted with his right-hand man, and they came to the conclusion that there could be no higher dream for a convict-engineer. As for shortening his sentence or releasing him altogether, the chief would not even dream of asking Moscow about that in such troubled political times. A slave should be satisfied with his master's old shoes and suit.

All Kolyma buzzed about these presents—literally all Kolyma. The local foremen received more than enough medals and official expressions of gratitude, but an American suit and American shoes with thick soles were in the same category as a trip to the moon or another planet.

The solemn evening arrived, and the cardboard boxes gleamed on a table covered with a red cloth.

The chief of Far Eastern Construction read from a paper in which Kipreev's name was not mentioned, could not be mentioned. Then he read aloud the list of those who were to receive presents. Kipreev's name came last in the list. The engineer stepped up to the table which was brightly lit—by his lightbulbs—and took the box from the hands of the chief of Far Eastern Construction.

Enunciating each word distinctly, Kipreev said in a loud voice: "I won't wear American hand-me-downs." Then he put the box back on the table.

Kipreev was arrested on the spot and sentenced to an additional eight years. I don't know precisely which article of the criminal code was cited, but in any case that is meaningless in Kolyma and interests no one.

But then, what sort of article could have covered the refusing of American presents? And that wasn't the only thing. There was more. In concluding the case against Kipreev, the investigator said: "He said that Kolyma was Auschwitz without the ovens."

Kipreev accepted his new sentence calmly. He was aware of the likely consequences when he refused the American presents. Nevertheless, he did take certain measures to ensure his personal safety. These measures consisted of asking a friend to write to his wife on the mainland to tell her that he had died. Second, he himself gave up writing letters.

The engineer was removed from the factory and sent to hard labor. The war was soon over, and the system of camps became even more complex. As a persistent offender, Kipreev knew he would be sent to a secret camp with no address—merely a number.

The engineer fell ill and ended up in the central prison hospital. There was a compelling need for Kipreev's skills there: an X-ray machine had to be assembled from old machine parts and junk. The chief physician, whose name was "Doctor," promised to get Kipreev released or at least to get his sentence shortened. Engineer Kipreev had little faith in such promises, because he was classified as a patient, and special work credit could be received only by staff employees of the hospital. Still, it was tempting to believe in this promise, and the X-ray lab was not the gold mine.

It was here that we learned of Hiroshima.

"That's the bomb we were working on in Kharkov."

"That's why Forrestal* committed suicide. He couldn't bear all those telegrams."

"Do you understand why? It's a very hard thing for a Western intellectual to make the decision to drop the bomb. Psychic depression, insanity, and suicide is the price that the Western intellectual pays for decisions like that. A Russian Forrestal wouldn't have lost his mind."

"How many good people have you met in your life? I mean real people, the kind you want to imitate and serve."

"Let me think: Miller, the engineer arrested for sabotage, and maybe five others."

"That's a lot."

The General Assembly signed the agreement on genocide.

"Genocide? Is that something they serve for dinner?"

We signed the convention. Of course, 1937 was not genocide. It was the destruction of the enemies of the people. There was no reason not to sign the convention.

"They're really tightening the screws. We cannot be silent. It's just like the sentence in the child's primer: "We are not slaves; no one's slaves are we." We have to do something, if only to demonstrate to ourselves that we are still people."

"The only thing you can demonstrate to yourself is your own stupidity. To live, to survive—that's the task at hand. We mustn't stumble. Life is more serious than you think."

Mirrors do not preserve memories. It is difficult to call the object that I keep hidden in my suitcase a mirror. It is a piece of glass that looks like the surface of some muddy river. The river has been muddied and will stay dirty forever, because it has remembered something important, something eternally

* First American secretary of defense. Committed suicide on 5/22/1949.—TRANS.

important. It can no longer be the crystal, transparent flow of water that is clear right down to its bed. The mirror is muddied and no longer reflects anything. But once the glass was a real mirror—a present unselfishly given that I carried with me through two decades of camp life, through civilian life that differed little from the camps, and everything that followed the twentieth party congress, when Khruschev denounced Stalin.

The mirror that Kipreev gave me was not part of any business scheme on his part. It was an experiment conducted in the darkness of the X-ray room. I made a wooden frame for this piece of mirror. That is, I ordered it; I didn't make it myself. The frame is still in one piece. It was made by a Latvian carpenter who was a patient recovering in the hospital. He made it in exchange for a ration of bread. At that time I could permit myself to give up a ration of bread for such a purely personal, totally frivolous wish.

I am holding the mirror in front of me right now. The frame is crudely made, painted with the oil paint used for floors; they were renovating the hospital, and the carpenter asked for a "smidgen" of paint. Later I shellacked the frame, but the shellac wore off long ago. You can't see anything in the mirror anymore, but I used to shave before it at Oimyakon, and all the civilian employees envied me. They envied me until 1953 when some civilian, some smart civilian, sent a package of cheap mirrors to the village. These tiny mirrors—some round and some square—should have cost a few kopecks, but they were sold for sums reminiscent of the prices paid for electric lightbulbs. Nevertheless, everyone withdrew his money from his savings account and bought them. The mirrors were sold in a day, in an hour. After that, my home-made mirror ceased to be the envy of my guests.

I keep the mirror with me. It is not an amulet. I don't know whether it brings luck. Perhaps the mirror attracts and reflects rays of evil, keeping me from dissolving in the human stream, where no one except me knows Kolyma and the engineer, Kipreev.

Kipreev was indifferent to his surroundings. A thief, a hardened criminal with a modicum of education, was invited by the administration to learn the secrets of the X-ray laboratory. It is always hard to tell if the criminals in camp are using their own real names, but this one called himself Rogov, and he was studying under Kipreev's tutelage. The hope was that he would learn to pull the right levers at the right time.

The administration had big plans, and they certainly weren't terribly concerned about Rogov, the criminal. Nevertheless, Rogov ensconced himself in the lab together with Kipreev, and watched him, reported on his actions, and participated in this governmental function as a proletarian friend of the people. He was constantly informing and made conversation and visits impossible. Even if he didn't interfere, he was constantly spying and was a model of vigilance.

This was the primary intent of the administration. Kipreev was to prepare his own replacement—from the criminal world. As soon as Rogov acquired the necessary skills, he would have a lifelong profession, and Kipreev would be sent to Berlag, a nameless camp identified only by number and intended for recidivists.

Kipreev realized all of this, but he had no intention of opposing his fate. He instructed Rogov without any concern for himself.

Kipreev was lucky in that Rogov was a poor student. Like any common criminal, Rogov knew what was most important—that the administration would not forget the criminal element under any circumstances. He was an inattentive student. Nevertheless, his hour came, and Rogov declared that he could do the job, and Kipreev was sent off to a numbered camp. But the X-ray lab somehow broke down, and the doctors had Kipreev returned to the hospital. Once more the lab began to function.

It was about this time that Kipreev began experimenting with the optic blind.

The dictionary of foreign words published in 1964 defines the "blind" as follows: "a diaphragm (a shutter with variable-size opening) which is used in photography, microscopy, and fluoroscopy."

Twenty years earlier the word "blind" was not listed in the dictionary of foreign words. It is a creation of the war period, an invention having to do with electron microscopes.

Somewhere Kipreev found a torn sheet from a technical journal, and the blind was used in the X-ray laboratory in the convict hospital on the left bank of the Kolyma River.

The blind was Kipreev's pride and joy—his hope, albeit a weak hope. A report was given at a medical conference and also sent to Moscow. There was no response.

"Can you make a mirror?"
"Of course."
"A full-length mirror?"
"Any kind you like, as long as I have the silver for it."
"Will silver spoons do?"
"They'll be fine."

Thick glass intended for the desks of senior bureaucrats was requisitioned from the warehouse and brought to the X-ray laboratory.

The first experiment was unsuccessful, and Kipreev fell into a rage and broke the mirror with a hammer. One of the fragments became my mirror—a present from Kipreev.

On the second occasion everything worked out successfully, and the bureaucrat realized his dream—a full-length mirror.

It never occurred to the bureaucrat to thank Kipreev. Whatever for? Even a literate slave ought to be grateful for the privilege of occupying a hospital bed. If the blind had attracted the attention of the higher-ups, the bureaucrat would have received a letter of commendation, nothing more. Now, the mirror—that was something real. But the blind was a very nebulous thing. Kipreev was in total agreement with his boss.

But falling asleep at night on his cot in the corner of the lab and waiting for the latest woman to leave the embraces of his pupil, assistant, and informer, Kipreev could not believe either himself or Kolyma. The blind was not a joke. It was a technical feat. But neither Moscow nor Magadan was in the least interested in engineer Kipreev's invention.

In camp, letters are not answered, nor are reminders of unanswered letters appreciated. The prisoner has to wait—for luck, an accidental meeting.

All this was wearing on the nerves—assuming they were still whole, untorn, and capable of being worn out.

Hope always shackles the convict. Hope is slavery. A man who hopes for something alters his conduct and is more frequently dishonest than a man who has ceased to hope. As long as the engineer waited for a decision on the damned blind, he kept his mouth shut, ignoring all the appropriate and inappropriate jokes that his immediate superior permitted himself— not to mention those of his own assistant who was only waiting for the hour and the day when he could take over. Rogov had even learned to make mirrors, so he was guaranteed a "rake-off."

Everyone knew about the blind, and everyone joked about Kipreev—including the pharmacist Kruglyak, who ran the Party organization at the hospital. This heavy-faced man was not a bad sort, but he had a bad temper, and—mainly—he had been taught that a prisoner is scum. As for this Kipreev. . . . The pharmacist had come to the hospital only recently, and he did not know the history of the electric lightbulbs. He never gave any thought to the difficulties of assembling an X-ray laboratory in the taiga, in the Far North.

As the pharmacist phrased it in the slang of the criminal world that he had recently acquired, Kipreev's invention was a "dodge."

Kruglyak sneered at Kipreev in the procedure room of the

surgical ward. The engineer grabbed a stool and was about to strike the Party secretary, but the stool was ripped from his hands, and he was led away to the ward.

Kipreev either would have been shot or sent to a penal mine, a so-called special zone, which is worse than being shot. He had many friends at the hospital, however, and not just because of his mirrors. The affair of the electric lightbulbs was well known and recent. People wanted to help him. But this was Point Eight of Article Fifty-Eight—terrorist activities.

The women doctors went to the head of the hospital, Vinokurov. Vinokurov had no use for Kurglyak. Moreover, he valued Kipreev and he was expecting a response to his report on the blind. And, mainly, he was not a vicious person. He was an official who didn't use his position to do evil. A careerist who feathered his own bed, Vinokurov did not go out of his way to help anyone, but he did not wish them evil either.

"All right, I won't forward the papers to the prosecutor's office under one condition," Vinokurov said. "Provided there isn't any report from the victim, Kurglyak. If he submits a report, the matter will go to trial. And a penal mine is the least Kipreev can get."

Kruglyak's male friends spoke to him.

"Don't you understand that he'll be shot? He has none of the rights that we have."

"He raised his hand at me."

"He didn't raise his hand, no one saw that. Now if I had a disagreement with you, I'd let you have it in the snout after two words. Don't you ever quit?"

Kruglyak was not really a bad person, and he certainly wouldn't do as a bigwig in Kolyma. He agreed not to send in a report.

Kipreev remained in the hospital. A month passed, and Major General Derevyanko arrived. He was second-in-charge to the chief of Far Eastern Construction, and he was the supreme authority for the prisoners.

High-placed officials liked to stop at the hospital. They

could always find quarters, and there was no shortage of food, liquor, and relaxation.

Major General Derevyanko donned a white coat and strolled from one ward to another to stretch his legs before dinner. The major general was in a good mood, and Vinokurov decided to take a chance.

"I have a prisoner here who has performed an important service for the state."

"What sort of service is that?"

The head of the hospital explained roughly what a blind was.

"I want to request that he be granted an early release."

The major general asked about the prisoner's background, and when he heard the answer, he grunted.

"The only thing that I can tell you," the major general said, "is that you should forget about any blinds, and send this engineer. . . . Korneev. . . ."

"Kipreev, sir."

"That's right, Kipreev. Ship him off to where his papers say he should be."

"Yes, sir."

A week later Kipreev was sent off, and in another week the X-ray machine broke down, so that he had to be recalled to the hospital.

It was no joking matter now, and Vinokurov lived in fear of the major general's anger. He would never believe that the X-ray machine had broken down. Kipreev's papers were again prepared for him to be sent off, but he fell ill and remained.

It was now utterly impossible for him to return to the X-ray laboratory. He realized this quite clearly.

Kipreev had mastoiditis; he had picked up the inflamation from sleeping on a camp cot. His condition was critical, but no one wanted to believe his temperature or the reports of the doctors. Vinokurov raged and demanded that the operation be performed as soon as possible.

The hospital's best surgeons prepared to perform Kipreev's mastoidectomy. The surgeon, Braude, was virtually a specialist in mastoidectomies. There were more than enough colds in Kolyma, and Braude had had the experience of performing hundreds of such operations. But Braude was only the assistant. Novikov, a well-known otolarynogologist and a student of Volchek, had worked for Far Eastern Construction for many years, and she was to perform the operation. Novikov had never been a prisoner nor was she after the hardship pay (commonly referred to as "the long ruble"), but there, in Kolyma, she was not condemned for her entrenched alchoholism. After her husband's death, this talented and beautiful woman had wandered for years about the Far North. She would begin things brilliantly but then would lose control for weeks on end.

Novikov was about fifty, and there was no one more qualified than she. At this moment she was dead drunk, but she was coming out of it, and the head of the hospital allowed Kipreev's operation to be held up for a few days.

Novikov sobered up, her hands stopped shaking, and she performed Kipreev's operation brilliantly. It was a parting gift, a purely medical gift to her former X-ray technician. Braude assisted her, and Kipreev recuperated in the hospital.

Kipreev realized that there was nothing left to hope for and that he would not be kept in the hospital for even one extra hour.

A numbered camp waited for him, where convicts walked in rows of five, elbow to elbow, with thirty dogs surrounding a column of prisoners.

Even in this hopeless state Kipreev did not betray himself. The head of the ward prescribed a special diet for the convict-engineer recovering from a mastoidectomy, a serious operation. Kipreev declared that there were many patients more seriously ill than he among the ward's three hundred patients and that they had a greater right to a special diet.

And they took Kipreev away.

For fifteen years I searched for engineer Kipreev and finally dedicated a play to his memory—an effective way of guaranteeing a man's involvement with the netherworld.

But it was not enough to write a play about Kipreev and dedicate it to his memory. A woman friend of mine was sharing an apartment in the center of Moscow, and it wasn't until she got a new neighbor through an ad in the paper that I finally found Kipreev.

The new woman came out of her room to become acquainted with her neighbors and saw the play dedicated to Kipreev. She picked it up: "The initials are the same as those of a friend of mine. But he's not in Kolyma; he's in a different place." My friend phoned me. I refused to continue the conversation. It was an error. Besides, in the play the hero is a doctor. Kipreev was a physical engineer.

"That's right, a physical engineer."

I got dressed and went to see my friend's new neighbor.

Fate weaves complex patterns. Why? Why did the will of fate have to be so clearly demonstrated by this series of coincidences? We seek each other little, but fate takes our lives in her hands.

Engineer Kipreev was alive in the Far North. He had been released ten years earlier. Before that, he had been brought to Moscow and had worked in secret camps. When he was released, he returned to the North. He wanted to remain there until he reached pension age.

Engineer Kipreev and I met.

"I'll never be a scientist—just an ordinary engineer. How could I return, stripped of all my rights and ignorant of what has happened in my field? The people I studied with are all laureates of various prizes."

"But that's nonsense!"

"No, it's not nonsense. I breathe easier in the North. And I'll continue breathing easier right up to my pension."

Mister Popp's Visit

>>

MR. POPP WAS DIRECTOR OF an American firm that was installing gasholders in the initial construction phase of the Berezniki Chemical Factory. It was a large order, the work was
going well, and the vice-president considered it essential to be
present in person when the equipment was to be turned over
to its new owners.

Various firms were participating in the construction of the
factory. Granovsky, the construction director, called it a capi-
talist international. The Germans were installing "Hanomag"
boilers; the English firm "Brown & Bovery" was building the
steam engines; and the Americans were installing the gasholders. The Germans were behind schedule; later this was
declared to be sabotage. At the Central Power Station, the
English were also behind schedule; later this too was declared
to be sabotage.

At the time I was working at the Central Power Station,
and I remember well the arrival of Mr. Holmes, chief engineer
of the firm Babcock & Wilcox. Holmes was met by Granovsky
at the train station, but instead of going to his hotel, the
English engineer went straight to where the boilers were
being installed. One of the English installers helped Holmes
out of his coat and gave him some working clothes, and
Holmes spent three hours in the boiler listening to the
mechanic's explanations. That evening there was a conference. He responded to all the comments and reports with one
short word which the interpreter rendered as: "Mr. Holmes is
not concerned with that." Nevertheless, Holmes spent about
two weeks at the factory, and the boiler began to function at
20 percent of planned capacity. Granovsky signed a report to
that effect, and Holmes flew back to London.

A few months later the boiler's output began to diminish, and a Soviet engineer, Leonid Ramzin, was called in for consultation. Ramzin had been arrested and tried for conspiracy to overthrow the government. He had been sentenced to death, but the sentence was commuted to ten years' imprisonment with confiscation of property. While serving his sentence, Ramzin was allowed to continue work on the development of a new water-tube boiler which he had designed in 1930, and he was also frequently called on as a consultant. His trial had attracted a lot of attention in the newspapers. Ramzin had not yet been released, had not yet received the Order of Lenin or the Stalin Prize. All that was to come later, but Ramzin already knew about it and conducted himself in a quite independent fashion at the power station. He didn't arrive alone, but with a companion whose appearance was singularly revealing. When Ramzin was done, the man left with him. Ramzin did not crawl into the boiler as Mr. Holmes had done but sat in the office of the station's technical director, Kastenner, who had also been exiled and sentenced for sabotage in the mines of Kizel.

The nominal director of the power station was a certain Rachov. He had, in the past, been active in the Party, but he wasn't a bad sort and didn't interfere in matters he didn't understand. At that time, I was working in the efficiency engineer's office, and for many years afterward I carried around with me the written complaint the boiler stokers had sent to Rachov. On the letter, in which the stokers had listed their numerous requests, Rachov had scrawled a characteristically straightforward resolution: "To the head of the power plant. Look into the matter and refuse them as much as possible."

Ramzin gave some practical advice but did not have a very high opinion of Holmes's work.

Mr. Holmes had always appeared at the station, accompanied not by Granovsky but by his deputy, the chief engineer Chistyakov. Nothing in this life is more dogmatic than diplomatic etiquette. Although Granovsky had all the free time in the world, he considered it beneath him to accompany the foreign firm's chief engineer around the construction site. Of course, if the firm's president were to come. . . .

Mr. Holmes was escorted around the site by the engineer, Chistyakov, a heavy, massive man of the type depicted in novels about the Russian gentry. At the factory Chistyakov had an enormous office opposite that of Granovsky. Chistyakov spent many hours there locked up with his young female courier.

I was young then and didn't understand the physiological law that dictated that superiors sleep with their couriers, stenographers, and secretaries in addition to their wives. I often had business with Chistyakov, and I spent a lot of time swearing outside his locked door.

I then lived next to the soda factory in the same hotel where the writer, Konstantin Paustovsky, composed his *Kara-Bugaz*. Judging by what Paustovsky wrote about that period—1930–1931—he failed to observe the events which, in the eyes of all our countrymen, colored those years and laid their stamp on the entire history of our society.

Here, right before Paustovsky's eyes, there took place an enormous experiment in the corruption of human souls, an experiment that was to be repeated throughout the country and which would well up in a fountain of blood in 1937. This experiment was the newly developed system of labor camps with its "reforging" of human souls, food rations, work days dependent on work accomplished, and the practice of prisoners guarding each other. This system flowered with the construction of the White Sea Canal and collapsed with the construction of the Moscow Canal where to this very day human bones are found in mass graves.

The experiment in Berezniki was conducted by Berzin*. It was not, of course, his personal invention. Berzin could always be counted on to carry out other people's ideas, whether or not they involved the shedding of blood. Berzin

* Shot during the purge of 1938.—TRANS.

was also the director of the Vishera Chemical Factory. Filippov was his subordinate in the camps, but the Vishera camp, which encompassed both Berezniki and Solikamsk with its potassium mines, was enormous. Berezniki alone had three or four thousand people.

It was here that the question of the camps' very existence was decided. Only after the Vishera experiment was judged profitable by the higher-ups did the camps spread all over the Soviet Union. No region was without a camp, no construction site was without convicts. It was only after Vishera that the number of prisoners in the country reached 12 million. Vishera blazed the trail to new areas of confinement. The prisons were handed over to the NKVD, the secret police, whose feats were sung by poets, playwrights, and film producers. Engrossed in his *Kara-Bugaz*, Paustovsky saw none of this.

Toward the end of 1931 I shared a room in the hotel with a young engineer by the name of Levin. He worked at the Berezniki Chemical Factory as an interpreter for the German engineers. When I asked Levin why he worked as a simple interpreter for a salary of only 300 old-style rubles a month when he was a chemical engineer, he answered: "It's better this way. I don't have any responsibility. The factory opening might be delayed for the tenth time, and a hundred people might be arrested, but that doesn't concern me, because I'm just a translator. Besides, I don't have much to do, so I have all the free time I need, and I make good use of it." Levin smiled.

I smiled back.

"You don't understand?"

"No."

"Haven't you noticed that I don't get back till morning?"

"No, I never noticed."

"You're not very observant. I have a job that brings me all the money I need."

"What's that?"

"I play cards."

"Cards?"

"Yes, poker."

"With foreigners?"

"Why should I play with foreigners? The only thing I could get out of that would be a court trial."

"With Russians?"

"Of course. There are a lot of bachelors here. And the stakes are high. So I have all the money I need. I get along fine and thank my father every day. He taught me to play poker. Want to try? I'll teach you in no time at all."

"No thanks."

I've inserted Levin by accident. I just can't get started on the story of Mr. Popp.

The work of the American firm was moving along at a rapid pace, the order was a large one, and the vice-director decided to come to Russia himself. M. Granovsky, director of the Berezniki Chemical Factory, was informed in advance a thousand times of Mr. Popp's arrival. Granovsky decided that diplomatic protocol would not permit him to go in person to meet Mr. Popp. After all, Granovsky was a Party member of long standing, construction chief of the largest project undertaken during the first five-year plan, and he ranked higher than the American businessman. It just wasn't proper. So Granovsky decided to meet him in his office, and not at the railroad station, Usolye, later renamed Berezniki.

Granovsky knew that the American guest was arriving by special train—just a locomotive and one car. Three days in advance the chief of construction was informed by telegram from Moscow of the arrival time at the Usolye station.

The protocol of meeting was worked out beforehand: the chief of construction's personal car was to be sent to pick up the guest and take him directly to the hotel for foreigners. For the past three days, the director of the hotel, a party lackey by the name of Tsyplyakov, had been keeping the best room vacant. After freshening up and having breakfast, Mr. Popp was to be brought to the office where the business part of the meeting had been scheduled to the minute.

The special train with the guest from beyond the seas was to arrive at nine in the morning, and on the previous evening Granovsky's personal chauffeur had been called up, instructed, and sworn at repeatedly.

"Comrade supervisor, maybe I ought to take the car to the station the night before and spend the night there," the chauffeur fretted.

"Nothing doing. We have to show them that we do everything to the minute. The train whistle blows, and you pull up just as the train pulls in. That's the only way to do things."

"Yes, sir, comrade supervisor."

To rehearse the plan, the car was sent empty to the station ten times, and the exhausted chauffeur calculated the exact speed and time. On the night before Mr. Popp's arrival, Granovsky's chauffeur fell asleep and dreamt he was on trial. . . .

The chief of construction hadn't honored the garage man with any confidential chats; he awakened the chauffeur when the phone rang with a call from the station.

Granovsky was an active man. He arrived in his office at six A.M. that day, conducted two meetings, and issued three official reprimands. He listened closely to every tiny noise from below, opened the curtains, and peered out the window at the road. There was no guest from beyond the seas.

At nine-thirty the man on duty, the chief of construction, called from the station. Granovsky picked up the receiver and heard a rasping voice with a strong foreign accent. The voice expressed surprise that Mr. Popp was inadequately received. There was no car. Mr. Popp asked that one be sent.

Granovsky fell into a satanic rage. Rushing down the stairs two at a time, he reached the garage, breathing heavily.

"Your chauffeur left at seven-thirty, comrade supervisor."

"What do you mean at seven-thirty?"

At that moment the car horn honked, and the chauffeur stepped over the threshold of the garage with a drunken grin.

"What the hell are you doing, you . . ."

But the chauffeur explained. At seven-thirty the Moscow passenger train had arrived. The head of bookkeeping, Grozovsky, had arrived on it with his family from their vacation and, as always, had taken Granovsky's car. The chauffeur tried to explain about Mr. Popp, but Grozovsky replied that it was all a mistake, that he knew nothing about any of it. He ordered that the car be sent directly to the station, and the chauffeur went after him. The chauffeur thought the whole business with the foreigner had been canceled, and, besides, what with all these Grozovskys and Granovskys, he didn't know whom to obey. So they all went to the new settlement four kilometers from the station where Grozovsky's new apartment was located. The chauffeur helped them carry in their things, and they treated him to some vodka.

"We'll talk about this later. We'll see who's important— Grozovsky or Granovsky? But for now get your ass down to the station."

The chauffeur screeched into the station just before ten. Mr. Popp was not in a good mood.

The chauffeur, too drunk even to recognize the road, nevertheless rushed Mr. Popp straight to the hotel for foreigners. Mr. Popp was shown his room, where he washed up, changed clothes, and calmed down.

Now the nervous one was Tsyplyakov, commandant of the hotel. That was his title—not "director" or "administrator" but "commandant." I don't know whether it took more pull to get that position than, say, "director of the water tower," but that was the title of his position.

Mr. Popp's secretary appeared on the threshold of the commandant's office: "Mr. Popp would like breakfast."

The hotel commandant put two large unwrapped pieces of candy, two sandwiches with preserves and two with sausage, and two glasses of watery tea on a tray and took it to Mr. Popp's room.

The secretary immediately brought the tray back out and set it on the table in the corridor. He was certain Mr. Popp would never eat that.

Tsyplyakov rushed off to report to the chief of construction, but Granovsky already knew everything—he had been informed by telephone.

"You old bitch," Granovsky roared into the receiver. "You're shaming me and the government. You just lost your job! This time you'll learn what work means! I'll send you to shovel sand in the quarries! Saboteurs! Bastards! You'll rot in the camps!"

The gray-haired Tsyplyakov waited for his boss to get his fill of swearing and thought to himself: "He'll probably do it too."

It was time to begin the business part of the meeting, and Granovsky calmed down a little. The firm had done good work at the site. Gas holders had been installed in Berezniki and Solikamsk. Mr. Popp was sure to want to see Solikamsk. That was why he had come, and he had no wish to give the impression that he was upset. Why, he wasn't upset at all. Surprised, maybe, but that was a trivial matter.

Casting aside his diplomatic reservations and canceling all his meetings, Granovsky accompanied Mr. Popp personally to the construction site. Granovsky also accompanied Mr. Popp to Solikamsk and returned with him. The appropriate documents were signed, and a gratified Mr. Popp was ready to return home to America.

"I have some extra time," Mr. Popp said to Granovsky. "I've saved two weeks, thanks to the excellent work of our engineers." Here he paused, then continued: "And yours too. The Kama is a beautiful river, and I'd like to take a boat trip down it to Perm—or, maybe, to Nizhny Novgorod. Is that possible?"

"Of course," Granovsky said.

"Can I rent a boat?"

"No. Our system of government is different from yours, Mr. Popp."

"Could I buy one?"

"No, you can't buy one either."

"Well, I guess I can understand that I can't buy a passenger ship. That might hinder navigation on an important body of water. But how about a tug? Something like that *Chaika* over there?" Mr. Popp pointed at a tug passing by the windows of the chief of construction's office.

"No, a tug is out of the question too. You have to understand . . ."

"Yes, I've heard a lot. . . . Buying one would be the simplest way. I'd leave it in Perm. I'd make a present of it to you."

"No, Mr. Popp, we can't accept such gifts."

"But what can I do then? It's absurd. Here we have summer and beautiful weather. This is one of the finest rivers in the world. It's a real Volga—I read about it. Besides, I have the time. And I can't leave. Ask Moscow."

"Moscow's far away," Granovsky quoted from habit.

"Well, you decide. I'm your guest. I'll do whatever you think best."

Granovsky asked for a half hour to think things over. He summoned to his office the chief of navigation and Ozols, the local head of the OGPU (the secret police). Granovsky told them about Mr. Popp's desire.

There were only two passenger ships that passed Berezniki—*The Red Urals* and *The Red Tataria*. They connected Cherdyn and Perm. Mironov said that *The Red Urals* was far downstream and couldn't arrive with any speed. Farther upstream, *The Red Tataria* was approaching Cherdyn. If she turned around right away and made no stops, she could be in Berezniki tomorrow. "Your boys would have to help out, Ozols." In a word, Mr. Popp could have his trip.

"Get on the telegraph, and tell your boys to get moving. Let one of them get on the boat to make sure they don't stop off somewhere and waste time. Tell them it's an important government assignment."

Ozols contacted Annov, Cherdyn's dock, and *The Red Tataria* left Cherdyn.

"Get a move on!"

"We are."

The chief of construction visited Mr. Popp at his hotel, where the commandant had already been replaced. He announced that a passenger boat would arrive at about two o'clock the next day and would have the privilege of taking an honored guest on board.

"No," Mr. Popp said. "Give me the exact time so I won't have to wait around on shore."

"At five o'clock then. I'll send a car for your things at four o'clock."

At five o'clock Granovsky, Mr. Popp, and his secretary arrived at the landing. There was no boat.

Granovsky excused himself and rushed off to the OGPU telegraph.

"They haven't even reached Icher yet."

Granovsky groaned. Icher was at least two hours away.

"Maybe we ought to return to the hotel and have a snack. We'll come back when the boat arrives," Granovsky suggested.

"You mean breakfast," Mr. Popp said expressively. "No thank you. It's a beautiful day with a great sun and sky. We'll wait here on shore."

Granovsky remained at the landing with his guest, smiled, made small talk, and kept glancing toward the promontory upstream, where the boat was to appear.

In the meantime Ozols and his men were on the telegraph demanding that things be speeded up.

At eight o'clock *The Red Tataria* appeared from behind

the promontory and slowly approached the landing. Granovsky smiled, expressed his thanks, and said good-by. Mr. Popp
returned the thanks without a trace of a smile.

As the boat approached the landing, there occurred the
difficulty, the delay that almost sent Granovsky and his weak
heart to the grave. The difficulty was resolved by the experienced and efficient chief of the regional office, Ozols.

The boat was packed with passengers. These crafts did
not run frequently, and there were so many people on board
that all the decks, all the cabins, and even the engine room
was full. There was no room on *The Red Tataria* for Mr. Popp.
Not only were all the cabin tickets sold, but each contained
secretaries of regional committees, shop supervisors, and
directors of important factories going to Perm for the holidays.

Granovsky felt that he was about to lose consciousness,
but Ozols was more experienced in such matters. He went up
to the top deck with four of his men, all armed and in uniform.

"Everybody get off! Take your things with you!"

"But we have tickets! To Perm!"

"To hell with you and your tickets! Go down below, to the
hold. You have three minutes to think it over."

"The guards will travel with you to Perm, I'll explain
along the way."

Five minutes later, Mr. Popp stepped onto the empty deck
of *The Red Tataria*.

Descendant of a Decembrist*

>>>

MANY BOOKS have been written about Mixail Lunin, the first hussar and a famous Decembrist. In the destroyed chapter of *Eugene Onegin*, Pushkin wrote:

Friend of Mars, Bacchus, and Venus . . .

He was a true knight, an intelligent, well-informed man who not only spoke up for his cause but worked actively toward it. It was indeed a great cause! In due course I will tell you everything I know about the second hussar, his descendant.

Hungry and exhausted, we leaned into a horse collar, raising blood blisters on our chests and pulling a stone-filled cart up the slanted mine floor. The collar was the same device used long ago by the ancient Egyptians. I saw it, experienced it myself. Throughout Kolyma the mine was notorious.

The cruel, snowless Kolyma winter of 1940–41 was approaching. Cold crushed the muscles and squeezed a man's temples. Iron stoves were placed in the tarpaulin tents that served as our shelter in the summer months, but the tents, a mass of holes, could not retain the "free air."

Our inventive bosses were preparing people for the winter. Inside each tent a second, smaller frame was constructed that was designed to trap a layer of air about four inches thick. This frame was covered, all but the ceiling, with roofing material. The resulting double tent was slightly warmer than the single canvas one.

The very first nights spent in these tents made it clear

* The Decembrists were a group of Russian officers who unsuccessfully attempted to stage a coup in December of 1825. Most were exiled to Siberia, accompanied by their wives.—TRANS.

that this arrangement meant doom, and a quick doom at that. I had to get out of there—but how? Who would help? Five miles from us was a large camp, Arkagala, where miners worked. Our group was considered a part of that camp. I had to get transferred there, to Arkagala.

But how?

Convict tradition demands that in such instances, a prisoner first of all approach a doctor. There was a first-aid station at Kadychkan run by a former student of the Moscow Medical Institute who hadn't finished his course of study. At least, that was the rumor in our tent.

It required enormous will power to find the strength to go to the first-aid station. I didn't have to get dressed or put on my boots, of course, since I wore them constantly from one bathhouse day to the next. But I just didn't have the strength. Why should I waste my rest period on this "visit" to the doctor, when it might result only in mockery or even a beating. (Such things happened.) But the main consideration was the hopelessness, the slimness of the chance of success. Nevertheless, I couldn't afford to lose even the slightest chance in the search for luck—this judgment came from my body and its exhausted muscles, not from experience or intelligence.

As in beasts, the will was subordinate to instinct.

On the other side of the road from our tent was a small hut used by geologists, exploring parties, secret police, and military patrols. The geologists had left long ago, and the hut had been converted into an outpatient medical facility with a cot, a cupboard with medications, and a curtain made from an old blanket. The blanket concealed the area where the "doctor" lived.

Right down the middle of the road was a line of people queuing up in the bitter cold to be examined.

I squeezed my way into the hut, and the heavy door, closing behind me, pushed me right in. The doctor had blue eyes, a large forehead with two bald spots, and hair. He had to have hair; hair was an existential statement. Hair in camp is a testimony to importance. Almost everyone was shaved bald, so that anyone who had hair was the object of general envy. Combed hair was a perculiar form of protest against life in the camps.

"From Moscow?" the doctor asked me.

"From Moscow."

"Let's get acquainted."

I gave him my name and shook his outstretched hand. It was cold and somewhat moist.

"Lunin."

"That's a proud name," I said with a smile.

"I'm his great-grandson. In our family the oldest son is always called either Mixail or Sergei. We alternate. Pushkin's Lunin was Mixail Sergeevich."

"I know." Somehow this, our first discussion, didn't smack at all of the camps. I forgot about my request, since I didn't want to introduce an inappropriate note into our conversation.

"Have a smoke!"

I began to roll a cigarette with my rosy, frost-bitten fingers.

"Take more, don't be bashful."

"Back at home I have a whole library of books about my great-grandfather. I'm a medical student. But I was arrested and didn't graduate. Everyone in our family was in the military except me. I became a doctor. And I don't regret it."

"So much for Mars. A friend of Aesculapius, Bacchus, and Venus."

"I don't know about the Venus part, but it certainly is true about Aesculapius—except I don't have a diploma. If I did, I'd really show them."

"How about Bacchus?"

"Well, of course, I do have grain alcohol here. But all I need is one shot glass. I get drunk easily. But you know how things are—I take care of the civilian village as well. Come back again sometime."

On the point of leaving, I opened the door slightly with my shoulder.

"You know," Lunin said, "Muscovites like to talk about their town—the streets, the skating rinks, the houses, the Moscow River—more than Kievans or Leningraders do. . . . You people like to talk about the city even more, and they remember it better. . . ."

I dropped by several times in the evening when Lunin had finished attending to patients. I'd smoke a homemade cigarette but never got up the nerve to ask for bread.

Sergei Mixailovich, like everyone who either through luck or profession had an easy time of it in camp, didn't think much about others and couldn't really understand hungry people. His sector—Arkagala—was getting enough to eat, and the mine catastrophes had bypassed the town.

"If you like, I'll operate on you—remove that cyst from your finger."

"All right."

"Just don't ask me to release you from work. You know yourself it's not really convenient for me to do that."

"But how can I work with my finger all cut up?"

"You'll manage."

I agreed, and Lunin did a good job of removing the cyst and gave it to me as a "keepsake." Many years later my wife and I were to meet, and in the first minute of our meeting she squeezed my fingers, feeling in amazement for that cyst.

I realized that Sergei Mixailovich was simply very young, that he needed an educated person to talk to, that his views of the camps and his idea of "fate" were no different from those of any civilian supervisor, that he was even capable of admiring the camp thugs, and that the brunt of the storm of '38 had passed over him.

I treasured every day, every hour of rest; exhausted from life in the gold mines, my muscles demanded a respite. I treasured every piece of bread, every bowl of soup; my stomach demanded food, and my will was not strong enough to keep my eyes from wandering over the shelves in search of bread. But I forced myself to remember Moscow's Chinatown (which has no Chinese) and the Nikitsky gates where the writer Andrei Sobol shot himself and where Stern shot at the German ambassador's car. It is that part of Moscow's street history which will never be written down.

"Yes, Moscow, Moscow. Tell me, how many women have you had?"

It was senseless for a half-starved man to keep up this conversation, but the young surgeon listened only to himself and wasn't offended by my silence.

"Sergei Mixailovich, our fates are a crime—the greatest crime of the age."

"I'm not sure of that," Sergei Mixailovich said with an expression of displeasure. "It's just the kikes muddying the water."

I shrugged my shoulders.

Soon Sergei Mixailovich got his transfer to Arkagala, and I thought—without any sadness or feeling of injustice—that one more person had left my life forever and that parting was, in reality, an easy thing. But matters worked out differently.

The supervisor of the sector where we worked harnessed to an Egyptian yoke like slaves was Pavel Ivanovich Kiselev. A middleaged engineer, he was not a Party member. He beat his prisoners daily. Whenever the supervisor set foot in the sector, there were beatings, blows, and shouting.

Was it because he had no fear of being punished? Was there a blood lust lurking in the depths of his soul? Or perhaps a desire to distinguish himself in the eyes of the senior supervisors? Power is a terrible thing.

Zelfugarov, a counterfeiter from my work gang, lay in the snow, spitting out his broken teeth.

"All my relatives were shot for counterfeiting, but I was a minor, so I got off with only fifteen years' hard labor. My father offered the prosecutor half a million rubles—real ones, in cash—but he wouldn't go for it."

There were four of us working the shift, harnessed to the horse collar and walking around the post. We stopped near Zelfugarov. There was Korneev, a Siberian peasant; Lenya Semenov, a thief; the engineer Vronsky; and myself. Semenov said:

"It's only in camp that you learn to work with machinery. Try your hand at any kind of work—what do you care if you break a crane or a winch?" This point of view was popular even among many of the young surgeons in Kolyma.

Vronsky and Korneev were my acquaintances. We were not friends, but we had known each other since we had been together at Black Lake—an assignment where I returned to life. Without getting up, Zelfugarov turned his bloodied face with its swollen, dirty lips to us.

"I can't get up, guys. He hit me under the ribs."

"Go tell the paramedic."

"I'm afraid to, that will only make things worse. He'll tell the supervisor."

"Listen," I said. "There's no end to this. We have only one way out. As soon as the coal production chief or some other bigwig comes, someone must step forward and hit Kiselev right on the snout. People will talk about it all over Kolyma, and they'll have to transfer Kiselev. Whoever hits him will have his sentence lengthened. How many years will they give for Kiselev?"

We returned to our work, leaned into the horse collar, went back to the barracks, had supper, and prepared to go to sleep. The "office" sent for me.

Kiselev was sitting in the office, staring at the floor. He was no coward and didn't fear threats.

"So that's it?" he said cheerfully. "All Kolyma will talk about it? I could have you put on trial—for an attempt on my life. Get out of here, you bastard."

The only one who could have turned me in was Vronsky, but how? We were together the entire time.

After that, life at the work site became easier for me. Kiselev didn't even approach our collar and came to work with a small-caliber rifle. He didn't descend into the test pit either.

Someone entered the barracks.

"The doctor wants to see you."

The "doctor" who replaced Lunin was a certain Kolesnikov, a tall young student who had also been arrested and thus had never finished his course of study.

When I arrived, I found Lunin sitting at the table in his overcoat.

"Get your things ready. We're leaving for Arkagala. Kolesnikov, make up a transfer sheet."

Kolesnikov folded a piece of paper several times and tore off a tiny fragment that was hardly larger than a postage stamp. On it he wrote in microscopic handwriting: "Transferred to medical section, Arkagala."

Lunin took the paper and ran off.

"I'll have Kiselev issue a travel permit."

He was upset when he returned.

"He won't let you go. He says you threatened to hit him in the face, and he absolutely refuses to agree."

I told Lunin the story.

"It's your own fault," he said. "What do you care about Zelfugarov and all these. . . . They weren't beating you."

"I was beaten before."

"Well, I'm off. The truck is leaving. We'll think of something." And Lunin got into the cab.

A few days passed, and Lunin appeared again.

"I'm here to see Kiselev. About you."

He returned in a half-hour.

"Everything's in order. He agreed."

"How?"

"I have a method for taming the heart of the rebellious." And Sergei Mixailovich acted out the conversation with Kiselev:

"What brings you back to these parts. Sergei Mixailovich? Sit down and have a smoke."

"Sorry, I don't have the time, Pavel Ivanovich. These petitions accusing you of beatings have been forwarded to me. But before signing them, I decided to ask you if they were accurate."

"It's a lie, Sergei Mixailovich. My enemies will say anything. . . ."

"That's what I thought. I won't sign them. What difference would it make, Pavel Ivanovich? What's done is done, and there's no replacing teeth that have been knocked out."

"That's right, Sergei Mixailovich. Why don't you come home with me? My wife has made some brandy. I was saving it to celebrate the New Year, but on such an occasion. . . ."

"I'm sorry, Pavel Ivanovich, I just can't. But I do want to ask one favor in return. Let me take Andreev to Arkagala."

"That's one thing I'll never do. Andreev is, how should I put it? . . ."

"Your personal enemy?"

"Precisely."

"Well, he's my personal friend. I thought you would be more receptive to my request. Take a look at these petitions."

Kiselev fell silent:

"Okay, he can go."

"Make up the transfer papers."

"Have him come for them himself."

I stepped across the threshold of the "office." Kiselev was staring at the floor.

"You're going to Arkgala. Here are your transfer papers."

Lunin had already left, but Kilesnikov was waiting for me.

"You can leave this evening—about nine o'clock. Right now we have a case of acute appendicitis." He handed me a slip of paper.

I never saw either Kiselev or Kolesnikov again. Kiselev was soon transferred to Elgen, where he was accidentally killed a few months after arriving. A thief broke into his house at night. Hearing steps, Kiselev grabbed the double-barreled shotgun from the wall, cocked it, and attacked the thief. The thief tried to get out the window, and Kiselev struck him in the back with the butt of the shotgun. The gun went off, and Kiselev took both barrels right in the stomach.

Every convict in every coal-mining area of Kolyma was delighted. The newspaper with the announcement of Kiselev's funeral passed from hand to hand. In the mines the wrinkled scrap of paper was held up to the battery light. People read it, rejoiced, and shouted: "Hurrah! Kiselev died! So there is a God!"

It was from this Kiselev that Sergei Mixailovich had saved me.

Convicts from Arkagala worked the mine. For every hundred men working underground, there were a thousand working in support groups.

Hunger had reached Arkagala. And, of course, it reached the political prisoner barracks first.

Sergei Mixailovich was angry:

"I'm not the sun that can warm everybody. I got you a job as an orderly in the chemical laboratory, so you have to figure out for yourself how to live—camp-style, you understand?" Sergei Mixailovich patted me on the shoulder. "Dmitri worked here before you. He sold all the glycerine—both barrels. He got twenty rubles for a half-liter bottle. Said it was honey. Ha-ha-ha. These convicts will drink anything."

"That's not my way."

"Just what is your way?"

The orderly's job wasn't reliable. There were strict orders regarding me, and I was quickly transferred to the mine. The desire to eat grew stronger.

Sergei Mixailovich rushed about the camp. Our doctor had one passion: he was immensely attracted by camp officials of all types. Friendship or even a shade of friendship with any camp official was a source of unbelievable pride for him. He attempted to demonstrate his intimacy with the camp authorities in any way possible and was capable of bragging for hours about this intimacy.

I went to see him in his office. Hungry but afraid to ask for a piece of bread, I sat and listened to his endless bragging.

"As for the camp authorities, they have real power. There is no power not given by the Lord. Ha-ha-ha! All you have to do is please them, and everything is fine."

"I'd like to punch each and every one of them in the face."

"That's just your trouble. Listen, let's make an agreement. You can come to see me; I know its boring in the regular barracks."

"Boring?"

"Sure. You can drop by, have a smoke. No one will give you a smoke in the barracks. I know what things are like over there—you light up, and a hundred eyes are watching you. Just don't ask me to release you from work. I can't do that. That is, I can, but it's awkward. I won't interfere in that respect. As for food, I depend on my orderly for that. I don't stand in line myself for bread. So if you need bread, ask my orderly, Nikolai. How is it that after all your years in the camps you can't lay your hands on some bread? You know what Olga Petrovna, the chief's wife, told me today? They're inviting me for dinner. There'll be booze too."

"I have to go, Sergei Mixailovich."

Hungry and terrible days ensued. Once, no longer able to struggle with hunger, I went to the first-aid station.

Sergei Mixailovich was sitting on a stool, clipping the dead nails from the frost-bitten fingers of a dirty, hunched man. The nails fell with a click, one after the other, into an empty basin. Sergei Mixailovich noticed me.

"I collected half a basin of these yesterday."

A woman's face looked out from behind the curtain. We rarely saw women, let alone this close and in the same room. She looked beautiful to me. I bowed and said hello.

"Hello," she said in a low, wonderful voice. "Sergei, is this your friend, the one you told me about?"

"No," Sergei Mixailovich said, tossing his snips into the basin and walking over to the sink to wash his hands.

"Nikolai," he said to his orderly, who had just come in, "take this basin away and bring some bread for him." He nodded in my direction.

I waited until the bread was brought and left for the barracks. As for the woman, whose tender and beautiful face I remember to this day, I never saw her again. She was Edith Abramovna, civilian, Party member, a nurse from the Olchan Mine. She had fallen in love with Sergei Mixailovich, taken up with him, got him transferred to Olchan, and obtained for him an early release while the war was still going on. She traveled to Magadan to present Sergei Mixailovich's case to Nikishov, the head of Far Northern Construction. She was expelled from the Party for being involved with a prisoner; it was the usual method for putting a stop to such affairs. She got Lunin's case transferred to Moscow, had his sentence canceled, and even managed to get permission for him to take his medical examinations at Moscow University, from which he graduated and had all his civil rights reinstated. And she married him formally.

And when this descendant of a Decembrist received his medical degree, he abandoned Edith Abramovna and demanded a divorce.

"She's got a pack of relatives, like all those kikes! I don't need that."

He left Edith Abramovna, but he didn't manage to leave Far Northern Construction. After graduation, he had to return to the Far North for at least three years. As a licensed doctor, Lunin used his connections with camp authorities to land an unexpectedly important appointment—chief of surgery at the Central Prison Hospital on the Left Bank of the Kolyma River in the village of Debin. It was 1948, and by that time I was senior orderly of the surgical ward.

I met Lunin on the stairway. He had a habit of blushing

when he was embarrased. His face became very red when he saw me, but he treated me to a cigarette, congratulated me on my successes and my "career," and told me about Edith Abramovna.

Lunin's appointment was like a thunderbolt. Rubantsev had been in charge of surgery. A front-line surgeon and a major in the medical service, he was an experienced, no-nonsense type who had moved here after the war—and not just for three days. Some didn't like Rubantsev. He didn't get along with camp authorities, couldn't stand toadying and lying, and had terrible relations with Scherbakov, chief of sanitation in Kolyma.

Rubantsev had signed a contract and had been warned that the prisoners were his enemies. Being a man of independent mind, however, he soon saw that he had been lied to during his "political" preparation. Rogues, embezzlers, slanderers, and loafers were his colleagues at the hospital. It was the prisoners with their many skills (including medicine) who ran the hospital. Rubantsev realized where the truth lay, and he was not about to hide it. He applied to be transferred to Magadan, where there was a high school for his son. He was denied the transfer orally. After considerable effort, he managed to send his son to a boarding school fifty miles from Debin. This took several months, and by that time he was running his ward confidently and dismissing loafers and thieves. News of these threatening activities was immediately sent to Scherbakov's office in Magadan.

Scherbakov didn't like to stand on ceremony with his subordinates. Cursing, threats, and prison sentences worked fine with prisoners, but they wouldn't do for a former front-line surgeon who had received medals in the war and who was working under contract.

Scherbakov dug up Rubantsev's old application and had him transferred to Magadan. And although the academic year had already begun and the surgical ward was working smoothly, he had to abandon everything. . . .

Rubantsev left, and three days later a drunken party was held in the treatment room. Even the principal doctor, Kovalev, and the hospital director, Vinokurov, helped themselves to the surgical alcohol. They hadn't visited the surgical ward earlier, because they were afraid of Rubantsev. Drunken parties began in all the doctors' offices, and nurses and cleaning women were invited. In a word, there were a lot of changes. Secondary adhesion began to occur in operations in the surgical ward, since precious grain alclohol could not be wasted on patients. Half-drunk hospital officials strolled back and forth through the ward.

This was my hospital. After I finished my courses in 1946, I was sent here with a group of patients. The hospital grew before my eyes. It had been a regimental headquarters formerly, but after the war a specialist on camouflage had judged it unsuitable because of its prominent location. Indeed, it could be seen for tens of miles, and so it was converted into a prison hospital. On leaving the three-story building, the former owners, the Kolyma Regiment, had ripped out all the plumbing and sewer pipes. All the chairs in the auditorium had been burned in the boiler. The walls were full of holes, and the doors were broken. The Kolyma Regiment had left Russian-style. We had to repair everything—screw by screw, brick by brick.

The doctors and assistants were doing their best to do a good job. For many of them it was a sacred duty—to pay for their medical education by helping people.

All the loafers raised their heads when Rubantsev left.

"Why are you stealing alcohol from the medicine cabinets?"

"Go to hell," a nurse answered me. "Thank God that Rubantsev is gone, and Lunin is in charge now."

I was amazed and depressed at Lunin's conduct. The party continued.

At the next brief meeting, Lunin laughed at Rubantsev: "He didn't do a single ulcer operation. And he's supposed to be a surgeon."

This was nothing new. It was true that Rubantsev hadn't done any ulcer operations. The patients in the therapeutic wards who had this diagnosis were emaciated, undernourished prisoners who didn't have the slightest chance of surviving the operation. "The background isn't right," Rubantsev would say.

"He's a coward," Lunin shouted and transferred twelve such patients to his ward from the therapeutic ward. All twelve were operated on, and all twelve died. The hospital doctors remembered Rubantsev's experience and kindness.

"Sergei Mixialovich, this is no way to work."

"Don't tell me what to do!"

I made up a report asking that a commission be sent from Magadan. I was transferred to a tree-cutting group in the forest. They wanted to send me to a penal mine, but the senior official of the local Party chapter talked them out of it: "This isn't '38 anymore. It's not worth the risk."

A commission was sent, and Lunin was "fired" by Far Northern Construction. Instead of three years, he only had to serve one and a half.

A year later, when the hospital administration had been replaced, I returned from my paramedic job in the forest to take charge of admitting patients to the hospital.

Once, in Moscow, I met the descendant of a Decembrist. We didn't say hello.

Sixteen years later I learned that Edith Abramovna had gotten Lunin reinstated in his job at Far Northern Construction. She had gone with him to the Chukotka Peninsula, to the village of Pevek. Here they talked things out for the last time, and Edith Abramovna died; she drowned herself in the Pevek River.

Sometimes my tranquilizers don't work, and I wake up at night. I remember the past and a woman's beautiful face; I hear her deep voice: "Sergei, is that your friend?"

The Seizure

>>>

THE WALL LURCHED, and nausea welled up in my throat, sickeningly sweet. For the thousandth time a burned-out match floated past me. I stretched out my hand to grab the annoying match, and it disappeared. Sight had left me. But the world had not yet abandoned me—I could still hear the far-off, insistent voice of the nurse somewhere out on the street. Then hospital gowns, the corner of a building, and the starry sky flashed by. . . . An enormous gray turtle with a cold gleam in its eyes rose up before me. Someone had broken a hole through its ribs, and I crawled into the hole, clutching and pulling myself up with my hands. I trusted only my hands.

I remembered someone's insistent fingers skillfully easing my head and shoulders onto the bed. Everything fell quiet, and I was alone with someone as enormous as Gulliver. Insectlike, I lay on a board, and someone examined me intently through a magnifying glass. I squirmed, but the terrible glass followed all my movements. Only when the orderlies had transferred me to a hospital cot and the blissful calm of solitude had followed did I realize that Gulliver's magnifying glass had not been a nightmare—I had been looking at the on-duty doctor's glasses. This pleased me.

My head ached and whirled at the slightest movement, and it was impossible to think. I could only remember, and remote frightening pictures began to appear in black and white like scenes from a silent movie. The cloying nausea so similar to the effect of ether would not go away. I had experienced that sensation before. . . . I recalled how, many years before, in the Far North, a day off had been declared for the first time in six months. Everybody wanted to lie down, simply to lie prone, not to mend clothing, not to move. . . . But everyone was awakened early in the morning and sent for firewood. Five miles from the village was a forest-cutting area, and we were each to select a log commensurate with our strength and drag it home to the barracks. I decided to go off in a different direction to a place a little more than a mile away where there were some old log stacks and where I could find a log I could handle. Climbing the mountain was exhausting, and when I reached the stack, I couldn't find a light log. Higher up I could see collapsed stacks of black logs, and I started to make my way up to them. There was only one log there that was slender enough for me to carry, but one end of it was pinned under the stack, and I didn't have the strength to pull it free.

After several attempts I became totally exhausted. Since it was impossible to return empty-handed, however, I gathered my strength and crawled still higher to a stack covered with snow. It took me a long time to clear away the loose, squeaky snow with my hands and feet. I finally managed to yank a log free, but it was too heavy.

I wore a dirty towel around my neck that served as a scarf. I unwound it, tied it to the tip of the log, and started dragging the log away. The log slid downhill, banging against trees, bumps, and my legs, sometimes even getting away from me. Octopuslike, the dwarf cedar grasped at the log, but it would tear itself free from the tree's black tentacles, gather speed, and then get stuck in the snow. I would crawl down to it and again force it to move. While I was still high up on the mountain, it became dark, and I realized that many hours had passed, and the road back to the village and the camp area was still far away. I yanked at the scarf, and the log again hurtled downward in jerks. I dragged the log out onto the road. The forest lurched before my eyes, and a sickening sweet nausea welled up from my throat. I came to in the crane operator's shed; he was rubbing my face and hands with stinging snow.

All this I saw projected once again on the hospital wall.

But instead of the crane operator, a doctor was holding my hand.

"Where am I?"

"In the Neurological Institute."

The doctor asked me something, and I answered with difficulty. I was not afraid of memories.

PART FOUR

MARRYING

Captain Tolly's Love

>>

IN THE GOLD-MINE WORK GANG, the easiest job was that of
carpenter. He would nail boards together to make a walkway
for wheelbarrows loaded with earth for the washer. These
wooden "whiskers" stretched out in all directions from the
central walkway. From above, that is from the gold washer,
the walkway looked like a monstrous centipede, flattened,
dried, and nailed forever to the gold mine's open workings.

The carpenter had a "pushover" job compared with that
of the miner or the wheelbarrow man. The carpenter's hands
knew neither the handle of the wheelbarrow, the shovel, the
feel of a crowbar, nor the pick. An ax and a handful of nails
were his only tools. Normally the gang boss would rotate men
on this crucial job to give everyone at least a slight chance to
rest up. Of course, fingers clutched in a death grip around a
shovel or pick handle cannot be straightened out by one day of
easy work. A man needs to be idle for at least a year for that to
happen. But there is, nevertheless, some measure of justice in
this alternation of easy and hard labor. The rotation was not
rigid: a weaker person had a better chance of working a day as
a carpenter. One didn't have to be a cabinetmaker or carpenter
to hew boards and drive nails. People with a university education coped with the job quite well.

In our work gang this pushover job wasn't evenly distributed. The job of carpenter was always filled by one and the
same person—Isaiah Davidovich Rabinovich, former director
of Soviet government insurance. Robinovich was sixty-eight
years old, but the old man was in good health and hoped to
survive his ten-year sentence. In camp it is the work that kills,
and anyone who praises it is either a scoundrel or a fool.
Twenty-year-olds, thirty-year-olds died one after the other,

and that was why they were brought to this "special zone," but Rabinovich, the carpenter, lived on. He evidently knew someone among the camp higher-ups, had some mysterious pull. He even got office jobs. Isaiah Rabinovich understood that every day and every hour spent some place other than the mine promised him life and salvation, whereas the mine offered him only doom and death. There was no reason to bring pensioners to the special zone. Rabinovich's nationality had brought him here to die.

But Rabinovich was stubborn and did not want to die.

Once we were locked up together, "isolated" for the first of May. It happened every year.

"I've been observing you for a long time," Robinovich said, "and I was pleased to know that someone was watching me, studying me, and that it was not someone who was doing it as part of his job."

I smiled at Rabinovich with a crooked smile that ripped open my wounded lips and tore my gums, which were already bloody from scurvy.

He said, "You're probably a good person. You don't speak degradingly of women."

"I hadn't noticed, Isaiah Davidovich. Can it be that they really talk about women here?"

"They do, but you don't take part."

"To tell the truth, Isaiah Davidovich, I consider women to be better than men. I understand the dual unity of man and woman, of husband and wife, etc. And then there's motherhood and labor. Women even work better than men."

"That's true," said Beznozhenko, a bookkeeper who was sitting next to Rabinovich. "Every Saturday when they make you work without pay you're better off not being next to a woman. She'll work you to death. And every time you want to take time out for a smoke, she'll get mad."

"That too," Rabinovich said distractedly, "probably, probably. . . . Well, here we are in Kolyma, and a lot of women have come to find their husbands. Theirs is a terrible lot, what with all those syphilitic higher-ups exploiting them. You know that just as well as I do. But no man has ever come out here to follow a convicted, exiled wife. I wasn't director of government insurance for long, but it was enough to get ten years. For many years I was in charge of the overseas division of government insurance. Do you know what that means?"

"I understand," I said without thinking, for I had no idea what that meant.

Rabinovich smiled very properly and very politely.

"Aside from my work for government insurance abroad . . ."

And glancing suddenly into my eyes, Rabinovich sensed that I was not interested in anything. At least not until dinner.

The conversation was renewed after a mouthful of soup.

"If you like, I'll tell you about myself. I lived abroad a lot, and everywhere I've been—in the hospital or the barracks—they always ask me to describe one thing: how, where, and what I ate over there. A sort of culinary motivation. Gastronomic dreams and nightmares. Would you like that kind of story?"

"Yes," I said.

"Good. I was an insurance agent in Odessa. I worked for the Russia, an insurance agency. I was young and tried to work well and honestly for the owner. I learned languages. He sent me abroad. I married the owner's daughter. I lived abroad right up to the revolution. The owner was like Savva Morozov;* he was laying his bets on the Bolsheviks. I was abroad during the revolution with my wife and daughter. My father-in-law died an accidental death; it had nothing to do with the revolution. I knew a lot of people, but none of them had any influence after the October Revolution. Do you understand me?"

"Yes."

"The Soviet government was just getting on its feet. People came to see me. Russia, the Russian Soviet Federated

* An extremely wealthy man before the revolution.—TRANS.

Socialist Republic, was making its first purchases abroad and
needed credit. But the word of the State Bank wasn't sufficient
collateral for a loan. A note from me, however, my recommen-
dation, was enough. So I fixed up Kreiger, the match king,
with the Russian Soviet Federated Socialist Republic. After a
few deals like that they let me come home. And I had some
delicate problems to work on here at home as well. Have you
heard anything about Spitzbergen and how the deal was paid
for?"

"A little."

"Well, I was the one who loaded the Norwegian gold onto
our schooner in the North Sea. So aside from handling foreign
accounts, I had a number of assignments of that sort. The
Soviet government was my new boss, and I served it just as I
had the insurance agency—honestly."

Rabinovich's calm, intelligent eyes peered directly at me.

"I'm going to die. I'm already an old man. I've seen life.
But I feel sorry for my wife. She's in Moscow. My daughter's
in Moscow too. They haven't been picked up yet as members
of the family . . . I guess I'll never see them again. They write
to me often, send packages. How about you? Do you get packages?"

"No, I wrote that I didn't want any packages. If I survive,
it'll be without anyone's help. I'll be obligated only to myself."

"There's something noble in that. But my wife and
daughter would never understand."

"Nothing noble at all. You and I are not only beyond good
and evil, we're also beyond anything human. After all that I've
seen, I don't want to be obligated to anyone—not even my own
wife."

"I can't say that I understand that; as for myself, I write
and ask for more. The packages mean a job in bookkeeping
for a month. I gave my best suit for that job. You probably
thought the director felt sorry for an old man. . . ."

"I thought you had an 'in' with the camp administration."

"So I'm a stool pigeon? But who needs a seventy-year-old

stool pigeon? No, I simply gave a bribe, a big bribe. And I'm not sharing the rewards of that bribe with anyone—not even you. I get my packages, write, ask for more."

After that first of May we returned to the same barracks, and our berths, something like those in a railroad car, were next to each other. I had accumulated a lot of experience in the camps, and the old man, Rabinovich, had a young man's curiosity for life. When he saw that my rage could not be contained, he began to have a certain respect for me—nothing more than respect. Maybe it was an old man's longing to talk about himself to anyone he might meet on a train, about the life he wanted to leave behind him on earth.

Lice did not frighten us. Precisely when I met Isaiah Rabinovich, my scarf was stolen. It was only a cotton scarf, of course, but it was, nevertheless, a real knitted scarf.

We were being led out to work. The method they used to hurry things along was called "last man out." The overseers would grab people, and the guards would push them with their rifle butts, driving the crowd of ragged men down the icy hill. The last man would be grabbed by the hands and feet and thrown down the hill. Both Rabinovich and I tried to jump down as quickly as possible and get in formation on the area below, where the guards were already dealing out blows to speed up the process. Most of the time we managed to roll down the hill without anything happening to us and to reach the mine alive. Once we got there, it was up to God.

The last man in formation was tossed from the icy hill, tied to the horse sleigh, and dragged to the work site. Both Rabinovich and I were fortunate enough to avoid that fatal trip.

The camp zone was selected so as to force us to climb upward when we returned from work, scrambling up the steps, grabbing at the remains of naked, broken shrubs. One might think that after a day in the gold mine, people would not have the strength to crawl upward. But they crawled— even if it took them a half-hour to reach the camp gates and the barracks zone. The usual inscription hung over the gates: "Labor is honor, glory, nobility, and heroism."* They would go to the cafeteria and drink something from bowls. From there they would go to the barracks to sleep. In the morning it would all begin again.

Not everyone was hungry here—just why, I never learned. When it got warmer, in the spring, the white nights began, and they started playing a terrible game in the camp cafeteria called "bait-fishing." A ration of bread would be put on the table, and everyone would hide around the corner to wait for the hungry victim to approach, be enticed by the bread, touch it, and take it. Then everyone would rush out from around the corner, from the darkness, from ambush, and there would commence the beating to death of the thief, who was usually a living skeleton. I never ran into this form of amusement anywhere except at Jelhala. The chief organizer was Dr. Krivitsky, an old revolutionary and former deputy commissar of defense industries. His accomplice in the setting out of these terrible baits was a correspondent from the news-paper *Izvestia*—Zaslavsky.†

I had my knitted cotton scarf. The paramedic in the hospital had given it to me when I was checking out. When our group reached the Jelhala mine, a gray, unsmiling face, crossed and crisscrossed with northern wrinkles and scarred with the marks of old frostbite, confronted me.

"Let's trade!"

"No."

"Sell it to me!"

"No."

All the locals—about twenty of them had come running up to our truck—stared at me, amazed at my rashness, foolishness, pride.

---

* Compare with: *Arbeit macht frei.*—TRANS.
† A journalist by that name wrote some of the most vicious attacks on Pasternak.—TRANS.

"He's a convict like us, but he's the group leader," someone prompted me, but I shook my head.

The brows shot upward on the unsmiling face. He nodded to someone and pointed to me.

But they lacked the nerve for open banditry in this camp. They had another, more simple way—and I knew it, so I tied the scarf around my neck and never took it off again—not in the bathhouse, not at night, never.

It would have been easy to keep the scarf, but the lice wouldn't leave me in peace. There were so many lice in the scarf that it moved all by itself when I took it off just for a minute to shake myself free of lice and put it on the table beside the lamp.

For two weeks I struggled with the shadows of thieves, trying to convince myself that these were shadows and not thieves.

At the end of two weeks I hung the scarf, on one occasion, in front of me, turned around to pour myself a mug of water, and the scarf immediately disappeared, plucked away by the hand of an experienced thief. The theft, which I knew was coming, which I felt, which I foresaw, demanded so much of my energy that I was glad I no longer had to struggle to keep the scarf. For the first time since arriving at Jelhala, I fell into a sound sleep and had a good dream—perhaps because the thousands of lice had disappeared, and my body could relax.

Isaiah Rabinovich had observed my struggle with sympathy. Of course, he had not made the slightest effort to help me preserve the lousy scarf. In camp it was each man for himself, and I didn't expect any assistance.

But Isaiah Rabinovich had been working for several days in bookkeeping, and he slipped me a dinner coupon to console me for my loss. And I thanked Rabinovich.

After work everyone lay down to sleep, spreading their dirty workclothes under them.

Isaiah Rabinovich said:

"I want to ask your advice on a certain question. It has nothing to do with camp."

"About General de Gaulle?"

"Don't laugh. I've received an important letter. That is, it's important to me."

With my entire body I made an effort to drive away encroaching sleep, shook myself, and began to listen.

"I already told you that my wife and daughter are in Moscow. They haven't been touched. My daughter wants to get married. I got a letter from her. And from her fiancé—here it is." And Rabinovich took a package of letters from under his pillow—a package of pretty sheets with swift, precise handwriting. I looked and saw that the letters were Latin, not Cyrillic.

"Moscow permitted these letters to be sent on to me. Do you know English?"

"Me? English? No."

"This is in English. It's from her fiancé. He asks permission to marry my daughter. He writes: 'My parents have already given permission, and there remains only the permission of the parents of my future wife. . . .' And here is my daughter's letter. 'Papa, my husband, naval attache of the United States of America, Captain Tolly, asks your permission for our marriage. Papa, answer right away.'-"

"What sort of delirium is that?" I said.

"It's no delirium. It's a letter from Captain Tolly to me. And a letter from my daughter. And a letter from my wife."

Rabinovich slowly searched out a louse under his shirt, pulled it out, and crushed it on the bunk.

"Your daughter wants your permission to get married?"

"Yes."

"Your daughter's fiancé, the naval attache of the United States, Captain Tolly, wants permission to marry your daughter?"

"Yes."

"So run to the camp director and request that a special delivery letter be sent."

"But I don't want to give my permission for this marriage. That's exactly what I wanted to ask your advice about."

I was simply dumbfounded by these letters, these stories, this act.

"If I agree to the marriage, I'll never see her again. She'll go away with Captain Tolly."

"Listen, Isaiah Davidovich, you're going to be seventy soon. I consider you a reasonable person."

"Those are just my feelings, and I haven't thought the matter out yet. I'll send a letter tomorrow. It's time to go to sleep."

"Let's celebrate this event tomorrow. We'll eat our kasha before the soup. And the soup—after the kasha. We can even roast some bread. Make toast. We'll boil the bread in water. What do you say to that, Isaiah Davidovich?"

Even an earthquake could not have kept me from sleep, from the unconsciousness of dream. I closed my eyes and forgot about Captain Tolly.

The next day Rabinovich wrote the letter and dropped it in the mailbox near the guard post.

Not long after that I was taken away for trial. They tried me and returned me to the same camp. I didn't have a scarf, but then the group leader was gone as well. I arrived just like any other emaciated prisoner. But Isaiah Rabinovich recognized me and brought me a piece of bread. He had nailed down his job in bookkeeping and had learned not to think about tomorrow. The mine had taught Rabinovich a lesson.

"I believe you were here when my daughter was getting married?"

"Of course."

"Let's have it."

"Captain Tolly married my daughter. I believe that was where we stopped." Rabinovich resumed his tale. His eyes smiled. "Captain Tolly stayed for three months, and then he got a position on a battleship in the Pacific Ocean and left on his assignment. My daughter, Captain Tolly's wife, wasn't allowed to leave. Stalin viewed these marriages with foreigners as a personal insult, so the People's Commissariat of Foreign Affairs whispered to Captain Tolly: 'Go on alone, have a good time. What's keeping you? Get married again.' In a word, the final answer was that my daughter was sent to work in Stockholm at the Swedish Embassy."

"As a spy? A secret assignment?"

Rabinovich looked at me in displeasure at my chatter.

"I don't know. I don't know what sort of work. She was in the embassy. My daughter worked for a week there. Then a plane came from America, and she flew away to her husband. Now I'll be expecting letters from places other than Moscow."

"And what about the local camp authorities?"

"They're afraid. They don't dare to have an opinion on such matters. An investigator came from Moscow to question me. And he left."

Isaiah Rabinovich's happiness didn't stop there. The greatest miracle was that his sentence ended when it was supposed to—to the day, without figuring in his workdays.

The body of the former insurance agent was strong enough for him to get a job as a financial inspector in Kolyma. They did not let Rabinovich go back to the mainland. He died about two years before the Twentieth Party Congress where Khrushchev gave his famous de-Stalinization speech.

The Lepers

>>

IMMEDIATELY AFTER the war a drama was played out at the hospital. Or, to be more precise, it was the conclusion of a drama.

The war had dragged out into the light of day whole strata of life that always and everywhere remain at the bottom. The actors were not criminals or underground political groups.

In the course of military actions the leprosariums had been destroyed, and the patients had merged with the rest of the population. Was this a secret war or an open one? Was it chemical or bacteriological?

People ill with leprosy easily passed themselves off as wounded or maimed in war. Lepers mixed with those fleeing to the east and returned to a real, albeit terrible life where they were accepted as victims or even heroes of the war.

These individuals lived and worked. The war had to end in order for the doctors to remember about them and for the terrible card catalogues of the leprosariums to fill up again.

Lepers lived among ordinary people, sharing the retreat and the advance, the joy and the bitterness of victory. They worked in factories and on farms. They got jobs and even became supervisors. But they never became soldiers—the stubs of the fingers that appeared to have been damaged in the war prevented them from assuming this last occupation. Lepers passed themselves off as war invalids and were lost in the throng.

Sergei Fedorenko was a warehouse manager. A war invalid, he was sufficiently able to command the disobedient stumps of his fingers to do his job well. He was forging a career for himself and expected to become a member of the Party, but when he got too close to money, he began to drink and run around with women and got arrested. He arrived in Magadan on one of the Kolyma ships as a common criminal with a sentence of ten years.

Here Fedorenko switched his diagnosis. Although there were more than enough persons maimed either by war or their own hand, it was more advantageous, more fashionable, and less noticeable to dissolve in the sea of frostbite cases.

That was how I met him in the hospital—with supposedly third- to fourth-degree frostbite, a wound that wouldn't heal, one foot and the fingers on both hands reduced to stumps.

Fedorenko was undergoing treatment—without any results. But then every patient tried his utmost to resist treatment so as not to go back to the mines. After many months of tropic ulcers, Fedorenko was released from the hospital. Not wanting to leave, he became an orderly and was ultimately promoted to senior orderly in the surgical ward with three hundred beds. This was the central hospital with a thousand convict-prisoners. One floor of one wing was reserved for civilian employees.

Somehow it happened that the doctor who was normally in charge of Fedorenko's case fell ill, and Doctor Krasinsky, an old military doctor and a lover of Jules Verne (Why?) was handling his patients for him. Kolyma life had not yet beaten out of him the desire to chat, gossip, and discuss cases.

In examining Fedorenko, Krasinsky experienced a feeling of surprise, but he couldn't put his finger on just what it was. He had known this feeling of anxiety from time to time ever since he was a student. No, this was not a tropic ulcer, not a stub left by an explosion or an ax. The flesh was slowly decomposing. Krasinsky's heart began to beat. He called Fedorenko over to the window, to the light, and greedily peered into his face, unable to believe what he saw. It was leprosy! A line from a medical school text ran through Krasinsky' mind—"The human face begins to resemble that of a lion"—and Fedorenko's face was a lion's mask! Feverishly Krasinsky leafed through his textbooks. He took a large needle and poked one of the numerous white spots on Fedorenko's skin several times. There was no sensation of pain!

Sweating, Krasinsky wrote a report to his superiors. The patient, Fedorenko, was isolated in a separate room, and samples of his skin were sent for biopsies to Magadan, and from there to Moscow. The response came in about two weeks. Leprosy! It was as if Krasinsky were celebrating his birthday. The hospital authorities wrote to still-higher authorities about sending Fedorenko to the Kolyma leprosarium, which was situated on an island with machine guns trained on the crossing. There was a guard, there had to be a guard.

Fedorenko did not deny that he had been in a leprosarium and that the patients, left to their own devices, had fled to freedom. Just as in ordinary life, some followed the retreating army, and others went forward to meet the Germans. Fedorenko calmly began to wait to be sent off, but the hospital was in an uproar. People were shouting and cursing Fedorenko. Everyone feared leprosy, even those who had been beaten during questioning and whose souls had been ground into dust by a thousand interrogations, whose bodies were broken and tormented by unbearable labor, who had sentences of twenty-five years' hard labor capped with five years' exile—sentences they could never serve or survive. . . .

The same psychic phenomenon was at work that forced a man to postpone a well-planned escape simply because there would be tobacco or commissary privileges that day. There are as many strange and illogical instances as there are camps. Human shame, for example. How does one measure it, what are its limits? People whose lives are ruined, whose past and future have been trampled on, suddenly find themselves in the grip of some trivial prejudice, some nonsense that they for some reason can neither ignore nor deny. And the sudden appearance of shame is the most subtle of human emotions, to be remembered for one's entire life as something real and infinitely precious.

There was an incident in the hospital when an orderly,

who was not yet an orderly and was simply helping out, was assigned to shave a newly arrived group of women. The administration was amusing itself by assigning men to shave women and women to shave men. But this man begged his superior to classify the affair as "sanitary treatment." He just could not accept that his life was ruined, that these amusements of the camp authorities were nothing but a dirty foam in a terrible kettle where he himself was being boiled away.

This amusing, tender human streak reveals itself suddenly.

The hospital was in a panic. After all, Fedorenko had been working there for several months. Unfortunately, the "prodromal period" of the illness, which precedes the appearance of any external symptoms, can last for several years. Those inclined to suspect the worst were doomed to retain this fear in their souls forever, whether they were civilian employees or convicts.

The hospital was in a panic. The doctors searched their own bodies and those of their patients for white, insensitive spots. A needle joined the phonendoscope and small rubber hammer as standard equipment for any doctor conducting a preliminary examination.

The patient, Fedorenko, was brought before the orderlies and doctors and undressed. An overseer with a pistol stood near the patient. Doctor Krasinsky, armed with an enormous pointer, gave a lecture on leprosy, pointing his stick alternately at the leonine face of the former orderly, at the fingers that were on the verge of falling off, and at the shiny white spots on his back.

All residents, without exception, civilian and convict, were reexamined, and suddenly a white spot insensitive to pain was discovered on the back of Shura Leschinskaya, a nurse from the front lines on duty in the women's ward. Leschinskaya, who had been in the hospital for only a few months, had no lion's mask. Her conduct had been neither stricter nor looser than that of any "nurse" recruited from among the former prisoners.

Leschinskaya was locked up in one of the rooms of the women's ward, and a sample of her skin was sent to Magadan and from there to Moscow for analysis. The answer came: leprosy!.

Disinfection after leprosy is quite difficult. Regulations require that the house in which a leper has lived be burned. That was what the textbooks said. But how could one of the wings of a gigantic two-storied hospital be burned? No one could make up his mind to do that. It was something like disinfecting expensive furs. To preserve the value of their furs, the owners are willing to risk leaving the infection in them. They sprinkle some chemical symbolically on the precious furs, because steaming would destroy not only the microbes but the fur as well. The administration would have remained silent even if it had been a matter of plague or cholera.

Someone assumed responsibility for not burning the wing, and even the room in which Fedorenko was kept under lock and key was not burned. They simply soaked everything with phenol and carbolic acid and sprayed repeatedly.

Downstairs, in the basement, two tiny rooms were constructed for the patients. Fedorenko and Leschinskaya were transferred there. Guards were stationed beside the heavy padlocked doors, and the couple was left there to await an order or a detachment of guards from the leprosarium.

Fedorenko and Leschinskaya spent one day in their cells, and when the guards were changed at the end of the day, the cells were found to be empty. Panic ensued in the hospital. Every window and door in the cells was intact. Krasinsky was the first to figure out how they had fled. They had escaped through the floor.

Fedorenko had used his enormous strength to pry the logs apart and had broken into the bread-slicing room and the operating room of the surgical ward. They had gathered up all the grain alcohol, and the narcotics from the cupboards, and made off with their loot to an underground den.

They had selected a spot, barricaded it, and thrown blankets and mattresses on top to wall themselves off from the world, the guards, the hospital, and the leprosarium. They lived there as man and wife for several days—three days, I believe.

On the third day guards with dogs found the two lepers. I was a member of the group that searched the tall basement of the hospital. The foundation was very high at that spot. The guards removed the logs and exposed the two lepers lying naked. They didn't get up. Fedorenko's dark, mutilated hands were around Leschinskaya's gleaming body. Both were drunk.

They were covered with blankets and carried away to one of the two cells, no longer separated.

Who covered them with a blanket, who touched their terrible bodies? A special janitor was found in the civilian hospital and, with the permission of higher authorities, given a credit of seven working days for each one spent with the lepers. That is more than they give people for working in the tungsten mines, the lead mines, or the uranium mines. Seven days for one. The article of the penal code under which the man was sentenced was not taken into consideration. They found a soldier, arrested at the front and sentenced to twenty-five years of hard labor and five years of exile, who naïvely assumed that his heroism would shorten his sentence and bring nearer the day of his liberation.

Convict Korolkov, a wartime lieutenant, stood guard at the cell round the clock. He even slept before the door. And when the guards arrived from the "island" (on which the leprosarium was located), convict Korolkov was taken with the two lepers to tend to their needs. I never heard anything more of Korolkov, or of Fedorenko, or of Leschinskaya.

PART FIVE

STEALING

The Red Cross

>>>

LIFE IN CAMP is so arranged that only medical personnel can give the convict any real help. The protection of labor depends on the protection of health, and the protection of health means the protection of life. The camp director and the overseers who work under him, the head of the guard and the guards themselves, the head of the Divisional Office of the Ministry of Internal Affairs and all his staff of investigators, the chief of culture and education with all his inspectors—these are only some of the numerous varieties of camp authority. Regulation of life in the camps consists of carrying out the will—good or bad—of these people. In the eyes of the convict they are all symbols of oppression and compulsion. All these people force the convict to work, guard him day and night to keep him from escaping, check to see that he doesn't eat or drink too much. Daily, hourly, all these people repeat to the convict: "Work! Work more!"

Only one person in the camp does not say these terrible, hated words to the convict. That is the doctor. The doctor uses other words: "Rest," "You're tired," "Don't work tomorrow," "You're sick." Only the doctor has the authority to save the convict from going out into the white winter fog to the icy stone face of the mine for many hours every day. The doctor is the convict's official defender from the arbitrary decisions of the camp authorities, from excessive zeal on the part of the more veteran guards.

At one time, large printed notices hung on the walls of the camp barracks: "The Rights 9 obligations of the Convict." Obligations were many and rights few. There was the right to make a written request to the head of the camp—as long as it was not a collective request . . . there was the right to send letters to one's relatives through the camp censors . . . and the right to medical aid.

This last right was extremely important, although in many of the first-aid stations at the mines, dysentery was cured with a solution of potassium permanganate, while the same solution—just a little thicker—was smeared on abscessed wounds and frostbite cases.

A doctor could officially free a man from work by writing in a book: "Hospitalize," "Send to health clinic," or "Increase rations." And in a "working" camp the doctor's most important job was to determine "labor categories," the degree to which a prisoner was capable of working. The setting of the different labor categories also determined the work norm of each prisoner. A doctor could even free a man—by declaring him an invalid under the authority of the famous Article 458. Once a person was freed from work because of illness, no one could make him work. The doctor could not be controlled in these instances; only medical personal higher up on the administrative ladder could do that. As far as treatment was concerned, the doctor was subordinate to no one.

It is important to remember that the doctor was also responsible for what went into the food—with regard both to quantity and quality.

The convict's only defender in any real sense was the camp doctor. The latter's power was considerable, since none of the camp authorities could control the actions of a specialist. An inaccurate, unconscientious diagnosis made by a doctor could only be determined by a medical worker of an equal or higher rank—that is, another doctor. Relations were almost inevitably hostile between camp authorities and their medical personnel. The very nature of their duties pulled them in different directions. The authorities always wanted group B (temporarily relieved from work because of illness) to be smaller so that the camp would have as many people as possible working. The doctor, on the other hand, saw that the bounds of good and evil had long since been passed, that people being sent to work were sick, tired, and exhausted, and had a right to be freed from work in much greater numbers than the camp authorities desired.

If he had a strong enough will, the doctor could insist that people be relieved from work. Without a doctor's sanction, no camp administrator could send people to work.

A doctor could save a convict from heavy labor. All convicts were divided, like horses, into categories of labor. There might be four, three or five such labor categories, although this term sounds as if it comes from a dictionary of philosophy. That is one of life's witticisms or, rather, mockeries.

To give a man an "easy" labor category often meant saving him from death. The saddest of all were those convicts who attempted to deceive the doctor and get into an easy labor category, and who were, in fact, more seriously ill than they themselves believed.

A doctor could release a man from work, send him to the hospital, and even classify him as an "invalid," thus returning him to the mainland. True, the bed in the hospital and actually getting sent back didn't depend on the doctor, but it was at least a start.

All this and many other things relating to everyday routine were understood perfectly and exploited by the criminal element in the camp. The thieves' code of morality prescribed a special attitude toward the doctor. Aside from legends about "prison rations" and the supposed "gentleman thief," the legend of the "Red Cross" was prevalent in the criminal world. The Red Cross was a criminal term, and I tense up every time I hear it.

The camp criminals openly demonstrated their respect for medical personnel, promised them their support, and made a distinction between doctors and "politicals."

A legend grew up, which is still told in the camps today, of how a doctor was robbed by petty thieves, and how other, more important criminals found the stolen goods and returned them with an apology.

But this went further than mere stories. The criminals genuinely did not steal from doctors, or at least tried not to. Doctors, if they were civilians, were given presents of objects or money. If the doctors were convicts, the method would be persistent requests for treatment and threats to kill. Doctors who rendered assistance to criminals were praised.

To have a doctor "on the hook" was the dream of every band of criminals. A criminal could be crude and insolent with any supervisor (he was even obliged to make a show of this sort of spirit under certain circumstances), but he would fawn, even cringe before a doctor. No criminal would allow a harsh word to be said about a doctor unless he realized that his complaint was not believed and that the doctor did not intend to satisfy his insolent demands.

No medical worker, the criminals believe, should be concerned about his fate in the camp. They assist him both in a material and a moral sense. Material assistance consists of stolen clothing. The criminal renders moral support by bestowing his conversation on the doctor, visiting him, being pleasant.

It is easy for a doctor to send some robust murderer and extortionist to the hospital instead of a sick political prisoner exhausted by excessive work. It is easy to send him there and keep him there until the criminal himself is ready to check out.

It is easy to send criminals to other hospitals for treatment if they need to go there for their own criminal, "higher" purposes.

It is easy to cover up for criminals who fake illness, and all the criminals are fakers and malingerers with their eternal trophic ulcers on shin and hip, with their trivial but impressive slashes on the stomach, and so on.

It is easy to hand over all the codeine and caffeine supplies together with the entire supply of drugs and alcoholic tinctures for use by one's "benefactors."

For many years I was responsible for admitting new

patients to the camp hospital. One hundred percent of the fakers officially sent by doctors were thieves. They either bribed the local doctor or threatened him, and he would make out the false medical slips.

Sometimes the local doctor or the local camp head would try to get rid of an annoying or dangerous element in his "household" by sending criminals to the hospital. They hoped at least to get a rest from them, if not to dispose of them altogether.

If a doctor was bribed, that was bad, very bad. But if he was frightened, that could be forgiven, for the criminals did not make empty threats. Once a doctor was sent from the hospital to the first-aid clinic of the Spokoiny Mine, where there was a large number of criminals. His name was Surovoy, and he had recently graduated from the Moscow Medical Institute. He was a young doctor, and—more important—he was a young convict doctor. Surovoy's friend tried to persuade him not to go. He could have refused and been sent to a general work gang instead of taking on this patently dangerous work. Surovoy had come to the hospital from a general work gang; he was afraid to return to it and agreed to go to the mine and work at his profession. The camp authorities gave him instructions but no advice on how to conduct himself. He was categorically forbidden to send healthy thieves from the mine to the hospital. Within a month he was killed while admitting patients; on his body were fifty-two knife wounds.

In the women's zone of another mine an elderly woman doctor, Spizel, was cut down with an ax by her own orderly, a female criminal named "Cooky" who was carrying out the "sentence" passed by the other criminals. That was what the expression "Red Cross" meant in those instances when the doctors could not be frightened or bribed.

Naïve doctors sought an explanation for these contradictions from the ideologists of the criminal world. One of the chief ideological leaders was a patient at the time in the surgical ward. Two months earlier he had used the usual foolproof method of getting himself out of solitary confinement: he sprinkled powder from a styptic pencil in his eyes—both of them, just to be sure. It just so happened that medical aid was late in arriving, and he was blinded. He was a bed-ridden invalid in the hospital and was to be shipped back to the mainland. But like Sir Williams from *Rocambole*, he continued— even though blind—to take part in making plans for future crimes, and in criminal "courts of honor" was considered an incontestable authority. In response to a doctor's question about the Red Cross and the murder of medical personnel by thieves, Sir Williams answered with that peculiar accent characteristic of so many of the thieves: "In life there are a number of situations in which the law should not be applied." He was a real specialist on dialectics, this Sir Williams.

In his "Notes from the House of the Dead," Dostoevsky never knew anyone from the true criminal world. He would never have allowed himself to express sympathy for that world.

The evil acts committed by criminals in camp are innumerable. The unfortunates are those from whom the thief steals their last rags, confiscates their last coin. The working man is afraid to complain, for he sees that the criminals are stronger than the camp authorities. The thief beats the working man and forces him to work. Tens of thousands of people have been beaten to death by thieves. Hundreds of thousands of people who have been in the camps are permanently seduced by the ideology of these criminals and have ceased to be people. Something criminal has entered into their souls forever. Thieves and their morality have left an indelible mark on the soul of each.

The camp administrator is rude and cruel; the persons responsible for propaganda lie; the doctor has no conscience. But all this is trivial in comparison with the corrupting power of the criminal world. In spite of everything, the authorities are still human beings, and the human element in them does survive. The criminals are not human.

The influence of their morality on camp life is boundless and many-sided. The camps are in every way schools of the negative. No one will ever receive anything useful or necessary from them—neither the convict himself, nor his superiors, nor the guard, nor the inadvertent witnesses (engineers, geologists, doctors), nor the camp administrators, nor their subordinates.

Every minute of camp life is a poisoned minute.

There is much there that a man should not know, should not see, and if he does see it, it is better for him to die.

There a convict learns to hate work. He does not and cannot learn anything else. He learns flattery, lying, petty acts and major villainies. He becomes totally engrossed in himself.

When he returns to "freedom," he sees that he has not only failed to grow during his years in camp but his interests have narrowed, become impoverished and crude. Moral barriers have somehow been pushed aside.

It is possible to commit base acts—and live.

It is possible to lie—and live.

It is possible to give a promise and not fulfill that promise—and live.

It is possible to drink up a friend's money.

It is possible to beg for charity—and live! Yes, even this is possible!

A person who has committed a base act doesn't die.

In camp a human being learns sloth, deception, and viciousness. In "mourning his fate," he blames the entire world.

He rates his own suffering too highly, forgetting that everyone has his own grief. He has forgotten empathy for another's sorrow; he simply does not understand it and does not desire to understand it.

Skepticism is by no means the worst aspect of the camp heritage. There a human being learns to hate. He is afraid; he is a coward. He fears repetitions of his own fate. He fears betrayal, he fears his neighbors, he fears everything that a human being should not fear. He is morally crushed. His concepts of morality have changed without his having noticed this change.

A camp supervisor learns to wield limitless power over the prisoners, he learns to view himself as a god, as the only authorized representative of power, as a man of a "superior race."

What will the guard tell his fiancée about his work in the Far North—the guard who often held human lives in his hands and who often killed people who stepped outside the "forbidden zone"? Will he tell her how he used his rifle butt to beat hungry old men who could not walk?

The young peasant who has become a prisoner sees that in this hell only the criminals live comparatively well, that they are important, that the all-powerful camp administrators fear them. The criminals always have clothes and food, and they support each other.

The young peasant cannot but be struck by this. It begins to seem to him that the criminals possess the truth of camp life, that only by imitating them will he tread the path that will save his life. He sees, moreover, that there are people who can live even on the very bottom of existence. And the peasant begins to imitate the conduct of the criminals. He agrees with their every word, is ready to carry out all their errands, speaks of them with fear and reverence. He is anxious to adorn his speech with their slang; no member of either sex, convict or civilian, who had been to Kolyma had failed to carry away from Kolyma the peculiar slang of the criminals.

These words are a poison that seeps into the soul. It is this mastery of the criminal dialect itself that marks the beginning of the noncriminal's intimacy with the criminal world.

The intellectual convict is crushed by the camp. Everything he valued is ground into the dust while civilization and culture drop from him within weeks. The method of persuasion in a quarrel is the fist or a stick. The way to induce someone to do something is by means of a rifle butt, a punch in the teeth.

The intellectual becomes a coward, and his own brain provides a "justification" of his own actions. He can persuade himself of anything, attach himself to either side in a quarrel. The intellectual sees in the criminal world "teachers of life," fighters for the "people's rights." A blow can transform an intellectual into the obedient servant of a petty crook. Physical force becomes moral force.

The intellectual is permanently terrified. His spirit is broken, and he takes this frightened and broken spirit with him back into civilian life.

Engineers, geologists, and doctors who have come to Kolyma to do contract work for Far Northern Construction are quickly corrupted. The sources of this corruption are many: a desire for money, rationalizations that the "taiga is the law," cheap and convenient slave labor, a narrowing of cultural interests. No one who has worked in the camps ever returns to the mainland. He would be worthless there, for he has grown accustomed to a "rich," carefree life. It is this very depravity that is described in works of literature as "the call of the North."

The criminal world, the habitual criminals whose tastes and habits are reflected in the total life pattern of Kolyma, are mainly responsible for this corruption of the human soul.

Women in the Criminal World

➤➤➤➤➤➤➤➤➤➤➤➤➤➤➤➤➤➤➤➤➤➤➤➤ ➤➤ ➤➤➤➤➤➤➤➤ ➤➤➤➤➤➤➤➤➤➤

AGLAYA DEMIDOVA was brought to the hospital with false documents. Neither her "case history" nor her convict passport were forged. No, these were in order. But the folder containing her papers was new and yellow—testimony of a recent sentencing. She arrived under the same name that she had used when she had been brought to the hospital two years earlier. Nothing in her situation had changed except her sentence. Two years ago her folder had been dark blue, and the sentence had been ten years.

A three-digit number had been added to the short list of two-digit figures listed in the column headed "Article of Criminal Code." It was her medical documents that were forged— the history of the illness, the laboratory tests, the diagnosis. They were forged by people who occupied official posts and who had at their disposal rubber stamps and their own good (or bad—who cares?) names. The head of medical services at the mine spent many truly inspired hours inventing a false case history.

The diagnosis of tuberculosis followed logically from the cleverly invented daily records. It was all there—the thick sheaf of temperature charts filled out to mimic typical tubercular curves and the forms testifying to impossible lab tests with threatening prognoses. It was the work of a doctor who, as if taking a medical examination, had been asked to describe the progress of a tubercular condition which had reached the point where immediate hospitalization was essential.

The work might have been done out of a sporting urge— just to show the central hospital that people back at the mines also knew their jobs. It was pleasant to remember, in the correct order, everything you had once learned at medical school. Of course, you never thought you would have occasion to apply your knowledge in such an unusual, "artistic" fashion. The main thing was that Demidova be accepted at the hospital—no matter what. The hospital could not refuse, had no right to refuse, this kind of patient, even if the doctors had a thousand doubts.

Suspicions cropped up right away, and Demidova sat alone in the hospital's enormous reception room while the question of her admission was discussed in local "higher circles." True, she was alone only in the Chestertonian sense of the word. The attendant and the orderlies didn't count, nor did the two guards who were never more than a step away from her. A third guard was off picking his way through the thickets of the hospital bureaucracy.

Demidova did not even bother to take off her cap and unbuttoned only the collar of her sheepskin coat. She smoked hurriedly, one cigarette after another, tossing the butts into a wooden ashtray filled with wood shavings. As she paced about the reception room from the narrow barred windows to the doors, her guards followed her, imitating her movements.

When the doctor on duty returned with a third doctor, the northern darkness had already fallen, and the lights had to be turned on.

"They won't take me?" Demidova asked the guard.

"No, they won't," the guard answered gloomily.

"I knew they wouldn't. It's all Kroshka's fault. She knifed that woman doctor, and they're taking it out on me."

"No one's taking anything out on you," the doctor said.

"I know better."

Demidova left ahead of the guards, the outside door slammed, and the truck engine roared.

Immediately a door opened from the corridor, and the head of the hospital entered with a whole retinue of security officers.

"Where is she? Where is Demidova?"

"They've already taken her away, sir."

"That's a shame, a real shame. I wanted to get a look at her. It's all your fault, Peter Ivanovich—you and your jokes." And the director and his companions left the reception room.

The director wanted at least to get a glance at the famous Demidova, a thief with a truly unusual story.

Aglaya Demidova had been sentenced to ten years for killing a woman whose responsibility it was to make job assignments. Demidova strangled her victim with a towel for being too pushy. Six months ago Demidova was being taken from court to the mine. There was a single guard, since it was only a few hours by car from the local court where they tried her to the mine where she worked. Space and time are analogous in the Far North. Space is generally measured in units of time; such is the practice of the Yakut tribesmen, who calculate the distance from one mountain to another as, for example, six days. Those who lived near the main artery—the highway— measured distances by the length of time it took to get there by motor vehicle.

Demidova's guard was a young "old man" who had stayed on for a second hitch and who was used to the liberties and peculiarities of life as a guard, the total master of the prisoners' fates. It was not the first time that he had "accompanied" a woman, and this sort of trip promised a form of amusement that most soldiers in the North enjoyed only rarely.

The three of them—the guard, the driver, and Demi-dova—ate at a roadside cafeteria. The guard drank some grain alcohol to get up his courage (in the North only higher-ups drink vodka) and took Demidova into the bushes. Rose willow, aspen saplings, and willow thickets grow luxuriously around any taiga settlement.

When they entered the bushes, the guard laid his automatic rifle on the ground and approached Demidova. Demidova tore herself free, grabbed the rifle, and in two crisscrossing bursts riddled the body of the amorous guard with nine bullets. She then threw the rifle into the bushes, returned to the cafeteria, and hitched a ride on a passing truck. The driver sounded the alarm, and the body of the guard along with the rifle was soon found. Demidova herself was arrested a couple of days later only a few hundred miles from where her tryst with the guard had taken place. She was again brought to trial and this time sentenced to twenty-five years. Even before she had shown no willingness to work and had occupied herself with robbing her neighbors in the barracks, so the head of the mine decided to get rid of her at any

price. The hope was that she would not be returned to the
mine after the hospital but would be sent somewhere else.

Demidova specialized in robbing stores and apartments—
a "city girl" in the terminology of the criminal world. This
world acknowledges only two types of women: thieves, whose
profession, like the men's, is stealing, and prostitutes, the
men's sweethearts.

The first group is considerably smaller than the second
but enjoys a certain respect among criminals, who consider
women to be creatures of a lower order. Their professional
abilities and services, however, demand recognition. The
female companion of a thief will, not infrequently, participate
in working out the plans for a robbery and even in the robbery
itself, but she does not take part in the male "trials of honor,"
where criminals actually try and sentence each other for violating their own peculiar code of ethics. These special male
and female roles have been dictated in part by a life where
men are imprisoned apart from women—a circumstance that
has influenced the life-styles, habits, and rules of both sexes.
Women are not as hard as men, and their "trials" are neither
as bloody nor as cruel. In a thieves' den, the women commit
murder less frequently than their male comrades.

Prostitutes consitute the second and larger group of
women connected with the world of crime. They are the
thieves' companions, and they are the breadwinners. Naturally, they participate, when necessary, in break-ins, casing a
building and staking it out, concealing the stolen merchan-
dise, and eventually fencing it, but they by no means enjoy
equal rights with the men of the criminal world. Any celebration is unthinkable without their presence, but they can never
even dream of participating in "courts of honor."

A third- or fourth-generation criminal learns contempt for
women from childhood. "Theoretical" and "pedagogical" ses-
sions alternate with the personal example of his elders.
Woman, an inferior being, has been created only to satisfy the

criminal's animal craving, to be the butt of his crude jokes and the victim of public beatings when her thug decides to "whoop it up." She is a living object, used by the criminal on a temporary basis.

When a criminal needs to "get to" a camp official, it is considered quite normal and proper for him to send his prostitute-companion to the man's bed. She herself shares this view. Conversations on this topic are always extremely cynical, laconic in the extreme, and descriptive. Time is precious.

The criminal code of ethics renders jealousy and courtship meaningless. Time-honored tradition permits the leader of a gang to select the best prostitute as his temporary wife. And if only yesterday this prostitute had been considered the property of a different thug, property that he could loan to his comrades in crime, today all his rights transfer to the new owner. If he is arrested tomorrow, the prostitute will return ho her former companion. And if the latter, in turn, is arrested, she will be told who her new owner is to be—the master of her life and her death, her fate, her money, her actions, her body.

What place can there be for such a feeling as jealousy? It simply does not exist in the thug's ethical system.

A criminal, they say, is human, and no human feeling is alien to him. It may be that he regrets having to give up his woman, but the law is the law, and those responsible for observing "ideological" purity, the purity of criminal ethics (without any quotation marks), will immediately point out the jealous criminal's error to him. And he will yield to the law.

There are instances when hot tempers and the hysteria characteristic of all criminals will make him defend "his woman." On such occasions the question is taken up in a criminal court, and criminal prosecutors will cite age-old traditions, demanding that the guilty man be punishsd.

Usually the parties concerned do not come to blows, and the prostitute submits to sleeping with her new master. There are no *ménages à trois* in the criminal world, with two men sharing one woman. Nor is it possible for a female thief to live with a noncriminal.

Men and women are separated in the camps. However, there are hospitals, transit prisons, out patient clinics, and clubs where men and women can hear and see each other.

One cannot but be amazed at the inventiveness of the prisoners, their energy in reaching goals that they have set for themselves. The amount of energy expended in prison to obtain a piece of crumpled tin which can be transformed into a knife to commit murder or suicide is incredible.

The energy expended by a criminal intent on arranging a meeting with a prostitute is enormous. The most critical factor is finding a place to which to summon the prostitute; the criminal need have no doubt as to whether or not she will come. The hand of justice will always find the guilty woman. She will dress in men's clothing and have sexual relations an extra time with her supervisor—just to slip away at the appointed hour to her unknown lover. The love drama is played out quickly—the way grass drops its seed in the Far North. If seen by the overseer when she returns to the women's zone, she will be put in a punishment cell, sentenced to a month of solitary confinement, or sent to a penal mine. She will endure all this with complete submission and even be proud of her actions; she has fulfilled her duty as a prostitute.

There was an instance in a large northern hospital for convicts when a prostitute was sent to spend an entire night with an important thug who was a patient in the surgical ward. The attendant on duty was threatened with a knife, and a stolen suit was given to the civilian orderly. Finally, the woman had relations with all eight of the criminals who were sharing the room. The suit's real owner recognized it and presented a written complaint. Considerable effort was expended to conceal the affair.

The woman was not at all upset or embarrassed when she was found in a room in the men's hospital.

"The fellows asked me to help them out, so I came," she explained calmly.

It is not difficult to understand that almost all the criminals and their female companions become ill with syphilis, and chronic gonorrhea is endemic—even in this age of penicillin.

There is a well-known classic expression: "Syphilis is not a disease but a misfortune." Here syphilis is not viewed as a cause for shame but is considered to be the prisoner's luck rather than his misfortune. This is yet a further example of the notorious "shift of values."

First, all cases of venereal disease must be treated, and every thug is aware of that. He knows he can "brake" in the hospital and that he won't be sent to some God-forsaken place but will live and be treated in relatively comfortable settlements where there are venerologists and specialists. This is so well known that even those criminals whom God has spared the third and fourth cross of the Wasserman reaction claim that they have venereal disease. They also are well aware that a negative laboratory result is not always reliable. Self-induced ulcers and false complaints are encountered along with real ulcers and genuine symptoms.

Venereal patients are kept in special treatment areas. At one time no work was done in these areas, but this system converted them into virtual resorts, a sort of *mon repos*. Later these "zones" were set up in special mines and wood-felling areas, and the prisoners had to produce the normal work quotas, but received medication (salvarsan) and a special diet.

In point of fact, however, relatively little work was demanded of the prisoners in these zones, and life there was considerably easier than in the mines.

Male veneral zones were always the source from which the hospital admitted the criminals' young "wives" who had been infected with syphilis through the anus. Almost all the professional criminals were homosexuals. When no women were at hand, they seduced and infected other men—most often by threatening them with a knife, less frequently in exchange for "rags" (clothing) or bread.

No discussion of women in the criminal world is complete without a mention of the vast army of "Zoikas," "Mankas," "Dashkas," and other creatures of the male sex who were christened with women's names. Strangely enough the bearers of these feminine names responded to them as if they saw nothing unusual, shameful, or offensive in them.

It is not considered shameful to be kept by a prostitute, since it is assumed that the prostitute will value highly any contact with a professional criminal. Furthermore, young criminals who are just trying their wings are very much attracted by the prospect of becoming pimps:

> They'll be sentencing us soon,
> March us off into the mines;
> Working girls will sing a tune
> And get a package through the lines.

This is a prison song; the "working girls" are prostitutes.

There are occasions when vanity and self-pity, emotions that take the place of love, cause a woman in the world of crime to commit "unlawful acts."

Of course, more is expected of a thief than of a prostitute. A female thief living with an overseer is, in the opinion of the zealots of thug juris prudence, committing treason. The "bitch's" error might be pointed out to her by means of a beating, or they might simply cut her throat. Similar conduct on the part of a prostitute would be regarded as normal.

When a woman has such a "run-in" with the law, the question is not always resolved even-handedly, and much depends on the personal qualities of the person involved.

Tamara Tsulukidze, a twenty-year-old thief and former companion of an import mobster in Tiflis, took up with Grachov, the head of cultural activities. Grachov was thirty, a lieutenant, and a handsome bachelor with a gallant bearing.

Grachov had a second mistress in camp, a Polish woman

by the name of Leszczewska, who was one of the famous "actresses" of the camp theater. When the lieutenant took up with Tamara, she did not demand that he give up Leszczewska. The rakish Grachov thus lived simultaneously with two "wives," showing a preference for the Muslim way of life. Being a man of experience, he tried to divide his attention equally between the two women and was successful in his efforts. Not only love but also its material manifestations were shared; each edible present was prepared in duplicate. It was the same with lipstick, ribbons, and perfume; both Leszczewska and Tsulukidze always received the same ribbons, the same bottles of perfume, the same scarves on the same day.

The impression this made was very touching. Moreover, Grachov was a handsome, clean-cut young man, and both Leszczewska and Tsulukidze (who lived in the same barracks) were ecstatic at their lover's tactful behavior. Nevertheless, they did not become friends, and Leszczewska was secretly delighted when Tamara was called to task by the hospital mobsters.

One day Tamara fell ill and was hospitalized. That night the doors of the women's ward opened, and an ambassador of the criminal world appeared on the threshold. He reminded Tamara of the property laws regarding women in the criminal world and instructed her to go to the surgical ward and carry out "the will of the sender." The messenger claimed there were people here who knew the Tiflis mobster whose companion Tamara had been. Here in camp he was being replaced by Senka, "the Nose." Tamara was to submit to his embraces.

Tamara grabbed a kitchen knife and rushed at the crippled thug. The attendants barely managed to save him. The man departed, threatening and cursing Tamara. Tamara checked out of the hospital the next morning.

There were several attempts—all of them unsuccessful—to return the prodigal daughter to the proud standards of the criminal world. Tamara was stabbed with a knife, but the wound was not serious. Her sentence ended, and she married an overseer—a man with a revolver—and the criminal world saw no more of her.

The blue-eyed Nastya Arxarova, a typist from the Kurgansk Oblast, was neither a prostitute nor a thief, but she voluntarily linked her fate to the criminal world.

Even as a child, Nastya had been surrounded by a suspicious respect, a sinister deference for the criminal world, whose figures seemed to have come from the pages of the detective novels she read. This respect, which Nastya had observed while still in the "free world," was present in prison and in the camps as well—wherever there were criminals.

There was nothing mysterious about this; Nastya's older brother was a well-known burglar in the Urals, and, since childhood, Nastya had bathed in the rays of his criminal glory. Without even noticing it, she found herself surrounded by criminals, became involved in their interests and affairs, and did not refuse to hide stolen goods for them. Her first three-month sentence angered and hardened her, and she became part of the criminal world. As long as she remained in her home town, the criminals were reluctant to declare their property rights to her for fear of her brother. Nastya's "social" position was more or less that of a thief; she had never been a prostitute and was sent as a thief on the usual long trips at the expense of the mob. She had no brother on these trips to protect her. On her first release from prison, the leader of a local mob in the first town she came to made her his wife and in the process infected her with gonorrhea. He was soon arrested and crooned a criminal parting song to her: "My buddy will take you over." Nastya didn't stay long with the "buddy," since he too was soon arrested, and Nastya's next owner exercised his rights to her. Nastya found him physically repulsive, because he slobbered constantly and was ill with some form of herpes. She attempted to use her brother's name to defend herself, but it was pointed out to her that her brother had no right to violate the immortal rules of the criminal world. She was threatened with a knife, and her resistance ceased.

At the hospital, when "romance" was called for, Nastya showed up meekly and often spent time in the punishment cells. She cried a lot—either because it was in her nature or because her own fate, the tragic fate of a twenty-year-old girl, terrified her.

Vostokov, an elderly doctor at the hostpial, was touched by Nastya's lot, even though she was only one of thousands in such a situation. He promised to help her get a job as a typist at the hospital if she would promise to change her way of life. "That is not in my power," Nastya answered him in her beautiful handwriting. "I cannot be saved. But if you wish to help me, buy me a pair of nylon stockings, the smallest size. Ready to do anything for you, Nastya Arxarova."

The thief Sima Sosnovskaya was tattooed from her head to her feet. Her entire body was covered with amazing interwined sexual scenes of the most unusual sort. Only her face, neck, and arms below the elbow were free of tattoos. Sima had acquired fame in the hospital through a bold theft—she had stolen a gold watch from the wrist of a guard who had decided to exploit the attractive girl's favorable disposition. Sima was of a much more peaceable nature than was Aglaya Demidova, or else the guard would have lain in the bushes until the Second Coming. She viewed the incident as an amusing adventure and considered that a gold watch was not too high a price for her favors. The guard nearly went crazy and, right up to the last minute, demanded that Sima return the watch. He searched her twice—quite unsuccessfully. The hospital was near, and the group of convicts being taken there was small; the guard couldn't risk a scandal in the hospital. Sima remained in possession of the gold watch. It was not long before she had sold it for liquor, and all trace of the watch vanished.

The moral code of the professional criminal, like that of the Koran, prescribes contempt for women. Woman is a contemptible, base creature deserving beatings but not pity. This is true of all women without exception. Any female representative of any other, noncriminal world is held in contempt by the mobster. Group rape ("in chorus") is not at all rare in the mines of the Far North. Supervisors bring their wives to Kolyma under armed guard; no woman ever walks or travels anywhere alone. Small children are guarded in the same fashion, since the seduction of little girls is the perpetual dream of every thug. This dream does not always remain a mere dream.

Children in the criminal world are educated in a spirit of contempt for women. The criminals beat their prostitute companions so much that it is said that these women are no longer able to experience the fullness of love. Sadistic inclinations are honed by the ethics of the criminal world.

The criminal is not supposed to experience any comradely or friendly emotion for his "woman." Nor is he supposed to have any pity for the object of his underground amusements. No justice can be shown toward the women of this world, for women's rights have been cast out of the gates of the criminal's ethical zone.

There is, however, a single exception to this black rule. There is one woman whose honor is not only protected from any attacks but who is even put on a high pedestal. There is one woman who is romanticized by the criminal world, one woman who has become the subject of criminal lyrics and the folklore heroine of many generations of criminals.

This woman is the criminal's mother.

The thug sees himself surrounded by a vicious and hostile world. Within this world, populated by his enemies, there is only one bright figure worthy of pure love, respect, and worship: his mother.

According to his own ethics, the criminal's attitude to the female sex is a combination of vicious contempt for women in general and a religious cult of motherhood. Many empty words have been written about sentimentality in the prisons. In reality this is the sentimentality of the murderer who waters his rose garden with the blood of his victims, the sentimentality of a person who bandages the wound of some small bird and who, an hour later, is capable of tearing this bird to shreds, since the sight of death is the best entertainment he knows.

We should recognize the true face of those who originated this cult of motherhood, a face that has been concealed by a poetic haze.

The criminal deifies his mother's image, makes it the object of the most sensitive prison lyrics, and demands that all others pay her the highest respect in absentia. He does this with the same heedlessness and theatricality with which he "signs his name" on the corpse of a murdered renegade, rapes a woman before the eyes of anyone who may care to watch, violates a three-year-old girl, or infects some male "Zoika" with syphilis.

At first glance, the only human emotion that seems to have been preserved in the criminal's obscene and distorted mind is his feeling for his mother. The criminal always claims to be a respectful son, and any crude talk about anyone's mother is always nipped in the bud. Motherhood represents a high ideal and at the same time something very real to everyone. A man's mother will always forgive, will always comfort and pity him.

One of the classic songs of the criminal world is titled "Fate":

> Momma worked when it got bad,
> And I began to steal.
> "You'll be a thief,
> Just like your dad,"
> She cried, over our meal.

Knowing that his mother will remain with him till the end of his brief and stormy life, the criminal spares her his cynicism. But even this one supposed ray of light is false—like every other feeling in the criminal soul. The glorification of one's mother is camouflage, a means of deceit—at best, a more or less bright expression of sentimentality in prison.

Even this seemingly lofty feeling is a lie from beginning

to end—as is everything else. No criminal has ever sent so much as a kopeck to his mother or made any attempt to help her on his own, even though he may have drunk up thousands of stolen rubles. This feeling for his mother is nothing but a pack of lies and theatrical pretense. The mother cult is a peculiar smoke screen used to conceal the hideous criminal world. The attitude toward women is the litmus test of any ethical system. Let us note here that it was the coexistence of the cult of motherhood with contempt for women that made the Russian poet Esenin so popular in the criminal world. But that is another story.

Any female thief or thief's companion, any woman who has directly or indirectly entered the world of crime, is forbidden all "romance" with non criminals. In such cases the traitoress is not killed. A knife is too noble a weapon to use on a woman; a stick or a poker it sufficient for her.

It is quite another matter if a man becomes involved with a woman from the "free world." This is honor and glory, the subject of one man's boasting stories and another's envy. Such instances are not at all rare, but such exaggerated fairy tales surround them that it is extremely difficult to learn the truth. A typist becomes a prosecutor, a courier is transformed into the director of a factory, and a salesgirl is promoted to the rank of a minister in the government. Bald-faced lies crowd the truth to the back of the stage, into utter blackness, and it is impossible to make head or tail of the play's action.

It is undoubtedly true, however, that a certain percent of the criminals have families back home, families that have long since been abandoned by their criminal fathers. The wives must raise their children and struggle with life as best they can. Sometimes it does happen that husbands return from imprisonment to their families, but they do not usually stay long. The "wandering spirit" lures them to new travels, and the local police provide an additional incentive for a speedy departure. The children remain behind—children who are not horrified by their father's profession. On the contrary, they pity him and even long to follow in his footsteps, as the song "Fate" tells us:

> *So have the strength to fight your fate,*
> *Don't look around for friend or mate.*
> *I'm very weak, but I will have*
> *To follow my dead father's path.*

The cadre officers of the criminal world—its "leaders" and "ideologues"—are criminals whose families have practiced the trade for generations.

As for fatherhood and the raising of children, these questions are totally excluded from the Talmud of vice. The criminal automatically expects his daughters (if they exist somewhere) to adopt a career of prostitution and become the companions of successful thieves. In such instances the conscience of the criminal is not burdened in the slightest—even within the unique ethical code of the world of crime. As for his sons becoming thugs, this, to the criminal, is a perfectly natural turn of events.

PART SIX

ESCAPING

The Procurator of Judea

>>>

ON THE FIFTH OF DECEMBER 1947, the steamship *Kim* entered the port of Nagaevo with a human cargo. Winter was coming on and navigation would soon be impossible, so this was the last ship that year. Magadan met its guests with forty-below weather. These, however, were no guests but convicts, the true masters of this land.

The whole city administration had come down to the port. Every truck in town was there to meet the boat. Soldiers— conscripts and regulars—surrounded the pier, and the process of unloading began.

Responding to the summons of the telegraph, every truck not needed in the mines within a radius of 500 kilometers had arrived empty in Magadan.

The dead were tossed onto the shore to be hauled away to the cemetery and buried in mass graves without so much as identification tags. A directive was made up ordering that the bodies be exhumed at some later date.

Patients who were moderately ill were taken to the central Prison Hospital on the left bank of the Kolyma River. The hospital had just been moved there—500 kilometers away. If the *Kim* had arrived a year earlier, no one would have had to make the long trip to the new hospital.

The head of surgery, Kubantsev, had just been transferred from an army post. He had been in the front lines, but even so he was shaken by the sight of these people, by their terrible wounds. Every truck arriving from Magadan carried the corpses of people who had died on the way to the hospital. The surgeon understood that these were the transportable, "minor" cases, and that the more seriously ill had been left in the port.

The surgeon kept repeating the words of General Radis-
chev, who once said after the war: "Experience on the front
cannot prepare a man for the sight of death in the camps."

Kubantsev was losing his composure. He didn't know
what sort of orders to give, where to begin. But something had
to be done. The orderlies were removing patients from the
trucks and carrying them on stretchers to the surgical ward.
Stretchers with patients were crammed into the corridors.
Smells cling to memory as if they were poems or human faces.
That festering camp stench remained forever in Kubantsev's
memory. He would never forget that smell. One might think
that the smell of pus and death is the same everywhere. That's
not true. Ever since that day it always seemed to Kubantsev
that he could smell his first Kolyma patients. Kubantsev
smoked constantly, feeling he was losing control of himself,
that he didn't know what instructions to give to the orderlies,
the paramedics, the doctors.

"Aleksei Alekseevich," Kubantsev heard someone say his
name. It was Braude, the surgeon who had formerly been in
charge of this ward but who had been removed from his position by the higher-ups simply because he was an ex-convict
and had a German name to boot.

"Let me take over. I'm familiar with all this. I've been here
for ten years."

Upset, Kubantsev relinquished his position of authority,
and the work began. Three surgeons began their operations
simultaneously. The orderlies scrubbed down to assist. Other
orderlies gave injections and poured out medicine for the
patients.

"Amputations, only amputations," Braude muttered. He
loved surgery and even admitted to suffering when a day in
this life went by without an operation, without a single inci-
sion.

"We won't be bored this time," Braude thought happily.
"Kubantsev isn't a bad sort, but he was overwhelmed by all of
this. A surgeon from the front! They've got all their instructions, plans, orders, but this is life itself. Kolyma!"

In spite of all this, Braude was not a vicious person. Demoted for no reason, he did not hate his successor or try to trip him up. On the contrary, Braude could see Kubantsev's confusion and sense his deep gratitude. After all, the man had a family, a wife, a boy in school. The officers all got special rations, lofty positions, hardship pay. As for Braude, he had only a ten-year sentence behind him and a very dubious future. Braude was from Saratov, a former student of the famous Krause, and had shown much promise at one time. But the year 1937 shattered Braude's life. Why should he attempt to take revenge on Kubantsev for his own failures? . . .

And Braude commanded, cut, swore. Braude lived, forgetting himself, and even though he hated this forgetfulness in moments of contemplation, he couldn't change.

He had decided today to leave the hospital, to go to the mainland. The fairy tale seemed to be over, but we don't know even the beginning.

On the fifth of December 1947, the steamship *Kim* entered the port of Nagaevo with a human cargo—three thousand convicts. During the trip the convicts had mutinied, and the ship authorities had decided to hose down all the holds. This was done when the temperature was forty degrees below zero. Kubantsev had come to Kolyma to speed up his pension, and on the first day of his Kolyma service he learned what third- and fourth-degree frostbite were.

All this had to be forgotten, and Kubantsev, being a disciplined man with a strong will, did precisely that. He forced himself to forget.

Seventeen years later, Kubantsev remembered the names of each of the convict orderlies, he remembered all the camp romances and which of the convicts "lived" with whom. He remembered the rank of every heartless administrator. There was only one thing that Kubantsev didn't remember—the steamship *Kim* with its three thousand prisoners.

Anatole France has a story, "The Procurator of Judea." In it, after seventeen years, Pontius Pilate cannot remember Christ.

The Green Procurator

≫≫≫≫≫≫≫≫≫≫≫≫≫≫≫≫≫≫≫≫≫≫≫≫≫≫≫≫≫≫≫≫≫≫≫≫≫≫

VALUES SHIFT HERE, in Kolyma, and any one of our concepts—even though its name may be pronounced in the usual way and spelled with the usual letters—may contain some new element or meaning, something for which there is no equivalent on the mainland. Here everything is judged by different standards: customs and habits are unique, and the meaning of every word had changed.

When it is impossible to describe a new event, feeling, or concept for which ordinary human language has no word, a new term is created, borrowed from the language of the legislator of style and taste in the Far North—the criminal world.

Semantic metamorphoses touch not only such concepts as Love, Family, Honor, Work, Virtue, Vice, Crime, but even words that are quite specific to the world of the Far North and that have been born within its bowels—for example, ESCAPE. . . .

In my early youth I read about Kropotkin's escape, in 1876, from the Fortress of Peter and Paul. His was a classic escape: a daredevil cab at the prison gates, a lady with a revolver under her cape, an exact calculation of the number of steps from the guardhouse door, the prisoner's sprint under fire, the clatter of horse hooves on the cobblestone pavement.

Later I read memoirs of persons who had been sent to exile in Siberia under the czars. I found their escapes from Yakutia and Verxoyansk bitterly disappointing: a sleigh ride with horses hitched nose to tail, arrival at the train station, purchase of a ticket at the ticket window. . . . I could never understand why this was called an "escape." Such escapes were once called "unwarranted absence from place of residence," and I believe that this was a far more accurate description than the romantic word "flight." Even the escape of the

Social-Revolutionary Zenzinov did not give the feeling of a real escape like Kropotkin's. An American yacht simply approached the boat on which Zenzinov was fishing and took him on board.

There were always plenty of escape attempts in Kolyma, and they were all unsuccessful, because of the particularly severe nature of the polar region, which the czarist government never attempted to colonize with convicts—as it did Sakhalin.

Distances to the mainland ran in to thousands of miles; the nearest settlements were those surrounding the mines of Far Northern Construction and Aldan, and we were separated from them by a taiga vacuum of six hundred miles.

True, the distance to America was significantly shorter. At its narrowest point, the Bering Strait is only fifty-five miles wide, but the border was so heavily guarded as to be absolutely impassable.

The main escape route led to Yakutsk. From there travel had to be either by water or on horseback. There were no planes in those days, but even so it would have been a simple matter to "lock up" the planes reliably.

It is understandable that there were no escape attempts in the winter; all convicts (and not only convicts) dream fervently of spending the winter under a roof next to a cast-iron stove.

Spring presents an unbearable temptation; it is always that way. To the compelling meteorological factor is added the power of cold logic. A trip through the taiga is possible only during the summer, when it is possible to eat grass, mushrooms, berries, roots, or pancakes baked from moss flour, to catch field mice, chipmunks, squirrels, jays, rabbits. . . .

No matter how cold the summer nights are in the north, in the land of the permafrost, no experienced man will catch cold if he sleeps on a rock, makes a mattress of grass or branches, avoids sleeping on his back, and changes position regularly from one side to the other.

The choice of Kolyma as a camp location was a brilliant

one, because of the impossibility of escape. Nevertheless, here as everywhere, the power of illusion is strong, and the price of such an illusion is paid in bitter days spent in punishment cells, additional sentences, beatings, hunger, and frequently death.

There were many escape attempts, which always began when the first emeralds colored the fingernails of the larches.

The convicts who tried to escape were almost always newcomers serving their first year, men in whose hearts freedom and vanity had not yet been annihilated, men whose reason had not yet come to grips with Far North conditions so different from those of the mainland. Until then the mainland was, after all, the only world that they had known. Distressed to the very depths of their souls by everything they saw, the beatings, torture, mockery, degradation, these newcomers fled—some more efficiently, others less—but all came to the same end. Some were caught in two days, others in a week, still others in two weeks. . . .

At first there were no long sentences for escaped prisoners. Ultimately, however, they were tried under Point Fourteen of Article Fifty-Eight of the criminal code. Escape is a refusal to work and is therefore counterrevolutionary sabotage. Ten years was thus to become the minimal "supplementary" sentence for an escape attempt. Repeated attempts were punished with twenty-five years. This frightened no one, nor did it lessen the number of escape attempts or of burglaries. But all that was to come later.

The enormous staff of camp guards with their thousands of German shepherds combined efforts with the border patrol and the vast army stationed in Kolyma and masquerading under the title "The Kolyma Regiment." Together, these groups had more than enough manpower to catch one hundred out of every hundred escapees.

How could escape be possible, and wouldn't it have been simpler to beef up the camp guards rather than hunt down those who had already escaped?

Economic considerations justify maintaining a staff of "head hunters," since this is cheaper than setting up a "dead-bolt" system of the prison variety. It is extraordinarily difficult to prevent the escape itself. Even the gigantic network of informers recruited from the prisoners themselves and paid with cheap cigarettes and soup is inadequate.

This is a question of human psychology with its twists and turns, and it is impossible to foresee who will attempt an escape, or when, or why. What happens is often quite different from that which might have been expected.

Of course, all sorts of preventive measures can be taken—arrests, imprisonment in those prisons within prisons that are called "punishment zones," transfers of "suspicious" prisoners from one place to another. Many such measures have been worked out, and they probably lessen the number of escapes. There would have been even more attempts had it not been for these "punishment zones" situated deep in the taiga under heavy guard.

People do manage to escape even from punishment zones, however, while no one attempts to escape from unguarded work sites. Anything can happen in camp.

Spring is a time of preparation. More guards and dogs are sent in, and additional training and special instructions are the rule. As for the prisoners, they also prepare—hiding tins of food and dried bread, selecting "partners."

There is a single example of a classic escape from Kolyma, carefully prepared and executed in a brilliant, methodical fashion. It is the exception that proves the rule. Even in this escape, however, a tiny insignificant thread was left that led back to the escapee—even though the search took two years. Evidently it was a question of the professional pride of the investigators, Vidokov and Lekokov, and considerably greater attention, effort, and money were spent on it than was normally done.

It is curious that the escapee who demonstrated such energy and wit was neither a "political" nor a professional criminal, either of whom might have been expected to specialize in such affairs. He was an embezzler with a ten-year sentence.

Even this is understandable. An escape by a "political" is always related to the mood of the "outside" and—like a hunger strike in prison—draws its strength from its connection with the outside. A prisoner must know, and know well in advance, the eventual goal of his escape. What goal could any "political" have had in 1937? People whose political connections are accidental and insignificant do not flee from prison. They might try to escape to their family and friends, but in 1938 that would have involved bringing repressive measures down on the heads of anyone whom the escapee might have seen on the street.

In such instances there was no getting off with fifteen or twenty years. The "political" would have been a threat to the very lives of his friends and family. Someone would have had to conceal him, render him assistance. None of the "politicals" in 1938 tried to escape.

The few men who actually served out their sentences and returned home found that their own wives checked the correctness and legality of their release papers and raced their neighbors to the police station to announce their husbands' arrival.

Reprisals taken upon innocent persons were quite simple. Instead of being reprimanded or issued a warning, they were tortured and then sentenced to ten or twenty years of prison or hard labor. All that was left to such persons was death. And they died with no thought of escape, displaying once more that national quality of passivity glorified by the poet Tiutchev and shamelessly exploited on later occasions by politicians of all levels.

The professional criminals made no attempts to escape because they did not believe they could succeed in returning to the mainland. Moreover, experienced employees of the camp police and the Criminal Investigation Service claim to have a sixth sense that enables them to recognize professional criminals. It is as if the criminal were stamped with the indelible mark of Cain. The most eloquent example of the existence of this sixth sense occurred during a month-long search for an armed robber and murderer. The search was being conducted along the roads of Kolyma, and an order was issued that he be shot on sight.

The detective, Sevastyanov, stopped a stranger in a sheepskin coat standing beside a tank at a filling station. When the man turned around, Sevastyanov shot him in the forehead. Sevastyanov had never seen the bandit, who was fully dressed in winter clothing. It is impossible to examine tattoos on every passer-by, and the description given to Sevastyanov was very vague. The photograph was so inadequate that it too was of little assistance. In spite of all this, Sevastyanov's intuition did not fail him.

A sawed-off shotgun fell from beneath the dead man's coat, and a Browning pistol was found in his pocket. He had more than enough identification papers.

How should we regard this positive proof of a sixth sense? Another minute, and Sevastyanov himself would have been shot. But what if he had killed an innocent man?

The criminals had neither the strength nor the desire to return to the mainland. Having weighed all the pros and cons, they decided not to take any chances but to limit their activities to reorganizing their lives in this new environment. This was, of course, a rational decision. The thugs viewed escape attempts as bold adventures, but unnecessary risks.

Who would make a run for it? A peasant? A priest? I met only one priest who had attempted to escape—and that was before the famous meeting where Patriarch Sergei handed Bullitt, the first American ambassador, a list of all Orthodox priests serving sentences throughout the Soviet Union. Patriarch Sergei had had the opportunity to acquaint himself with the cells of Butyr Prison when he was Metropolitan. As a result of Roosevelt's intervention, all members of the clergy were released in a body from imprisonment and exile. The intention was to arrange a certain "concordat" with the church—an essential step in view of the approaching war.

Perhaps it would be a common criminal who would attempt to escape—a child molester, an embezzler, a bribe taker, a murderer? But there was no sense in these people's attempting to escape, since their sentences (which were called "terms" in Dostoevsky's time) were short, and they were given easy service jobs. In general they had no difficulty in obtaining "positions of privilege" in the camp administration. Workdays were generously credited to them and—most important—they were well treated when they returned to their hometowns and villages. This kindness could not be explained away as the Russian people's capacity to pity the "unfortunate." That attitude had long since become a thing of the past, a charming fairy tale. Times had changed, and the great discipline of the new society demanded that "the simple people" copy the attitude of the authorities in such matters. This attitude was usually favorable, since common criminals did not trouble the government. Only "Trotskyites" and "enemies of the people" were to be hated.

There was another significant factor that might explain the indifference of the populace to those who had returned from the prisons. So many people had spent time in prison that there probably was not a family in the country in which some family member or friend had not been "repressed." Once the saboteurs had been eliminated, it was the turn of the well-to-do peasants, who were called *kulaks* (the term meaning "fist"). After the *kulaks* came the "Trotskyites," and the "Trotskyites" were followed by persons with German surnames. Then a crusade against the Jews was on the point of being declared. All this reduced people to total indifference toward anyone who had been marked by any part of the criminal code.

Earlier anyone who had returned from prison to his native village inspired in others guarded feelings (concealed or openly displayed) of animosity, contempt, or sympathy, while now no one paid any attention to such persons. The moral isolation of those marked as convicts had long since disappeared.

Former prisoners were met in the most hospitable fashion—provided their return had been sanctioned by the authorities. Any child molester and rapist who had infected his young victim with syphilis could count on enjoying full freedom of action in those same circles where he had once "overstepped" the bounds of the criminal code.

The fictionalized treatment of legal categories played a significant role in this regard. For some reason writers and dramatists wrote many works having to do with the theory of law. The law book of the prisons and camps, however, remained locked up under seven seals. No serious conclusions that might touch upon the heart of the matter were reached on the basis of service reports.

Why should the criminal element in camp have attempted to escape? The idea was remote from their minds, and they relinquished their fates totally to the camp administration. In view of all these circumstances, Paul Krivoshei's escape was all the more remarkable.

Krivoshei's name meant "crooked neck" in Russian, and he was a stocky, short-legged man with a thick red neck that was all apiece with the back of his head. His name was no accident.

A chemical engineer from a factory in Kharkov, he spoke several foreign languages perfectly, read a great deal, had a good knowledge of painting and sculpture, and a large collection of antiques.

A prominent Ukrainian engineer, he did not belong to the Party and deeply despised all politicians. He was a clever and passionate man, but greed was not one of his vices. That would have been too crude and banal for Krivoshei, whose passion was for enjoying life as he understood it—indulging in relaxation and lust. Intellectual pleasures did not appeal to him. His culture and vast knowledge combined with material possessions provided him with many opportunities to satisfy his baser instincts and desires.

Krivoshei had studied painting simply to be able to enjoy a higher status among those who loved and appreciated art and not appear ignorant before the objects of his passion—be they male or female. Painting had never interested him in the slightest, but he considered it his obligation to have an opinion even on the square hall in the Louvre.

The same was true of literature, which he read primarily in French or English and primarily for language practice. In and of itself, literature was of little interest to him, and he could spend a virtual eternity reading a novel—one page a night before falling asleep. There cannot be a single book in this world that could have kept Krivoshei awake till morning. He guarded his sleep carefully, and no detective novel could have upset his even schedule.

Musically, Krivoshei was a total ignoramus. He had no ear, and he had never even heard of, much less felt, the sort of mystical reverence Blok had for music. Krivoshei had long since learned that the lack of a musical ear was "not a vice, but a misfortune," and he was quite reconciled to his ill luck. In any case, he possessed sufficient patience to sit to the end of some fugue or sonata and thank the performer—particularly if it was a woman. He enjoyed excellent health and was of a plump, Pickwickian build, in other words a shape that threatened no one in camp.

Krivoshei was born in 1900. He always wore either horn-rimmed glasses or glasses with round lenses and no rims at all. Slow and unhurried in composure with a high, arched, receding brow, he presented an extremely imposing figure. This too was probably intentional; his sedate bearing impressed the supervisors and lightened his lot in camp.

A man with no feeling for art and lacking that excitement characteristic of both the creator and the user of art, Krivoshei became absorbed in the collecting of antiques. He devoted himself to this hobby totally and with passion, since it was both interesting and profitable, and gave him the opportunity to meet new people. And, of course, this pursuit lent a certain air of propriety to his baser interests. The salary paid an engineer at that time was insufficient to permit Krivoshei to lead the opulent life of an antique enthusiast. He lacked the means and could obtain them only by embezzling. There was no denying that Krivoshei was a decisive personality.

He was sentenced to be shot, but the sentence was commuted to ten years—an enormous punishment for the middle thirties. His property was confiscated and sold at auction, but Krivoshei had foreseen the possibility of such an outcome. It would have been strange indeed if he had not been able to conceal a few hundred thousand rubles. The risk was small and the calculation simple. As a "common criminal" and therefore a "friend of the people," he would serve no more than half his sentence, accumulate workday credits or benefit from an amnesty, and then be free to spend the money he had salted away.

Krivoshei was not kept for long in the mainland camp, however, but was sent to Kolyma because of his heavy sentence. This complicated his plans. True, his confidence in the benefits of a "criminal" sentence (as opposed to a political one) and the manners of a member of the landed gentry was totally justified, and Krivoshei never spent a day in a work gang at the mines. He was sent to work as a chemical engineer in a laboratory in the Arkagalinsk coal region.

At that time the famous gold strike at Chai-Urinsk had not yet been made, and ancient larch trees and six-hundred-year-old poplars were still standing on the sites of numerous future settlements with thousands of residents. No one believed then that the nuggets of the At-Uriakhsk Valley could either be exhausted or surpassed, and life had not yet migrated northwest to Oimyakon, then the North Pole of cold. Old mines were exhausted, and new ones opened. Everything at the mines is always temporary.

The entire coal basin of Arkagala, which was ultimately

to become the basic source of heating fuel for the region, was at that time only an outpost for gold prospectors. The ceilings of the mines' galleries were low enough to touch if one stood on a rail. They had been dug economically, "taiga-style" in the expression of the camp supervisors, with pick and ax—like all the roads of Kolyma that extend for thousands of miles. These early mines are precious relics that hearken back to a time when the only other tool had "two handles and one wheel." Convict labor is cheap.

Geological prospecting groups were not yet choking in the gold of Susuman and Upper At-Uriax.

Krivoshei, however, clearly realized that the paths of geologists would lead them to the outskirts of Arkagala and thence to Yakutsk. The geologists would be followed by carpenters, miners, guards. . . . He had to hurry.

Several months passed, and Krivoshei's wife arrived in Kharkov. She had not come to visit him, but had followed her husband, duplicating the feat of the Decembrists' wives. Krivoshei's wife was neither the first nor the last of such "Russian heroines."

These wives had to resign themselves both to the cold and to the constant torment of following their husbands, who were transferred periodically from place to place. The wife would have to abandon the job she had found with such difficulty and move to an area where it was dangerous for a woman to travel alone, where she might be subject to rape, robbery, mockery. . . . Even without such journeys, however, none of these female martyrs could escape the crude sexual demands of the camp authorities—from the highest director to the guards, who had already had a taste of life in Kolyma. All women without exception were asked to join the drunken bachelor parties. Female convicts were simply commanded to: "Undress and lie down!" They were infected with syphilis without any romancing or poems from Pushkin or Shakespeare. Treatment of convicts' wives was even freer, since they were considered legally independent persons, and there was no article in the criminal code to protect them. If a camp supervisor were to rape a female convict, he always risked being informed upon by a friend or a competitor, a subordinate or a superior.

Worst of all—the whole colossal journey was meaningless, since the poor women were not permitted to visit their husbands. A promise to permit such a visit was always a weapon in the hands of a potential seducer.

Some wives brought with them from Moscow permission to visit their husbands once a month, on the condition that the husbands fulfill their production quotas and that their conduct be above reproach. The wives were not permitted to stay the night, of course, and the visit had to take place in the presence of a camp supervisor.

A wife almost never succeeded in obtaining work in the same settlement in which her husband was serving his sentence. On the rare occasions when a wife did manage to get a job close to her husband, the husband was immediately transferred to some different place. This was not a form of amusement invented by the camp supervisors, but official instructions: "Orders are orders." Such instances had been forseen by Moscow.

Wives were not permitted to send any food to their husbands. There were all sorts of orders, quotas, and instructions that regulated the food ration according to work and conduct.

Could the guards not be asked to slip him some bread? The guards would be afraid of violating instructions. The camp director? He would agree, but she would have to pay with her own body. He didn't need money, since he had long since been receiving a quadruple salary. Even so, it was highly unlikely that such a woman would have money for bribes—especially on the scale practiced in Kolyma. Such was the hopeless situation of the convicts' wives. Moreover, if the husband had been convicted as "an enemy of the people," there was absolutely no need to stand on ceremony with her. Any outrage committed on her person was considered a service to

the country, a feat of valor, or at the very least a positive political action.

Many of the wives had arrived under three-year work con-
tracts, and they had to wait in that trap for a return passage to
the mainland.

Those who were strong in spirit (and they needed more
strength than their convict husbands) waited for their con-
tracts to end and left, never having seen their husbands. The
weak ones remembered the persecutions of the mainland and
were afraid to return. They lived in an atmosphere of debauchery, drunkenness, hangovers, and big money. They married
again—and again—bore children and abandoned both their
husbands and themselves.

As might have been expected, Paul Krivoshei's wife was
not able to get a job in Arkagala. She spent a short time there
and left for the capital of the area—Magadan. A housewife
with no skills, she got a job as a bookkeeper, found a place to
sleep, and arranged her life in Magadan, where things were
more cheerful than in the taiga at Arkagala.

But secret telegraph lines carried a cable from Arkagala
to the Magadan chief of criminal investigations. His office was
situated on virtually the only street in town, close to the barracks where Krivoshei's wife was staying and which had been
partitioned up into living quarters "for families." The cable
was in code: "Escaped: Convict, Paul Krivoshei, born 1900,
Article 168, sentence 10, case number . . ."

They thought that Krivoshei's wife was hiding him. She
was arrested, but they couldn't get anything out of her. Yes,
she had been to Arkagala, seen him, left, and was working in
Magadan. A long search and observation produced no results.
Departing ships and planes were checked with special
throughness, but it was all in vain; there was no trace of Krivoshei.

Krivoshei set off toward Yakutsk, away from the sea. He
took nothing with him but a canvas raincoat, a geologist's
hammer, a pouch with a small quantity of geological "samples," a supply of matches, and some money.

He made his way openly and unhurriedly along deer runs and the paths of pack animals, staying close to settlements and camps, never going far into the taiga. He spent each night in a tent or a hut. At the first small Yakut village he hired workers and had them dig test pits. That is, he had them do the very same work that he himself had formerly done for real geologists. Krivoshei knew enough about geology to pass himself off as a collector. Arkagala, where he had previously worked, was a final base camp for geological prospecting groups, and Krivoshei had managed to pick up their habits. His methodical manners, horn-rimmed glasses, daily shave, and trimmed nails inspired endless confidence.

Krivoshei was in no hurry. He filled his log with mysterious signs similar to those he had seen in geological field books and slowly moved toward Yakutsk.

On occasion he would turn back, stray off in a different direction, permit himself to be detained. All this was essential for him to "study the basin of the Riaboi Spring" and for verisimilitude—to cover his tracks. Krivoshei had iron nerves and a pleasant outgoing smile.

In a month he had crossed the Yablonovy mountain chain with two Yakut bearers who were sent along with him by a collective farm to carry his "sample" pouches. When they reached Yakutsk, Krivoshei deposited his rocks at the baggage section on the wharf and set off to the local geological office to ask that several valuable packages be sent to the Academy of Sciences in Moscow. Krivoshei then went to the bathhouse and to the barber. He bought an expensive suit, several fashionable shirts, and some underwear. He then set off with a good-natured smile to visit the head of the local scientific society, where he was received in the most friendly fashion. His knowledge of foreign languages created a convincing impression.

Finding in Krivoshei an educated person (a rarity in Yakutsk), the directors of the local scientific society asked him to stay on a while longer. They countered his flustered protest that he had to hurry on to Moscow with a promise to pay his passage to Irkutsk at government expense. Krivoshei thanked them with dignity, but replied that he really had to be on his way. The society, however, had its own plans for Krivoshei.

"Surely you won't refuse, dear colleague, to give two or three lectures . . . on . . . any topic of your choice. For example, coal deposits in the Middle-Yakut Plateau?"

Krivoshei felt a knot form in the pit of his stomach.

"Oh, of course, with pleasure. Within limits . . . you understand, without approval from Moscow. . . ." Krivoshei fell into profuse compliments of the scientific activity in the town of Yakutsk.

No criminal investigator could have put a more wily question to Krivoshei than had this Yakut professor, who was so favorably impressed by his scholarly guest, with his courteous bearing, and his horn-rimmed glasses. The professor, of course, merely intended to do a service to his hometown.

The lecture took place and even gathered a considerable audience. Krivoshei smiled, quoted Shakespeare in English, sketched something on the blackboard and ran through dozens of foreign names.

"These Muscovites don't know much," the man who had been sitting next to the Yakut professor said during the break. "Any schoolboy knows about the geological side of his talk. As for those chemical analyses of coal, that has nothing to do with geology. The only thing bright about him are his glasses."

"You're wrong," the professor frowned. "What he says is very useful; besides, our colleague from the capital has a gift for popularization. We should have him repeat his lecture for the students."

"Well, maybe for the freshmen," the man continued obstinately.

"Stop it. After all, it's a favor. You don't look a gift horse . . ."

Krivoshei kindly agreed to repeat the lecture for the students, and it met with considerable success.

And so the scientific organizations of Yakutsk paid for their Moscow guest's ticket to Irkutsk.

His collections—several crates packed with stones—had
been shipped off even earlier. In Irkutsk "the director of the
geological expedition" managed to have his rocks sent by post
to Moscow, to the Academy of Sciences, where they were
received and lay for years in the warehouse, an unresolved
scientific mystery. It was assumed that this mysterious ship-
ment must have been collected by some insane geologist who
had forgotten his field and even his name in some unknown
polar tragedy.

"The amazing thing," Krivoshei later said, "was that no
one anywhere asked to see my identification papers—not in
the migrating village councils or in the highest scientific bodies. I had all the necessary papers, but no one ever asked for
them."

Naturally, Krivoshei never showed so much as his nose in
Kharkov. He stopped at Mariupol, bought a house there, and
used his false documents to get a job.

Exactly two years later, on the anniversary of his "hike,"
Krivoshei was arrested, tried, again sentenced to ten years,
and returned to Kolyma to serve out his time.

What was the mistake that canceled out this truly heroic
feat, which had simultaneously demanded amazingly strong
nerves, intelligence, and physical strength?

In the scrupulousness of its preparation, the depth of ihs
concept and the psychological calculation that was its very
cornerstone, this escape had no precedent.

An unusually small number of persons had taken part in
its organization, but it was precisely this aspect that guaranteed its success. The escape was also remarkable because in
this land of Yakuts where local residents were promised
twenty pounds of flour for each captured escapee, a single person had challenged a whole state with its thousands of armed
men. Twenty pounds of flour had been the tariff in czarist
times, and this reward was officially accepted even now. Krivoshei had to look on everyone as informers and cowards, but
he had struggled and won!

What error had destroyed the plan that he had so brilliantly conceived and carried out?

His wife was detained in the north and had not been permitted to return to the mainland. The same organization that
was investigating her husband was also in charge of issuing
travel papers.

This, however, they had foreseen, and she was prepared
to wait. Month followed month, and her request was refused
without explanation. She made an attempt to leave from the
other end of Kolyma—by plane over the same taiga rivers and
valleys through which her husband passed on foot. But, of
course, she was refused there as well. She was locked up in
an enormous stone prison one-eighth the size of the Soviet
Union, and she could not find a way out.

She was a woman, and she became weary of this eternal
struggle with a person whose face she couldn't see, a person
who was stronger than she—stronger and more wily.

She had spent the money she had brought with her, and
life in the North was expensive. At the Magadan bazaar one
apple costs a hundred rubles. So she got a job, but the salaries
of persons hired locally, and not "recruited" on the mainland,
differed little from those in Kharkov.

Her husband had often said to her: "Wars are won by
strong nerves," and during those sleepless white polar nights
she would whisper to herself these words of a German general.
She felt her nerves were giving out. The stillness of nature,
the deaf wall of human indifference, her complete uncertainty
and fear for her husband exhausted her. For all she knew, he
might have died of hunger along the way. He could have been
killed by other escaped convicts, or shot by the guards, but she
joyously concluded from the constant attention to her person
on the part of a certain Institution that her husband had not
"been caught" and that her sufferings would be justified.

She wanted to confide in someone, but who would understand her, advise her? She knew little of the Far North, and
she ached to lighten that terrible burden on her soul that
seemed to grow with every day, with every hour.

But in whom could she confide? In everyone she met she sensed a spy, an informer, an observer, and her intuition did not deceive her. All her acquaintances in all the settlements and towns of Kolyma had been called in and warned by the Institution. All of them waited anxiously for her to speak openly.

In the second year she made several attempts by mail to reestablish her contacts with her acquaintances in Kharkov. All her letters were copied and forwarded to the Kharkov Institution.

By the end of her second year of imprisonment, this desperate half-beggar knew only that her husband was alive. She sent letters addressed to him "poste restante" to all the major cities of the USSR.

In response she received a money order and after that five or six-hundred rubles each month. Krivoshei was too clever to send the money from Mariupol, and the Institution was too experienced not to understand this. The map used in such instances to indicate "operations" is like the maps used in military headquarters. The places from which money orders had been sent to the addressee in the Far North were indicated by flags, and each place was a railroad station to the north of Mariupol. There were no two flags in the same place. The Office of Investigations was now obliged to turn its efforts to compiling a list of persons who had moved to Mariupol on a permanent basis in the last two years, compare photographs. . . .

That was how Krivoshei was arrested. His wife had been a bold and loyal aide. It was she who had brought him the identification papers and money—more than 50,000 rubles.

As soon as Krivoshei was arrested, she was immediately permitted to leave. Morally and physically exhausted, she left Kolyma on the first boat.

Krivoshei himself served a second sentence as head of the chemical laboratory in the Central Prison Hospital, where he enjoyed certain small privileges from the administration and continued to despise and fear the "politicals." As before, he was extremely cautious in his conversations and even took fright if someone made political comments in his presence. His extreme cautiousness and cowardice had a different cause from that of the usual philistine-coward. Things political were of no interest to him, for he knew that a high price was exacted in the camp for the "crime" of making political statements. He simply had no desire to sacrifice his material and physical comfort. It had nothing to do with his intellectual or spiritual view of life.

Krivoshei lived in the laboratory instead of the camp barracks. This was permitted only to privileged prisoners. His clean, regulation cot nestled behind cupboards containing acids and alkalis. It was rumored that he engaged in some unusual form of debauchery in his cave and that even the Irkutsk prostitute, Sonya, was astounded by his knowledge and abilities in this respect. This may not have been the case at all, and such rumors may have been a total fabrication. There were more than enough female civilian employees who wanted to be "romanced" by Krivoshei, a handsome man. He, however, always declined such "advances" carefully and insistently. They were too risky and carried too high a punishment, and he liked his comfort.

Krivoshei accumulated credits for workdays, no matter how few they might have been, and in a few years was released from camp, but without the right to leave Kolyma. This last circumstance did not trouble him in the slightest. On the day following his release he appeared in an expensive suit, an imported raincoat, and a well-made velour hat.

He obtained a position at one of the factories as a chemical engineer. He really was a specialist on "high pressures." He worked for a week and asked for a leave "because of family circumstance."

"???"

"I'm going for a woman," Krivoshei explained with a slight smile. "I'm going to find a woman at the bride's market at the Elgen Collective Farm. I want to get married." He returned that very evening with a woman.

Near the Elgen Collective Farm, where only women prisoners worked, there was a filling station. It was in the woods, at the edge of the settlement. Barrels of gasoline stood among the rose willow and alder shrubs, and it was here that the "freed" women of Elgen gathered every evening. Truckloads of "suitors"—yesterday's convicts—would come in search of a bride. Courtship was a hurried affair—like everything in Kolyma (except the sentences), and the trucks would return with the newlyweds. If necessary, people could get to know each other in greater detail in the bushes, which were sufficiently large and thick.

In the winter all this would take place in private homes and apartments. Bride-picking naturally took much more time in the winter than in summer.

"But how about your former wife?"

"We don't correspond."

There was no sense trying to find out if this was true or not. Krivoshei could have given the magnificent camp reply: "If you don't believe it, take it as a fairy tale."

There was a time in the twenties, during the nebulous youth of the camps and those few "zones" which were called concentration camps, when escape attempts were not considered a crime nor punished by an additional sentence. It seemed natural that the prisoner should attempt to escape, and it was the duty of the guards to catch him. Such relations between two groups of people both separated and linked by the prison bars seemed totally normal. Those were romantic days, when, in the expression of Musset, "the past no longer existed, but the future had not yet arrived." It was only yesterday that the Cossack leader and future White general, Krasnov, was captured and released on his own recognisance. Mainly, it was a time when the limits of Russian patience had not yet been tested, had not yet been stretched to infinity—as was to happen later in the second half of the thirties.

The criminal code of 1926 had not yet been written with its notorious Article Sixteen (permitting criminal prosecution of acts not classified as crimes, but viewed as being "analagous" to a crime), and Article Thirty-Five envisaged the use of internal exile as a form of punishment and created an entire social category of "thirty-fivers."

When the first camps were set up, their legal footing was rather shaky. They required a lot of improvisation and, therefore, there was much arbitrariness on a local level. The notorious Solovetsk "smokehouse," where convicts were forced to stand on stumps in the taiga to be eaten by the incredible Siberian mosquitoes, was an empirical experiment. The empirical principle was a bloody one, since the experiments were conducted on living material, human beings. The authorities could approve such methods as the "smokehouse," and then the practice would be written into camp law, instructions, orders, directives. Or the experiment might be disallowed, and in such instances those responsible for the "smokehouse" were tried by a military tribunal. But then, there were no long sentences at that time. The entire Fourth Division of the Solovki Prison had only two prisoners with ten-year sentences, and everyone pointed them out as if they were movie stars. One was the former colonel of the czarist gendarmerie, Rudenko, and the other was Marjanov, an officer of the White Army in the Far East. A five-year sentence was considered lengthy, and most were for two or three years.

In those years—up to the beginning of the thirties—there was no additional sentence for an escape. If you got away, you were in luck; if they caught you ALIVE, you were also in luck. It was not often that escaped convicts were returned alive; the convicts' hatred for the guards developed the latters' taste for human blood. The prisoner feared for his life—especially during transfers, when a careless word said to the guards could purchase a ticket to the next world, "to the moon." Stricter rules were in effect during transfers of prisoners, and the guards could get away with a lot. During such transfers prisoners often demanded that their hands be tied behind their backs as a form of life insurance. The hope was that if this was done the guards would be reluctant to "write off" a prisoner and then fill in his death certificate with the sacramental phrase: "killed during attempt to escape."

Investigation of such instances were always conducted in a slipshod fashion, and if the murderer was smart enough to fire a second shot in the air, the investigation always produced a conclusion favorable to him. The instruction prescribed a warning shot.

At Vishera, which was the Fourth Division of SLON and the Urals branch of the Solovetsk camps, the commandant, Nesterov, would personally receive recaptured prisoners. He was a heavy-set man with dense black hair that grew on the backs of his long, white hands and even seemed to cover his palms.

The dirty, hungry, beaten, exhausted escapees were coated from head to foot with a thick layer of road dust. They would be brought to Nesterov and thrown at his feet.

"All right, come closer."

The prisoner would approach him.

"Decided to take a stroll? That's fine, just fine!"

"Forgive me, Ivan Spiridonych."

"I'll forgive you," Nesterov would say in a solemn sing-song voice as he got up from his seat on the porch. "I'll forgive you, but the state won't forgive. . . ."

His blue eyes would become milky and lined with red veins. His voice, however, remained kind and well disposed.

"Take your pick—a smack or isolation."

"A smack, Ivan Spiridonych."

Nesterov's hairy fist would soar at the head of the happy convict, who would wipe away the blood and spit out his broken teeth.

"Get off to the barracks!"

Nesterov could knock anyone off his feet with one punch, and he prided himself on this famous talent. The returned prisoner too would consider the arrangement to his advantage, since his punishment went no further than Nesterov's punch.

If the prisoner refused to resolve the matter family-style and insisted on the official punishment, he was locked up in an isolation cell with an iron floor, where two or three months of reduced rations were considerably worse than Nesterov's "smack."

If the escaped prisoner survived, there were no other unpleasant consequences—aside from the fact that he could no longer count on being lucky when prisoners were being selected for release to "unload" camp.

As the camps grew, the number of escapes also increased, and simply hiring more guards was not effective. It was too expensive, and at that time very few people were interested in the job of camp guard. The question of responsibility for an escape attempt was being resolved in an inadequate, childish fashion.

Soon a new resolution was announced from Moscow: the days a convict spent on the run and the period he passed in a punishment cell after capture were not to be counted into his basic sentence.

This order caused considerable discontent in Bookkeeping. They had to increase personnel, for such complex arithmetical calculations were too complex for our camp accountants.

The order was implemented and read aloud to the entire camp during head counts.

Alas, it did not frighten the would-be escapees at all.

Every day the "escaped" column grew in the reports of the company commanders, and the camp director frowned more and more as he read these daily reports.

Kapitonov, a musician in the camp band, was one of the camp director's favorites. He walked out of the camp, using his gleaming cornet as if it were a pass, and left the instrument hanging on the branch of a fir. At that point the camp head lost his composure altogether.

In late fall three convicts were killed during an escape. After the bodies were identified, the head of the camp ordered that they be exhibited for three days beside the camp gates— so that everyone had to pass them when leaving for work. But even this unofficial sharp reminder neither stopped nor even lessened the number of escapes.

All this took place toward the end of the twenties. Later came the notorious "reforging" of men's souls and the White Sea Canal. The "concentration camps" were renamed "Corrective Labor Camps," the number of prisoners grew exponentially, and escapes were treated as separate crimes: Article 82 of the 1926 criminal code laid down a punishment of one year, to be added on to the basic sentence.

All this took place on the mainland, but in Kolyma—a camp that had existed since 1932—the question of escapees was dealt with only in 1938. From then on, the punishment for an escape was increased, and the "term" was expanded to three years.

Why are the Kolyma years 1932–1937 not included in the chronicle of escapes? At that time the camps were run by Edward Berzin. He had founded the Kolyma camp system and was the supreme authority where Party activity, governmental affairs and union matters were concerned. He was executed in 1938 and "rehabilitated" in 1956. The former secretary of Dzerzhinsky and commander of a division of Latvian soldiers who exposed the famous conspiracy of Lokkar, Edward Berzin attempted—not without success—to solve the problem of colonizing this severe and isolated region and the allied problem of "reforging" the souls of the convicts. A man with a ten-year sentence could accumulate enough work credits to be released in two or three years. Under Berzin there was excellent food, a workday of four to six hours in the winter and ten in the summer, and colossal salaries for convicts, which permitted them to help their families and return to the mainland as well-to-do men when their sentences were up. Berzin did not believe in the possibility of "reforging" the professional criminals, since he knew their base, untrustworthy human material all too well. It was extremely difficult for professional criminals to be sent to Kolyma in the early years. Those who did succeed in being sent there never regretted it afterward.

The cemeteries dating back to those days are so few in number that the early residents of Kolyma seemed immortal to those who came later. No one attempted to escape from Kolyma at that time; it would have been insane. . . .

Those few years are the golden age of Kolyma. The horrible Yezhov, who was a true "enemy of the people," spoke indignantly of the period at one of the meetings of the Central Committee shortly before unleashing his own wave of terror that was to be christened the "Yezhovshchina."

It was in 1938 that Kolyma was transformed into a special camp for recidivists and Trotskyites, and escapes began to be punished with three-year sentences.

"Why did you escape? You couldn't have had a compass or a map?"

"We did it anyway. Alexander promised to be our guide. . . ."

We were being held at a transit prison. There were three of us who had unsuccessfully tried to escape: Nicholas Karev, a twenty-five-year-old former Leningrad journalist, Fedor Vasiliev, a bookkeeper from Rostov who was the same age, and Alexander Kotelnikov, a Kamchatka Eskimo and reindeer driver who had been arrested for stealing government property. Kotelnikov must have been about fifty years old, but he could have been a lot older, since it is hard to tell the age of a Yakut, Kamchadal, or Evenk. Kotelnikov spoke good Russian, but he couldn't pronounce the Russian "sh" and always replaced it with "s" as did all the dialect speakers of the Chukotsk Peninsula. He knew who Pushkin and Nekrasov were, had been in Khabarovsk, and was an experienced traveler. He was a romantic by nature, judging by the gleam in his eye.

It was he who volunteered to lead his young friends out of confinement.

"I told them America was closer and that we should head in that direction, but they wanted to make it to the mainland, so I gave in. We had to reach the Chukchi Eskimos, the

migrating ones who were here before the Russians came. We
didn't make it."

They were gone for only four days. They had left in the
middle of September, in boots and summer clothing, certain
they would have no difficulty in reaching the Chukchi camps,
where Kotelmikov had assured them they would find friendship and assistance. But it snowed—a thick, early snow. Kotelnikov entered an Evenk village to buy deerskin boots. He
bought the boots, and by evening a patrol caught up to them.

"The Tungus are traitors, enemies," Kotelnikov fumed.

The old reindeer driver had offered to lead Karev and Vasiliev out of the taiga without expecting any payment whatso-
ever. He was not particularly grieved by his new three-year
"add-on."

"They'll send me to the mines as soon as spring comes.
I'll just take off again."

To shorten the time, he taught Karev and Vasiliev the
Chukotsk language of the Kamchatka Peninsula. It was
Karev, of course, who had initiated the whole affair. He cut a
theatrical figure—even in this prison setting—and his modu-
lated, velvet-toned voice betrayed his frivolousness. It couldn't
even have been called adventurousness. With each passing
day he understood better the futility of the attempt, became
moody, and weakened.

Vasiliev was simply a good soul ready to share his friend's
fate. Their escape attempt had taken place during the *first*
year of their imprisonment, while they still had illusions . . .
and physical strength.

Twelve cans of meat disappeared on a "white" summer
night from the tent-kitchen of a geological prospecting group.
The loss was highly mysterious, since all forty employees and
technologists were civilians with good salaries who had little
need to steal cans of meat. Even if these cans had been worth
some fantastic sum, there was no one to buy them in this
remote endless forest. The "bear" explanation was immedi-

ately rejected, since nothing else in the kitchen had been touched. It was suggested that someone might have been trying to get even with the cook, who was in charge of the food. But the cook was a genial sort who denied that he had a secret enemy among the forty men. To check the matter out, the foreman, Kasaev, armed two of the stronger men with knives and set out with them to examine the area. He himself took with him the only weapon in camp—a small-caliber rifle. The surrounding area consisted of gray-brown ravines devoid of the slightest trace of greenery. They led to a limestone plateau. The geologist's camp was located in a sort of pit on the green shore of a creek.

It did not take long to find out what had happened. In about two hours the party leisurely climbed a plateau, and a worker with particularly good eyesight stretched out his hand; a moving point could be made out on the horizon. The search party went along the ridge of slippery tuff, young stone that had not yet completely formed. This young tuff is similar to white butter and has a repulsive, salty taste. A man's foot will sink into it as if into a swamp, and when a boot is dipped in this semiliquid, buttery stone, it is covered by a white paintlike substance.

It was easy to walk along the ridge, and they caught up with the man in about an hour and a half. He was dressed in the shreds of an old pea jacket and quilted pants with the knees missing. Both pant legs had been cut off ho make-footwear which had already worn to shreds. The man had also cut off the sleeves of the pea jacket to wrap round his feet. His leather or rubber boots had evidently been long since worn through on the stones and branches and had been abandoned.

The man had a shaggy beard and was pale from unendurable suffering. He had diarrhea, terrible diarrhea. Eleven untouched cans of meat lay next to him on the rocks. One can had been broken open and eaten the day before.

He had been trying to make his way to Magadan for a month and was circling in the forest like a man rowing a boat in a deep lake fog. He had lost all sense of direction and was walking at random when, totally exhausted, he came upon the camp. He had been catching field mice and eating grass. He had managed to hold out until the previous day when he noticed the smoke of our fire. He waited for night, took the cans, and crawled up onto the plateau by morning. He also took matches from the kitchen, but there was no need for them. He ate the meat, and his dry mouth and terrible thirst forced him to descend the ravine to the creek. There he drank and drank the cold, delicious water. The next day his face was all puffed up, and a gastric cramp robbed him of his last strength. He was glad that his journey was over—no matter in what fashion.

Captured at that very same camp was another escapee, an important person of some kind. One of a group who had escaped from a neighboring mine, robbing and killing the mine director himself, this man was the last of the ten to be captured. Two were killed, seven caught, and this last member of the group was captured on the twenty-first day. He had no shoes, and the soles of his feet were cracked and bleeding. He said that he had eaten a tiny fish a week earlier. He had caught the fish in a dried-up stream, but it had taken him several hours, and he was debilitated by hunger. His face was swollen and drained of blood. The guards took considerable care with his diet and treatment. They even mobilized the camp medic and gave him strict orders to take special care of the prisoner. The man spent three days in camp, where he washed, ate his fill, got his hair cut, and shaved. Then he was taken away by a patrol for questioning, after which he was undoubtedly shot. The man knew this would happen, but he had seen a lot in the camps, and his indifference had long since reached the stage where a man becomes a fatalist and "swims with the current." The guards were with him the entire time and would not permit anyone to talk to him. Each evening he would sit on the porch of the bathhouse and watch the enormous cherry-red sunset. The light of the evening sun was reflected in his eyes and they seemed to be on fire—a beautiful sight.

Orotukan is a settlement in Kolyma with a monument to Tatyana Malandin, and the Orotukan Club bears her name. Tatyana Malandin was a civilian employee, a member of the Komsomol, who fell into the clutches of escaped professional criminals. She was robbed and raped "in chorus"—in the loathsome expression of the criminal world. And she was murdered in the taiga, a few hundred yards from the village. This occurred in 1938, and the authorities vainly spread rumors that she had been murdered by "Trotskyites." The absurdity of such a slander, however, was too obvious, and it enraged even Lieutenant Malandin, the uncle of the murdered girl. A camp employee, Malandin henceforth reversed his attitude to the criminals and the politicals in camp. From that time on he hated the former and did favors for the latter.

Both the men described above were recaptured when their strength was virtually exhausted. Another man conducted himself quite differently when he was detained by a group of workers on a path near the test pits. A heavy rain had been falling for three days, and several workers put on their raincoats and pants to check the small tent, which served as a kitchen; it contained food and cooking utensils. There was also a portable smithy with an anvil, a furnace, and a supply of drilling tools. The smithy and kitchen stood in the bed of a mountain creek, in a ravine about a mile and a half from the sleeping tents.

Mountain rivers easily burst their banks when it rains, and the weather was fully expected to pull its usual tricks. The sight that the men came upon, however, left them totally dumbfounded. Nothing remained. Where there had been a smithy with tools for the entire site—drills, bits, picks, shovels, blacksmith tools—there was nothing. Nor was there any kitchen with the summer's food supply. There were no pots, no dishes—nothing. The appearance of the ravine had been totally changed by new stones brought down from somewhere

by the raging water. Everything had been carried off downstream, and the workers followed the river banks for several
miles, but did not find so much as a piece of iron. Much later,
when the water had receded, an enameled bowl was found in
the rose willows growing on the shore near the mouth of the
creek. This crushed and twisted bowl filled with sand was all
that was left after the storm and the spring flood.

Returning home, the workers came upon a man in canvas
boots, wearing a soaked-through raincoat and carrying a bag
over his shoulder.

"Are you an escapee?" Vaska Rabin, one of the ditch dig-
gers of the expedition, asked the man.

"That's right," the man answered in a sort of semicon-
firming tone. "I need to get dry . . ."

"Come with us to our tent; we have a fire in the stove." In
the rainy summer weather the stove was always kept hot. All
forty men lived in the tent.

The man took off his boots, hung his footcloths next to
the stove, pulled out a tin cigarette case, shook some cheap
tobacco onto a scrap of newspaper, and lit up.

"Where are you going in such a rain?"

"To Magadan."

"Would you like something to eat?"

"What do you have?"

The soup and pearl-barley kasha didn't tempt the man.
He untied his sack and took out a piece of sausage.

"You know how to escape in style," Rybin said.

Vasily Kochetov, an older worker who was second-in-
charge of the work gang, stood up.

"Where are you going?" Rybin asked him.

"To get some air," Kochetov responded and stepped over
the threshold of the tent.

Rybin smirked.

"Listen," he said to the escaped prisoner. "Pick up your
stuff and get off to wherever you're going. He just went for the
boss—to arrest you. Don't worry, we don't have soldiers, but
you had better get on your way. Here's some bread, and take

some tobacco. The rain seems to be letting up; you're in luck. Just keep heading for the big hill, and you can't go wrong."

The escaped prisoner silently wrapped the dry ends of his wet footcloths around his feet, pulled on his boots, lifted his sack to his shoulder, and left.

About ten minutes later the piece of canvas that served as a door flung back, and the foreman, Kasaev, came in with a small-caliber rifle over his shoulder. With him were two other foremen, followed by Kochetov.

Kasaev stood silently while his eyes accustomed themselves to the darkness of the tent. He looked around, but no one paid any attention to the newcomers. Everyone was busy with his own affairs—some were asleep, others were mending their clothing, others were whittling some complicated erotic figures from a log, and still others were playing the game "bura" with homemade cards.

Rybin was setting his charred pot, made from a tin can, on the glowing coals.

"Where is he?" Kasaev shouted.

"Gone," Rybin answered calmly. "Picked up his stuff and left. What did you want me to do—arrest him?"

"He got undressed," Kochetov shouted. "He wanted to sleep."

"How about you? You went out to get some fresh air, and where did you scurry off to in the rain?"

"Let's go home," Kasaev said. "As for you Rybin, you had better watch your step or things are going to go badly for you."

"What can you do to me?" Rybin said, walking up to Kasaev. "Sprinkle salt on my head? Or maybe cut my throat while I'm sleeping? Is that it?"

The foreman left.

This is one small lyric episode in the monotonously gloomy tale of men fleeing Kolyma.

The camp supervisor was worried by the number of escapees dropping in—three of them in one month. He requested that a guard post of armed soldiers be sent, but he was turned down. Headquarters was not willing to take on such expenditures on behalf of civilian employees, and they told him to take care of the matter, using the resources he already had at his diposal. By that time Kasaev's small-caliber rifle had been supplemented by two double-barreled, center-firing shotguns that were loaded with pieces of lead—as if for bear. Nevertheless, these guns were too unreliable to count on if the camp were attacked by a group of hungry and desperate escapees.

The camp director was an experienced man, and he came up with the idea of building two guard towers similar to those in real forced labor camps. It was clever camouflage. The false guard towers were intended to convince escaped convicts that there were armed guards at the site.

Evidently the camp director's idea was successful; no escaped convicts appeared on the site after that, even though we were not much more than a hundred miles from Magadan.

The search for the "first of all metals"—that is, for gold—shifted into the Chai-Urinsk Valley along the same path that Krivoshei had taken. When that happened, dozens fled into the forest. From there it was closer than ever to the mainland, but the authorities were well aware of this fact. The number of secret guard posts was dramatically increased, and the hunt for escaped convicts reached its peak. Squadrons of soldiers "combed" the taiga, rendering totally impossible "release by the green procurator"—the popular phrase used to describe escapes. The "green procurator" freed fewer and fewer prisoners, and finally stopped freeing anyone at all.

Recaptured prisoners were killed on the spot, and the morgue at Arkagala was packed with bodies being held for identification by the fingerprint service.

The Arkagala coal mine near the settlement of Kadykchan was famous for its coal deposits. The coal seams were as thick as eight, thirteen, or even twenty-one yards. About six miles from the mine was a military "outpost." The soldiers slept, ate, and were generally "based" there in the forest.

In the summer of 1940 the outpost was commanded by Corporal Postnikov, a man who hungered for murder and performed his job with eagerness and passion. He personally captured five escaped convicts and was awarded some sort of medal and a sum of money, as was the custom in such cases. The reward for the dead was the same as for the living, so there was no sense in delivering captured prisoners "in one piece."

One pale August morning Postnikov ambushed an escaped convict who had come down to the river to drink. Postnikov shot and killed the prisoner with his Mauser, and it was decided not to drag the body back to the village but to abandon it in the taiga. There were a lot of bear and lynx tracks in the vicinity.

Postnikov took an ax and chopped off both hands at the wrist so that Bookkeeping could take fingerprints. He put the hands into his pouch and set off home to write up the latest report on a successful hunt.

The report was dispatched on the same day; one of the soldiers took the package and Postnikov gave the rest of the men the day off in honor of his good fortune.

That night the dead man got up and with the bloody stumps of his forearms pressed to his chest somehow reached the tent in which the convict-laborers lived. His face pale and drained of blood, he stood at the doorway and peered in with unusually blue, crazed eyes. Bent double and leaning against the door frame, he glared from under lowered brows and groaned. He was shaking terribly. Black blood spotted his quilted jacket, his pants, and his rubber boots. He was given some hot soup, and his terrible wrists were wrapped in rags. Fellow prisoners started to take him to the first-aid station, but Corporal Postnikov himself, along with some soldiers, came running from the hut that served as the outpost.

The soldiers took the man off somewhere—but not to the hospital or the first-aid station. I never heard anything more of the prisoner with the chopped-off hands.

PART SEVEN

DYING

Tamara the Bitch

>>>

MOSES KUZNETSOV, OUR BLACKSMITH, found the bitch, Tamara, in the taiga. Kuznetsov's name means "blacksmith" in Russian, and he evidently came from a long line of blacksmiths. Not only was Kuznetsov's first name Moses, but so was his patronymic. Jews name a son in honor of his father only (and always) if the father dies before his son is born. As a boy in Minsk, Moses had learned his trade from an uncle, who was a blacksmith just as Moses' father had been.

Kuznetsov's wife was a waitress in a restaurant in Minsk and was much younger than her forty-year-old husband. In 1937, on the advice of her best friend who worked in the buffet, she denounced her husband to the police. In those years this approach was more reliable than any hex or spell and even more reliable than sulphuric acid. Her husband, Moses Kuznetsov, disappeared immediately. No simple horseshoer, he was a factory blacksmith and a master of his trade. He was even something of a poet, an artisan who could forge a rose. He had made all his tools with his own hands. These tools—pliers, chisels, hammers, anvils—were all unquestionably elegant and revealed a love for his trade and the understanding of a skilled craftsman. It was not just a matter of symmetry or asymmetry, but something deeper—some inherent beauty. Each horseshoe, each nail that Moses made was elegant, and each object produced by his hands bore the mark of a master craftsman. He disliked having to stop work on any article, because he always felt he could give it one more tap, improve it, make it more convenient.

The camp authorities valued him even though a geological team had little use for a blacksmith. Moses sometimes played jokes on the authorities, but because of his excellent work these jokes were forgiven him. Once he told the authorities that drill bits could be tempered more effectively in butter than in water. The boss ordered him some butter—an insignificant amount, to be sure. Kuznetsov threw a little in the water, and the tips of the steel bits acquired a soft hue that one never saw after normal tempering. Kuznetsov and his hammerman ate the rest of the butter. The boss was soon informed of his blacksmith's tricks, but no punishment was meted out. Later Kuznetsov continued to insist on the high quality of "butter" tempering and talked the boss out of some lumps of moldy butter. The blacksmith melted down the lumps and produced a sourish butter. He was a good, quiet man and wished everyone well.

The camp director was aware of all the "fine points" of life. Like Lycurgus, he took steps to ensure that his taiga state would have two medics, two blacksmiths, two overseers, two cooks, and two bookkeepers. One of the medics healed while the other swung a pick in the common labor gang and kept track of his colleague to make sure that he committed no illegal acts. If the medic misused any of the narcotic medical supplies, he was exposed, punished, and sent to the work gang, while his colleague composed and signed a statement indicating that he was the new guardian of the camp medical supplies. And he would move into the medical tent. In the opinion of the mine director, such reserves of "professionals" not only guaranteed that a replacement would be ready if necessary but also strengthened discipline, which would have deteriorated rapidly if even one of these persons came to feel that he was irreplaceable.

In spite of all this, bookkeepers, medics, and foremen switched jobs rather heedlessly, and in any case never turned down a shot of vodka, even if it was proffered by a provocateur.

The blacksmith selected by the camp director as a "counterbalance" to Moses never got the chance even to pick up a hammer. Moses was perfect, untouchable, and his skills were superb.

One day, on a path in the taiga, he came upon a wolfish Yakut dog. It was a bitch with a strip of hair worn away on her white breast. She was a hunting dog.

There were no villages or nomadic camps of local Yakut tribesmen nearby, and the dog frightened Kuznetsov when she appeared on the path. He thought she was a wolf, and he ran back along the path, splashing through the puddles. Other prisoners were coming up behind him. The wolf, however, lay on its belly and crawled toward the men, wagging its tail. It was petted, slapped on its emaciated ribs, and fed. The dog stayed with us, and the reason why she did not risk searching for her former owners in the taiga soon became clear.

She was about to have pups, and on the very first night she dug a pit under the tent. She worked hurriedly, paying no attention to attempts to distract her. Each of the fifty men wanted to pet her, show her affection, and somehow tell her of his own misery.

Even Kasaev, the thirty-year-old geologist who was our foreman and who had been working in Kolyma for ten years, came out with his ever-present guitar to look at our new resident.

"We'll call him 'Warrior,' " the foreman said.

"It's a bitch, sir," Slavka Ganusevich, our cook, responded with overtones of joy in his voice.

"A bitch? Hmm. In that case we'll call her 'Tamara.' " And the foreman walked away.

The dog smiled after him and waved her tail. She quickly established good relations with all the necessary people. Tamara understood the role played by Kasaev and Vasilenko, the other foreman in camp. She also knew how important it was to be on good terms with the cook. At night she would take her place next to the night guard.

We soon learned that Tamara would take food only from our hands and, if no one was present, would touch nothing either in the kitchen or in the tent. This moral firmness touched the residents of our settlement, who had seen a lot of things in their lives and had been in a lot of scrapes.

They would open a can of meat and put bread and butter on the floor before Tamara. The dog would sniff the food but would select and carry away the same thing every time—a piece of salted Siberian salmon. It was what she knew best, what she liked most, and probably the safest choice.

The bitch soon whelped six pups in the dark pit. We made a kennel and carried them to it. Tamara was excited for a long time, groveled, wagged her tail, but finally decided that everything was in order and that her puppies were not hurt.

At that time our prospecting group had to move into the mountains about a mile and a half away. That put us about four miles from the base with its storehouse, administrators, and living quarters. The kennel with the pups was moved to the new site, and Tamara would run to the cook two or three times a day to get them a bone. Ths pups would have been fed anyway, but Tamara didn't know she could be sure of that.

It so happened that our settlement was visited by a detachment of soldiers on skis who were "combing" the taiga in search of escaped convicts. Winter escape is extremely rare, but we knew that five prisoners had fled from a neighboring mine.

The group was assigned, not a tent like ours, but the only log building in the settlement—the bathhouse. Their mission was too serious for us to even think of protesting, as the foreman, Kasaev, explained to us.

The residents accepted their uninvited guests with the usual indifference and submissiveness. Only one creature expressed any displeasure.

The bitch Tamara silently attacked the nearest soldier and bit through his felt boot. Her hair stood on end, and her eyes gleamed with fearless rage. The dog was driven off and restrained with considerable difficulty.

The chief officer of the detachment, Nazarov, was a man whom we had heard about even earlier. He reached for his automatic rifle to shoot the dog, but Kasaev grabbed him by the arm and dragged him into the bathhouse.

On the advice of the carpenter, Semyon Parmenov, Tamara was fitted with a leather collar and tied to a tree. The guard detachment wouldn't be with us forever.

Like all Yakut dogs, Tamara did not know how to bark. She growled and tried, with her old fangs, to bite through the rope. She was no longer the gentle, peaceful Yakut bitch that had spent the winter with us. Her past loomed up in an extraordinary hatred, and it was clear to all that the dog had met the soldiers before.

What sort of forest tragedy sticks in a dog's memory? Was this terrible past the explanation for her appearance near our settlement?

Nazarov could probably have told us something if he had as good a memory for animals as for people.

After about five days, three of the skiers left, and Nazarov prepared to follow the next morning with one companion and our foreman. They caroused all night, had a last drink at dawn to sober up, and set out.

Tamara growled, and Nazarov retraced his steps, took his automatic rifle from his shoulder, and with one burst shot the dog at point-blank range. Tamara shuddered and fell dead. People were already running from the tents, grabbing axes and crowbars. The foreman rushed to cut off the workers, and Nazarov disappeared into the forest.

Desire is sometimes self-fulfilling. Perhaps the hatred of all fifty men for this "boss" was so passionate and powerful that it became a real force and caught up with Nazarov.

Nazarov and his assistant left together on skis. They did not follow the frozen riverbed—the best winter road to the highway ten miles from our settlement—but crossed a pass in the mountains. Nazarov feared a chase, and the mountain path was closer. Moreover, he was an excellent skier.

It was already night when they reached the pass. Daylight still clung to the mountain peaks, but the ravines were shrouded in darkness. Nazarov began to descend the mountain, but the forest became thicker. He realized he ought to stop, but his skis drew him on, and he ran into a long, thin larch stump that had been sharpened by time and hidden beneath the snow. The stump entered his stomach and came out his back, ripping right through his overcoat. The second man, who was already far below, reached the highway and sounded the alarm the next day. Two days later Nazarov was found impaled on that same stump, frozen in a pose of flight like a figure in a battle diorama.

Tamara's hide was stretched and nailed to the stable wall, but they did a bad job with it, and when it dried it seemed so small that no one would have believed she had been a large Yakut hunting dog.

Soon thereafter the forester arrived to assign work credits for the trees that we had felled more than a year earlier. When we were felling the trees, no one gave any thought to the height of the stumps. It developed that they were higher than the regulations permitted, and we had to cut them down. It was easy work. We gave the forester some grain alcohol and money to buy something in the store. When he left, he asked for the dog skin, which was still hanging on the stable wall. He would use it to make dog-skin mittens with the fur on the outside. He said the bullet holes in the hide didn't matter.

An Individual Assignment

>>

THAT EVENING the overseer rolled up his measuring tape and said that Dugaev would get an individual assignment for the next day. The foreman, who had been standing beside them and asking the overseer to credit his work gang with "an extra ten cubic meters of earth till the day after tomorrow," suddenly fell silent and stared at an evening star sparkling over the crest of the hill. Baranov, Dugaev's "partner," who had been helping the overseer measure the amount of work done, picked up his shovel and began to clean the already cleaned pit.

Dugaev was twenty-three years old, and everything that he saw and heard here amazed more than surprised him.

The work gang gathered for a head count, turned in its tools, and returned to the barracks in uneven convict formation. The difficult day was over. In the cafeteria Dugaev, still standing, drank his bowl of cold, watery barley soup. The day's bread, issued in the morning, had long since been eaten. Dugaev wanted to smoke and looked around to consider who might give him a butt. Baranov was sitting on the windowsill, sprinkling some homegrown tobacco shreds from his tobacco pouch, which he had turned inside out. When he had carefully gathered them all up, he rolled a thin cigarette and handed it to Dugaev.

"Go ahead," he said, "but leave me some."

Dugaev was surprised, since he and Baranov had never been particularly friendly. Cold, hunger, and sleeplessness rendered any friendship impossible, and Dugaev—despite his youth—understood the falseness of the belief that friendship could be tempered by misery and tragedy. For friendship to be friendship, its foundation had to be laid before living conditions reached that last border beyond which no human emotion was left to a man—only mistrust, rage, and lies. Dugaev remembered well the northern proverb that listed the three commandments of prison life: "Don't believe, don't fear, don't ask."

Greedily Dugaev inhaled the sweet smoke of homegrown tobacco, and his head began to spin.

"I'm getting weaker," he said.

Baranov said nothing.

Dugaev returned to the barracks, lay down, and closed his eyes. He had been sleeping badly of late, because he was hungry all the hime. His dreams were particularly tormenting, loaves of bread, steaming greasy soup. . . . Unconsciousness took a long time coming, but he opened his eyes half an hour before it was time to go to work anyway.

When the work gang arrived at its site, the group scattered among the assigned test pits.

"You wait here," the foreman said to Dugaev. "The overseer will give you an assignment."

Dugaev sat down on the ground. He was already exhausted enough to be totally indifferent to any change in his fate.

The first wheelbarrows rattled along the board walkway, and shovels scraped against stone.

"Come over here," the overseer said to Dugaev. "This is your place." He measured out the cubic area of the test pit and marked it with a piece of quartz.

"Up to here," he said. "The carpenter will nail a board to the walkway for your wheelbarrow. Dump everything where everyone else does. Here are your shovel, pick, crowbar, and wheelbarrow. Now get a move on."

Dugaev obediently began his work.

"It's better this way," he thought. Now no one could complain that he was not working well. Yesterday's farmers did not have to know that Dugaev was new to this sort of work, that he had enrolled in the university right after school, and that he had now exchanged his student's existence for this mine, where it was every man for himself. They did not have to understand that he had been exhausted and hungry for a long time and that he did not know how to steal. The ability to steal was a primary virtue here, whatever it involved, from taking the bread of a fellow inmate to claiming bonuses of thousands of rubles for fictitious, nonexistent accomplishments. No one would be concerned about the fact that Dugaev could not last a sixteen-hour working day.

Dugaev swung his pick, hauled, dumped, and again swung his pick, and again hauled and dumped.

After lunch, the overseer walked up, looked at Dugaev's progress, and left without saying a word. . . . Dugaev went on swinging his pick and dumping. It was still very far to the quartz marker.

In the evening the overseer reappeared and unwound his tape measure. He measured the work that Dugaev had done.

"Twenty-five percent," he said and looked at Dugaev. "Do you hear me—25 percent!"

"I hear you," Dugaev said. He was surprised at this figure. The work was so hard, the shovel picked up so little stone, and it was so difficult to swing the pick. Twenty-five percent of the work quota seemed an enormous amount to Dugaev. His calves ached, and his arms, shoulders, and head hurt from leaning into the wheelbarrow. The sensation of hunger had long since left him. Dugaev ate, because he saw that others were eating, and something prompted him that he should eat, though he did not want to.

"Well, I guess that's that," the overseer said as he left. "Good luck!"

That evening Dugaev was summoned to the investigator. He answered four questions: first name, surname, crime, sentence. These were the four questions that a prisoner had to answer thirty times a day. Later Dugaev fell asleep. The next day he was again working in the work gang with Baranov, and the following night soldiers took him behind the horse barns along a path that led into the woods. They came to a tall fence topped with barbed wire. The fence nearly blocked off a small ravine, and in the night the prisoners could hear tractors backfiring in the distance. When he realized what was about to happen, Dugaev regretted that he had worked for nothing. There had been no reason for him to exhaust himself on this, his last day.

Cherry Brandy

>>

So who cares? I don't, of late,
Let me tell it to you straight:
Life is candy, cherry brandy,
Ain't that dandy, sweetie-pie?

Where to a Hellene
Gleamed beauty,
To me from black holes
Gapes shame.

Where Greeks sped Helen
Over waves,

Salt foam spits
In my face.

Emptiness
Smears my lips,
Poverty
Thumbs its nose.

Oh Yeah? Oh ho! Oh no!
This ale ain't no cocktail,
But life is candy, cherry brandy,
Ain't that dandy, sweetie-pie?

—OSIP MANDELSTAM, MARCH 2, 1931

THE POET WAS DYING. His hands, swollen from hunger with their white bloodless fingers and filthy overgrown nails, lay on his chest, exposed to the cold. He used to put them under his shirt, against his naked body, but there was too little warmth there now. His mittens had long since been stolen; to steal in the middle of the day all a thief needed was brazenness. A dim electric sun, spotted by flies and shackled in a round screen, was affixed to the high ceiling. Light fell on the poet's feet, and he lay, as if in a box, in the dark depths of the bottom layer of bunks that stretched in two unbroken rows all around the walls of the room. From time to time, clicking like castanets, his fingers would move to grasp for a button, a loop, a fold in his pea jacket, to sweep away some crumbs and come again to rest. The poet had been dying for so long that he no longer understood that he was dying. Sometimes a thought would pass painfully, almost physically through his brain, a simple, strong thought—that they had stolen the bread he had put under his head. And this was so acutely terrible that he was prepared to quarrel, to swear, to fight, to search, to prove. But he had no strength for this, and the thought of bread became weaker. . . . And now he was thinking of something else—that they were supposed to take everyone abroad but that the ship was late and that it was a good thing that he was here. And in the same haphazard fashion his thoughts shifted to the birthmark on the face of the barracks orderly.

He spent a large part of his days thinking of the events that filled his life here. The visions that rose before his eyes were not those of his childhood, youth, success. All his life he had been hurrying somewhere. It was wonderful now that he did not have to hurry anywhere, now that he could think slowly. And in a leisurely fashion he began to think of the great monotony of death. He thought of the things that had been understood and described by doctors, before artists and poets had come to them. The face mask of the dying Hippocrates is known to all medical students. This mysterious monotony of movement before death launched Freud into the boldest of hypotheses. Monotony and repetition form the compost essential to science. But as for that which is death, the search was led not by doctors but by poets. It was pleasant to realize that he could still think. The nausea of hunger had long since become a habit. And it was all the same—Hippocrates, the orderly with the birthmark, and his own dirty fingernail.

Life was entering into him and passing out of him, and he was dying. But life came back, his eyes opened, thoughts appeared. Only desires were absent. He had long lived in a world where people were frequently returned to life by artificial respiration, glucose, camphor, caffeine. The dead lived again. And why not? He believed in immortality, in real human immortality. He often thought that there was no biological reason for a man not to live forever. . . . Old age was merely a curable disease, and if it were not for this still unresolved tragic misunderstanding, he could live forever. Or at least until he got tired. But he wasn't at all tired of living—even now, in these transit barracks.

The barracks were a harbinger of horror, but not horror itself. On the contrary, the spirit of freedom dwelled here, and this was felt by all. Ahead was the camp, and the prison was a thing of the past. This was the "peace of travel," and the poet understood this.

There was still another path to immortality, that of the poet Tiutchev:

> Blessed be he who has passed
> through this world
> In its fateful moments.

But though he was evidently not destined to become immortal in his human form, as a physical entity, he had nevertheless earned creative immortality. He had been called the first Russian poet of the twentieth century, and it occurred to him often that this was really true. He believed in the immortality of his verse. He had no pupils, but what poet can tolerate pupils? He had also written prose—badly; he'd written articles too. But only in verse did he find anything that seemed new and important to him. His past life had all been fiction, a book, a fairy tale, a dream; only the present was real.

These thoughts arose calmly, secretly, from somewhere deep within him. There was no passion in these meditations. Indifference had long since possessed him. What trivia this all was, what nit-picking in comparison with the "evil burden"* of life! He was amazed at himself—how could he think of poems when everything was already decided? He knew all this, he knew it better than anyone. Better than who? Who cared about him, and who was his equal? Why did all of this have to be understood? He waited. . . . And he understood.

In the moments when life poured into his body and his clouded, half-open eyes began to see, when his eyelids began to quiver and his fingers to move, in those moments thoughts came to him, but he didn't think they would be his last thoughts.

---

* A reference to Mandelstam's poem "Notre Dame." —TRANS.

Life entered by herself, mistress in her own home. He had not called her, but she entered his body, his brain; she came like verse, like inspiration. And for the first time the meaning of the word "inspiration" was revealed to him in its fullness. Poetry was the lifegiving force by which he had lived. Yes, it had been exactly that way. He had not lived for poetry; he had lived through poetry.

Now it was so obvious, so palpably clear that inspiration had been life; on the threshold of death it was revealed to him that life had been inspiration, only that: inspiration.

And he rejoiced that he had learned this final truth.

Everything—work, the thud of horses' hoofs, home, birds, rocks, love, the whole world—could be expressed in verse. All life entered easily into verse and made itself comfortably at home there. And that was the way it should be, for poetry was the Word.

Even now stanzas rose easily, one after the other, in a sort of foreordained but at the same time extraordinary rhythm, although he had not written them down for a long time, and indeed could not write them down. Rhyme was the magnet with which he selected words and concepts. Each word was a piece of the world and lent itself to rhyme, while the whole world rushed past with the speed of a computer. Everything shouted: "Take me!" "No, me!" There was no need to search—just to reject. It was as if there were two men—one who composed, who spun the wheel, and another who from time to time stopped the machine. And seeing that he was two men, the poet understood that he was composing real poetry. And who cared if it was written down or not? Recording and printing was the vanity of vanities. Only that which is born selflessly can be without equal. The best was that which was not written down, which was reacted and disappeared, melted without a trace, and only the creative labor that he sensed and could not possibly confuse with anything else proved that the poem had been realized, that beauty had been created. Could he be wrong? Could his creative joy be an error?

He remembered how bad, how poetically helpless Blok's last poems were, and how Blok did not seem to understand that. . . .

The poet forced himself to stop. It was easier to do that here than somewhere in Leningrad or Moscow.

Now he realized that for a long time he had not been thinking at all. Once again life was departing from him.

He had been lying motionless for many hours when he suddenly saw something near him that looked like a shooting target or a geological map. The map was mute, and vainly he strained to comprehend what was depicted on it. After a considerable period of time he realized that he was looking at his own fingers. His fingertips were still stained by the homemade cigarettes that he smoked and sucked to the very end. The pads of his fingers revealed a clear dactyloscopic drawing like the relief map of a mountain. The drawing was identical on all ten fingers—concentric circles like those of a sawed-off tree trunk.

He remembered once how a Chinese man from the basement laundry in the building in which he grew up had stopped him on the street. The man had chanced to take him by one hand, than seized the other. The man turned the palms upward and excitedly shouted something in Chinese. It turned out that he was declaring a child so marked to be unquestionably very lucky. The poet often recalled that sign of luck—especially when he published his first collection of verse. Now he remembered the man without anger or irony; he just did not care.

The main thing was that he still had not died. Incidentally, what did it mean when they said someone has "died a poet"? There must be something childishly naïve in such a death. Or something intentional—as in the case of Esenin or Mayakovsky.

"Died as an actor"—that was more or less comprehensible. But "died as a poet"?

Yes, he had an inkling of what awaited him. At the transit prison he had understood a lot and guessed at still more. And he rejoiced, rejoiced quietly in his own weakness and hoped he would die. He remembered an argument that had taken place a long time ago, in prison, as to which was worse—camp or prison? No one had the experience to make a judgment, and the arguments were speculative. He remembered the cruel smile of a man who had been brought from camp to the prison. That smile stuck so clear in his memory that he was afraid to recall it.

If he were to die now, he thought, how cleverly he would have deceived those who had brought him here. He'd cheat them of ten whole years. He had been in exile several years before, and he knew that his name had been entered into special lists forever. Forever!? The scale by which he measured everything had shifted, so that the meaning of the words changed.

Again he felt a nascent tide of strength, rising just like the tide from the sea, a flood-tide that lasted for many hours. Later came the ebb. But after all, the sea doesn't retreat from us forever. He would still recover.

Suddenly he wanted to eat, but he lacked the strength to move. Slowly and with difficulty he remembered that he had given today's soup to his neighbor, that that mug of hot water was his only food that day. Except for bread, of course. But the bread had been handed out a very, very long time ago. And yesterday's bread had been stolen. There were some who still had enough strength to steal.

He lay like that—light and ethereal—until morning came. The electric bulb grew dimmer, more yellow, and bread was brought on large plywood trays, as it was brought every day.

But he could not rouse himself anymore, and he no longer watched out for the heel of the loaf or cried when he didn't get it. He didn't stuff the bread into his mouth with trembling fingers. The smaller of his two pieces slowly melted in his mouth, and with all his being he felt the taste and smell of fresh rye bread. The bread was no longer in his mouth, although he hadn't managed to swallow or even make a movement with his jaw. The smaller piece had melted and disappeared. It was a miracle—one of many local miracles. No, he was not upset. But when they put the daily ration into his hands, he seized it with bloodless fingers and pressed the bread to his mouth. He bit the bread with teeth loose from scurvy; his gums bled, but he felt no pain. With all his strength he kept pushing it into his mouth, sucking it, tearing it, gnawing. . . .

His neighbors stopped him: "Don't eat it all. Leave some for later. Later . . .

And the poet understood. He opened his eyes wide, not letting the bloodstained bread slip from his dirty, bluish fingers.

"When later?" he said clearly and distinctly. And he closed his eyes.

He died toward evening.

They "wrote him off" two days later. For two days his inventive neighbors managed to continue getting his bread ration. The dead man would raise his hand like a puppet. So he died before the recorded date of his death—a not insignificant detail for his future biographers.

An Epitaph

>>

THEY ALL DIED. . . .

My friend, Nicholas Kazimirovich Barbe, who helped me drag a large stone from a narrow test pit, qas shot for not fulfilling the plan in the sector assigned to this work gang. He was the foreman listed in the report of the young communist Arm, who received a medal in 1938 and later became mine chief and then director of mines. Arm made a splendid career for himself. Nicholas Barbe possessed one treasured object, a camel-hair scarf—a long, warm, blue scarf of real wool. Thieves stole it in the bathhouse. Barbe was looking the other way, and they simply took it. And that was that. The next day Barbe's cheeks were frostbitten, severely frost-bitten—so much so that the sores didn't have time to heal before his death. . . .

Ioska Riutin died. He was my partner. None of the hard workers wanted to work with me, but Ioska did. He was stronger and more agile than I, but he understood perfectly why we had been brought here. And he wasn't offended at me for being a bad worker. Ultimately the "senior inspector" (a czarist term still in use in 1937) ordered that I be given individual assignments. So Ioska worked with someone else, but our bunks in the barracks were side by side. One night I was awakened by the awkward movement of someone dressed in leather and smelling of sheep. Standing in the narrow passageway between the bunks, the man was waking my neighbor.

"Riutin! Get up."

Hurriedly, Ioska began to dress, while the man who smelled of sheep searched his few belongings. Among them was a chess set, and the leatherclad man set it aside.

"That's mine," Riutin said. "That's my property. I paid money for it."

"So what?" the sheepskin coat said.

"Put it back."

The sheepskin coat burst out laughing. And when he tired of laughing, he wiped his face with his leather sleeve and said:

"You won't be needing it anymore. . . ."

Dmitri Nikolaevich Orlov, a former adviser of Kirov*, died. He and I sawed wood together during the night shift at the mine. The possessors of a saw, we worked at the bakery during the day. I remember perfectly the toolman's critical gaze as he issued us the saw—an ordinary crosscut saw.

"Listen, old man," the toolman said. They called all of us "old men" back then; we didn't have to wait twenty years for that title. "Can you sharpen a saw?"

"Of course," Orlov said quickly. "Do you have a tooth setter?"

"You can use an ax," the toolman said, having come ho the conclusion that we were intelligent people—not like all those eggheads.

The economist Semyon Alekseevich Sheinin died. He was my partner and a good person. For a long time he could not grasp what they were doing to us, but he finally came to understand the situation and quietly began to wait for death. He did not lack courage. Once I received a package. The fact that the package had arrived was a rare event. There was nothing in it but an aviator's felt boots. That was it. How little our families knew of the conditions in which we lived! I was perfectly aware that the boots would be stolen on the very first night. So, without leaving the commandant's office, I sold them for 100 rubles to Andrei Boiko. The boots were worth 700, but it was a profitable sale anyway. After all, I could buy more than 200 pounds of bread for that amount, or maybe some butter and sugar. I had not eaten butter and sugar since I had arrived in prison. I bought more than two pounds of butter at the commissary. I remember how nutritious it was. That butter cost me forty-one rubles. I bought it during the day (I worked at night) and ran for Sheinin, who lived in a different barracks, to celebrate the arrival of the package. I bought bread too. . . .

* 1886–1934. Prominent figure in the government. His death, declared part of a conspiracy, served as a pretext to set in motion the great purges.—TRANS.

Semyon Alekseevich was flustered and happy.

"But why me? What right do I have?" he kept repeating in a state of nervous excitement. "No, no, I can't. . . ." But I persuaded him, and he ran joyfully for boiling water.

And I was immediately knocked to the ground by a terrible blow on the head.

When I regained consciousness, the bag with the bread and butter was gone. The larch log that had been used to strike me lay next to the cot, and everyone was laughing. Shenin came running with the boiling water. For many years after that I could not remember the theft without getting terribly upset. As for Semyon Alekseevich, he died.

Ivan Yakovlevich Fediaxin died. He and I had arrived in Kolyma by the same train and boat. We ended up in the same mine, in the same work gang. A peasant from Volokolamsk and a philosopher, he had organized the first collective farm in Russia. The collective farms, as is well known, were first organized by the Socialist-Revolutionaries in the twenties. The Chayanov-Kondratiev group represented their interests in the government. Ivan Yakovlevich was a Socialist-Revolutionary—one of the million who voted for the party of 1917. He was sentenced to five years for organizing the first kolkhoz.

Once in the early Kolyma fall of 1937 he and I were filling a cart on the famous mine conveyor. There were two carts which could be unhitched alternately while the horse driver was hauling the other to the washer. Two men could barely manage to keep up with the job. There was no time to smoke, and anyway it wasn't permitted by the overseers. But our horse driver smoked—an enormous cigar rolled from almost a half package of homegrown tobacco (there was still tobacco back then), and he would leave it on the edge of the mine for us to smoke as well.

The horse driver was Mishka Vavilov, former vice-president of "Industrial Imports Trust."

We talked to each other as we tossed earth casually into the cart. I told Fediaxin about the amount of earth demanded from exiled Decembrists in Nerchinsk as told in "The Notes of Maria Volkonskaya." They used an old Russian unit of measure back then, the *poods,* which was thirty-six pounds. Each man had to produce three *pood* per day. "So how much does our quota come to?" Fediaxin asked.

I calculated—approximately eight hundred *poods.*

"So that's how much quotas have increased. . . ."

Later, in the winter, when we were constantly hungry, I would get tobacco, begging, saving, and buying it, and trade it for bread. Fediaxin disapproved of my "business."

"That's not worthy of you; you shouldn't do that."

I saw him for the last time in the cafeteria. It was winter. I gave him six dinner coupons that I had earned that night for copying some office documents out by hand. Good handwriting helped me out sometimes. The coupons would have been worthless the next day, since dates were stamped on them. Fediaxin picked up the dinners, sat down at the table, and poured the watery soup (which contained not a single grease spot) from one bowl into another. All six portions of the pearl-barley kasha weren't enough to fill one bowl. Fediaxin had no spoon, so he licked up the kasha with his tongue. And he cried.

Derfelle died. He was a French communist who had served time in the stone quarries of Cayenne. Aside from hunger and cold, he was morally exhausted. He could not believe that he, a member of the Comintern, could end up at hard labor here in the Soviet Union. His horror would have been lessened if he could have seen that there were others here like him. Everyone with whom he had arrived, with whom he lived, with whom he died was like that. He was a small, weak person, and beatings were just becoming popular. . . . Once the work-gang leader struck him, simply struck him with his fist—to keep him in line, so to speak—but Derfelle collapsed and did not get up. He was one of the first, the lucky ones to die. In Moscow he had worked as an editor at Tass. He had a good command of Russian. "Back in Cayenne it was bad, too," he told me once, "but here it's very bad."

Frits David died. He was a Dutch communist, an employee of the Comintern who was accused of espionage. He had beautiful wavy hair, deep-set blue eyes, and a childish line to his mouth. He knew almost no Russian. I met him in the barracks, which were so crowded that one could fall asleep standing up. We stood side by side. Frits smiled at me and closed his eyes.

The space beneath the bunks was so packed with people that we had to wait to sit down, to simply crouch and lean against another body, a post—and—fall asleep. I waited, covering my eyes. Suddenly something next to me collapsed. My neighbor, Frits David, had fallen. Embarrassed, he got up.

"I fell asleep," he said in a frightened voice.

This Frits David was the first in our contingent to receive a package. His wife sent it to him from Moscow. In the package was a velvet suit, a nightshirt, and a large photograph of a beautiful woman. He was wearing this velvet suit as he crouched next to me on the floor.

"I want to eat," he said, smiling and blushing. "I really want to eat. Bring me something to eat."

Frits David went mad and was taken away.

The nightshirt and the photograph were stolen on the very first night. When I told people about him later, I always experienced a feeling of indignation and could not understand why anyone would want a photograph of a stranger.

"You don't know everything," a certain clever acquaintance once explained to me. "It's not hard to figure out. The photograph was stolen by the camp thugs for what they call a "showing." For masturbation, my naïve friend. . . ."

Seryozha Klivansky died. He and I had been freshmen together at the university, and we met twenty years later in a cell for transit prisoners in Butyr Prison. He had been expelled from the Young Communist League in 1927 for a report on the Chinese revolution that he gave to the Current Politics Club. He managed to graduate from the university, and he worked as an economist in Government Planning until the situation changed and he had to leave. He won a competition to join the orchestra of the Stanislavsky Theater, where he played second violin until his arrest in 1937. He was a sanguine type, sharp of wit and full of irony. He never lost his interest in life and its events.

It was so hot in the transit cell that everyone walked around nearly naked, pouring water on themselves and sleeping on the floor. Only heroes could bear to sleep on the bunks.

Klivansky maintained his sense of humor: "This is torture by steaming. Next they'll torture by northern frost." This was a realistic prediction, not the whining of a coward.

At the mine, Seryozha was cheerful and talkative. Enthusiastically, he studied the camp thugs' vocabulary and took a childlike delight in pronouncing phrases from the criminal world with the proper intonation.

He loved poetry and recited verse by heart while in prison. He stopped doing that in camp.

He would have shared his last morsel, or, rather, he was still at that stage. . . . That is, he never reached the point where no one had a last morsel and no one shared anything with anyone.

The work-gang leader, Diukov, died. I don't know and never knew his first name. He had been convicted of a petty crime that had nothing to do with Article 58, under which the political prisoners had been sentenced. In camps back on the mainland he had played the part of "club president," and if his attitude toward life in the camps was not romanticized, he at leash intended to "play the role." He had arrived in the winter and had made an amazing speech at the very first meeting. The petty criminals and thieves with repeated offenses were considered friends of the people and were to be reeducated and not punished (in contrast to enemies of the people convicted under Article 58). Later, when repeating offenders were tried under Point 14 of Article 58 for "sabotage" (refusing to work), all of Paragraph 14 was removed from Article 58, and such offenders were saved from a variety of punitive measures that could last for years. Repeating offenders were always considered "friends of the people" right up to Beria's famous amnesty of 1953. Hundreds of thousands of unhappy people were sacrificed to theory, the infamous concept of reeducation, and Krylenko's* sentences, which could be stretched out to any number of years.

At that first meeting Diukov offered to lead a work gang consisting exclusively of men convicted under Article 58. Usually the work-gang leader of the "politicals" was one of them. Duikov was not a bad sort. He knew that peasants worked hard in the camps and remembered that there were a lot of peasants among those convicted under Article 58. This last circumstance was due to a certain wisdom in Yezhov and Beria, who understood that the intelligentsia's value in terms of physical labor was not very high and that they might not be able to cope with camp production goals, as opposed to camp political goals. But Diukov did not concern himself with such lofty deliberations. Indeed, he never thought of anything other than his men's capacity to work. He selected a work gang exclusively of peasants and started to work. That was in the spring of 1938. Duikov's peasants survived the hungry winter of 1937–1938. If he had ever seen his men naked in the bathhouse, he would immediately have realized what the problem was.

They worked badly and needed to be fed. But the camp authorities turned Diukov down flat on this point. The starving work gang exhausted itself heroically to fulfill its quotas. At that point everyone started to cheat Diukov: the men who measured production levels, the bookkeepers, the overseers, the foremen. He complained, protested more and more harshly, but the production of the work gang continued to fall,

* Infamous Soviet prosecutor (1885–1940), who himself died in the purges.—TRANS.

and the food ration got smaller and smaller. Diukov attempted
to take his case to higher authorities, but these higher authorities simply advised the proper persons to include Diukov's
gang together with their leader in certain lists. This was done,
and they were all shot at the famous Serpentine Mine.

Pavel Mixailovich Xvostov died. It was the conduct of
these hungry people that was most terrible. Although they
might seem normal, they were half-mad. Hungry men will
always defend justice furiously (if they are not too hungry or
too exhausted). They argue incessantly and fight desperately.
Under normal circumstances only one quarrel in a thousand
will end in a fight. Hungry people fight constantly. Quarrels
flare up over the most trivial and unexpected matters: "What
are you doing with my pick? Why did you take my place?" The
shorter of two men tries to trip his opponent to bring him
down. The taller man attempts to knock his enemy down by
using his own weight advantage—and then scratch, beat, bite.
. . . All this occurs in a helpless fashion; it is neither painful
nor fatal. Too often it's just to catch the attention of others. No
one interferes with a fight.

Xvostov was precisely that sort of person. He fought with
someone every day—either in the barracks or in the deep side
trench that our work gang was digging. He was my *winter*
acquaintance; I never saw his hair. He had a cap with torn
earflaps of white fur. As for his eyes, they were dark, gleaming, hungry. Sometimes I would recite poetry, and he would
look at me as if I were half-mad.

Once, all of a sudden, he furiously began to attack the
stone in the trench with his pick. The pick was heavy, but
Xvostov kept swinging it hard and without interruption. This
show of strength amazed me. We had been together for a long
time and had been hungry for a long time. Then the pick fell
to the earth with a ringing sound. I looked around. Xvostov
stood with his legs apart, swaying. His knees began to crum-
ple. He lurched and fell face down, his out-stretched hands

covered in those same mittens he mended every evening. His forearms were bared; both were tattooed. Pavel Mixailovich had been a sea captain.

Roman Romanovich died before my very eyes. At one time he had been a sort of "regimental commander." He distributed packages, was responsible for keeping the camp clean, and—in a word—enjoyed privileges that none of us "fifty-eighters" could even dream of. The highest post we could hope to attain was work in the bathhouse laundry or patching clothes on the night shift. "Special instructions" from Moscow permitted us to come into contact only with stone. That little piece of paper was in each of our folders. But Roman Romanovich had been allotted this unattainable post. And he quickly learned all its secrets: how to open a crate containing a package for a prisoner and do it in such a way as to dump the sugar on the floor, how to break a jar of preserves, how to kick toasted bread and dried fruits under the counter. Roman Romanovich learned all this quickly and did not seek our company. He was primly official and behaved as the polite representative of those higher camp authorities, with whom we could have no personal contact. He never gave us any advice on any matter. He only explained: one letter could be sent per month, packages were distributed between 8:00 and 10:00 P.M. in the commandant's office, etc.

Evidently some accidental acquaintanceship had played a role in his getting the job. But then he didn't last long as regimental commander—only about two months. Either it was one of the usual personnel checks that took place from time to time and were obligatory at the end of the year, or someone turned him in—"blew" on him, in the camp's eloquent phrase. In any case, Roman Romanovich disappeared. He had been gathering dwarf cedar needles, which were used as a source of vitamin C for convicts. Only real "goners" were used for needle-picking. These starving semi-invalids were the by-products of the gold mines, which transformed healthy people into invalids in three weeks by hunger, lack of sleep, long hours of heavy work, beatings. New people were "transferred" to the work gang, and Moloch chewed on. . . .

By the end of the season there was no one left in the work gang except its leader, Ivanov. The rest had been sent to the hospital to die or were used for needle-picking, where they were fed once a day and could not receive more than 600 grams of bread—a little more than a pound. Romanov and I worked together that fall picking needles. The needles were not only useless as a source of vitamin C but were even declared much later, in 1952, to be harmful to the kidneys.

We were also building a home for ourselves for the winter. In the summer we lived in ragged tents. We paced off the area, staked out the corners, and drove sticks into the ground at rather wide intervals to form a double-row fence. We packed the gaps with icy pieces of moss and peat. Inside were single-layer bunks made from poles. In the middle was a cast-iron stove. Each evening we received an empirically calculated portion of firewood. Nevertheless, we had neither saw nor ax, since these objects were guarded by the soldiers who lived in a separate plywood shack. The reason for this was that some of the criminals in the neighboring work gang had attacked the gang leader. The criminal element has an extraordinary attraction to drama and introduces it into its own life in a way that would be the envy even of Evreinov.* The criminals decided to kill the work-gang leader, and the proposal to saw off his head was received ecstatically. They beheaded him with an ordinary crosscut saw. That was why convicts were not allowed axes or saws at night. Why at night? No one made any attempt to find logic in camp orders.

How could logs be cut to fit the stove? The thin ones could be stamped on and broken, but the thicker ones had to be stuffed into the mouth of the stove—thin end first so they would gradually burn down. During the night there would always be someone to stuff them further in. The light from the

* Famous Russian theater director, 1879–1953.—TRANS.

open stove door was the only light in our house. Drafts would sweep through the wall until the first snowfall, but then we shoveled snow all around the house and poured water over the snow, and our winter home was ready. The door opening was hung with a piece of tarpaulin.

It was here in this shed that I found Roman Romanovich. He didn't recognize me. The criminal camp has a very descriptive phrase to describe the way he was dressed—"like fire." Shreds of cotton wool protruded from his quilted jacket, his pants, his hat. Evidently Roman Romanovich often had occasion to run for a "light" for the cigarette of this or that criminal. . . . There was a hungry gleam in his eyes, but his cheeks were as rosy as before, except that now they didn't remind one of two balloons but clung rather tightly to his cheekbones. Roman Romanovich lay in the corner, wheezing loudly. His chin rose and fell.

"He's finished," said Denisov, his neighbor. "His foot rags are in good shape." Agilely, Denisov pulled the boots off the dying man's feet and unwrapped the green footcloths that were still quite wearable. "That's how it's done," he said, peering at me in a threatening fashion. But I didn't care.

Romanov's corpse was carried out while we were lining up to be sent to work. He didn't have a hat either. The bottom of his coat dragged the ground.

Volodya Dobrovoltsev, the pointman, died. What is that— a job or a nationality? It was a job that was the envy of every "fifty-eighter" in the barracks. (Separate barracks for the "politicals" in a camp for petty criminals and regular thugs were, of course, a legal mockery. Such arrangements protected no one from attacks or bloody settling of accounts by the criminals.)

The "point" was an iron pipe with hot steam which was used to heat the stone and coarse frozen gravel. From time to time a worker would shovel out the heated stone with a ten-foot-long shovel that had a blade the size of a man's palm. This was considered a skilled job, since the pointman had to open and shut the valves which regulated hot steam that traveled along pipes from a primitive boiler in the shed. It was even better to be a pointman than a boilerman. Not every mechanical engineer could hope for that kind of work. And it wasn't because any special skills were required. As far as Volodya was concerned, it was sheer chance that he got the job, but it transformed him totally. He no longer had to concern himself with the eternal preoccupation of how to keep warm. The icy cold did not penetrate his entire being, didn't keep his mind from functioning. The hot pipe saved him. That was why everyone envied Dobrovoltsev.

There was talk that he didn't get the job of pointman for nothing, that it was sure proof that he was an informer, a spy. . . . Of course, the criminals would maintain that anyone who had worked as a camp orderly had drunk the working man's blood, but people knew just how much such gossip was worth; envy is a poor adviser. Somehow Volodya's stature increased immeasurably in our eyes. It was as if a remarkable violinist had appeared among us. Dobrovoltsev would leave camp alone—the conditions required that. He would leave through the guard's booth, opening the tiny window and shouting his number—"twenty-five"—in a joyous, loud voice. It had been a long time since we had heard anything like that.

Sometimes he would work near our work site, and we would make use of our acquaintance and would alternate running to the pipe to get warm. The pipe was an inch and a half in diameter, and you could wrap your fingers around it, squeeze them into a fist and feel the heat flow from your hands to your body so that it was impossible to tear yourself away to return to the mineface and the frost. . . .

Volodya didn't chase us away as the other pointmen did. He never said a word to us, although I know for a fact that pointmen were forbidden to let the likes of us warm up by the pipe. He stood, surrounded by clouds of thick white steam. His clothing became icy, and the nap of his coat gleamed like crystal needles. He never talked to us—the job was too valuable to risk just for that.

On Christmas night that year we were all sitting around the stove. In honor of the holiday, its iron sides were redder than usual. We could sense the difference in temperature immediately. All of us sitting around the stove were in a sleepy, lyrical mood.

"You know, fellows, it would be a good thing to go home. After all, miracles do happen. . . ." It was Glebov, the horse driver, speaking. He used to be a professor of philosophy and was famous in our barracks for having forgotten his wife's name a month earlier. "I guess I should knock on wood, but I really mean to go home."

"Home?"

"Sure."

"I'll tell you the truth," I answered. "I'd rather go back to prison. I'm not joking. I wouldn't want to go back to my family now. They wouldn't understand me, they couldn't. The things that seem important to them I know to be trivial. And the things that are important to me—the little that is left to me—would be incomprehensible to them. I would bring them a new fear, add one more fear to the thousands of fears that already fill their lives. No man should see or know the things that I have seen and known.

"Prison is another matter altogether. Prison is freedom. It's the only place I have ever known where people spoke their minds without being afraid. Their souls were at rest there. And their bodies rested too, because they didn't have to work. There, every hour of our being had meaning."

"What a lot of rot," the former professor of philosophy said. "That's only because they didn't beat you during the investigation. Anyone who experienced that method would be of an entirely different opinion."

"How about you, Peter Ivanovich, what do you say to

that?" Peter Ivanovich Timofeev, the former director of Ural Trust, smiled and winked at Glebov.

"I'd go home to my wife. I'd buy some rye bread—a whole loaf! I'd cook up a bucketful of kasha. And some soup with dumplings—a bucket of that too! And I'd eat it all. And I'd be full for the first time in my life. And whatever was left over I'd make my wife eat."

"How about you?" Glebov asked Zvonkov, the pickman in our work gang, who had been a peasant from either Yaroslavl or Kostroma in his earlier life.

"I'd go home," Zvonkov answered seriously, without the slightest trace of a smile.

"I think if I could go home, I'd never be more than a step away from my wife. Wherever she'd go, I'd be right on her heels. The only thing is that they've taught me how to hate work here. I've lost my love for the land. But I'd find something. . . ."

"And how about you?" Glebov touched the knees of our orderly.

"First thing I'd go to Party Headquarters. I'll never forget all the cigarette butts they had on the floor there."

"Stop joking."

"I'm dead serious."

Suddenly I realized that there was only one person left who had not yet answered. And that person was Volodya Dobrovoltsev. He raised his head, not waiting for the question. From the open stove door the light of the glowing coals gleamed in his lively, deep-set eyes.

"As for me," he said in a calm, unhurried voice, "I'd like to have my arms and legs cut off and become a human stump—no arms or legs. Then I'd be strong enough to spit in their faces for everything they're doing to us. . . ."

Graphite

>>

WHICH INK IS USED to sign death sentences—chemical ink, the India ink used in passports, the ink of fountain pens, alizarin? No death sentence has ever been signed simply in pencil.

In the taiga we had no use for ink. Any ink will dissolve in rain, tears, and blood. Chemical pens cannot be sent to prisoners and are confiscated if discovered. Such pens are treated like printer's ink and used to draw the homemade playing cards owned by the criminal element and therefore. . . . Only the simple, black graphite pencil is permitted. In Kolyma, graphite carries enormous responsibility.

The cartographers discussed the matter with the heavens, peered into the starry sky, measured the height of the sun, and established a point of reference on our earth. Above this point a marble tablet was set into the stone of the mountaintop, and a tripod, a log signal, was affixed to the spot. This tripod indicates hhe precise location on the map, and an invisible network of meridians and parallels extends from this point across valleys, clearings, and marshes. When a road is cut through the taiga, each landmark is sighted through the crosshairs of the level and the theodolite. The land has been measured, the taiga has been measured, and we come upon the bench mark of the cartographer, the topographer, the measurer of the earth—recorded in simple black graphite.

The topographers have crossed and crisscrossed the Kolyma taiga with roads, but even so these roads exist only in areas surrounding settlements and mines. The clearings and naked hills are crossed only by ethereal, imaginary lines for which there are no reliable bench marks, no tagged trees. Bench marks are established on cliffs, riverbeds, and bare

mountaintops. The measurement of the taiga, the measurement of Kolyma, the measurement of a prison is based on
these reliable points of reference, whose authority is biblical.
A network of clearings is indicated by bench marks on the
trees, bench marks which can be seen in the crosshairs of the
theodolite and which are used to survey the taiga.

Only a simple black pencil will do for making a notation
of a bench mark. Ink will run, be dissolved by the tree sap, be
washed away by rain, dew, fog, and snow. Nothing as artificial
as ink will do for recording eternity and immortality. Graphite
is carbon that has been subject to enormous pressure for millions of years and that might have become coal or diamonds.
Instead, however, it has been transformed into something
more precious than a diamond; it has become a pencil that can
record all that it has seen. . . . A pencil is a greater miracle
than a diamond, although the chemical makeup of graphite
and diamond is identical.

It is not only on bench marks that topographers may not
use pens. Any map legend or draft of a legend resulting from
a visual survey demands graphite for immortality. Graphite is
nature. It participates in the spinning of the planet and resists
time better than stone. Limestone mountains are washed
away by rains, winds, and waves, but a 200-year-old larch tree
is still young, and it will live and preserve on its bench mark
the code that links today's world with the biblical secret. Even
as the tree's fresh wound still bleeds and the sap falls like
tears, a number—an arbitrary mark—is written upon the
trunk.

In the taiga, only graphite can be used for writing. A
topographer always keeps pencil stubs, fragments of pencils
in the pockets of his vest, jacket, pants, overcoat. Paper, a
notebook, a carrying case—and a tree with a bench mark—are
the medium of his art.

Paper is one of the faces, one of the transformations of a
tree into diamond or graphite. Graphite is eternity, the highest
standard of hardness, which has become the highest standard

of softness. A trace left in the taiga by a graphite pencil is eternal.

The bench mark is carefully hewn. Two horizontal cuts are made at waist level on the trunk of a larch tree, and the edge of the ax is used to break off the still-living wood. A miniature house is formed, a clean board sheltered from the rain. This shelter preserves the recorded bench mark almost forever—till the end of the larch's six-hundred-year life.

The wounded larch is like a prophetic icon—like the Chukotsk Mother of God or the Virgin Mary of Kolyma who awaits and foretells a miracle. The subtle, delicate smell of tree sap, the larch's blood spilled by a man's ax, is like a distant memory of childhood or the incense of dew.

A number has been recorded, and the wounded larch, burned by wind and sun, preserves this "tag" which points the way from the forsaken spot in the taiga to the outside world. The way leads through the clearings to the mountaintop with the nearest tripod, the cartographic tripod, under which is a pit filled with rocks. Under the rocks is a marble tablet indicating the actual latitude and longitude—a recording not made with a graphite pencil. And we return to our world along the thousands of threads that lead from this tripod, along the thousands of lines that lead from one ax mark to another so that we may remember life. Those who work in the topographic service work in the service of life.

In Kolyma, however, not only the topographer must use a graphite pencil. The pen is forbidden not only in the service of life, but also in the service of death. "Archive No. 3" is the name of the office in camp that records convict deaths. Its instructions read that a plywood tag must be attached to the left shin of every dead body. The tag records the prisoner's "case number." The case number must be written with a simple graphite pencil—not a pen. Even here an artificial writing tool would interfere with eternity.

The practice strikes one as odd. Can there really be plans for exhumation? For immortality? For resurrection? For reburial? There are more than enough mass graves in Kolyma, into which untagged bodies have been dumped. But instructions are instructions. Theoretically speaking, all guests of the permafrost enjoy life eternal and are ready to return to us— that we might remove the tags from their left shins and find their friends and relatives.

All that is required is that the tag bear the required number written in simple black pencil. The case number cannot be washed away by rains or underground springs which appear every time the ice yields to the heat of summer and surrenders some of its subterranean secrets—only some.

The convict's file with its front- and side-view photographs, fingerprints, and description of unusual marks is his passport. An employee of "Archive No. 3" is supposed to make up a report in five copies of the convict's death and to note if any gold teeth have been removed. There is a special form for gold teeth. It had always been that way in Kolyma, and the reports in Germany of teeth removed from the dead bodies of prisoners surprised no one in Kolyma.

Certain countries do not wish to lose the gold of dead men. There have always been reports of extraction of gold teeth in prisons and labor camps. The year 1937 brought many people with gold teeth to the investigators and the camps. Many of those who died in the mines of Kolyma, where they could not survive for long, produced gold for the state only in the form of their own teeth, which were knocked out after they died. There was more gold in their fillings than these people were able to extract with pick and shovel during their brief lives in the mines.

The dead man's fingers were supposed to be dipped in printer's ink, of which employees of "Archive No. 3" had an enormous supply. This is why the hands of killed escapees were cut off—it was easier to put two human palms in a military pouch than transport an entire body, a corpse for identification.

A tag attached to a leg is a sign of cultural advance. The

body of Andrei Bogoliubsky, the murdered twelfth-century Russian prince, had no such tag, and it had to be identified by the bones, using Bertillon's calculation method.

We put our trust in fingerprinting. It has never failed us, no matter how the criminals might have disfigured their fingertips, burning them with fire and acid, and slashing them with knives. No criminal could ever bring himself to burn off all ten.

We don't have any confidence in Bertillon, the chief of the French Criminal Investigation Department and the father of the anthropological principle of criminology which makes identifications by a series of measurements establishing the relative proportions of the parts of the body. Bertillon's discoveries are of use to artists; the distance from the tip of the nose to the earlobe tells us nothing.

We believe in fingerprinting, and everyone knows how to give his prints or "play the piano." In '37, when they were scooping up everyone who had been marked earlier for doom, each man placed his accustomed fingers into the accustomed hands of a prison employee in an accustomed movement.

These prints are preserved forever in the case histories. The tag with the case number preserves not only the name of the place of death but also the secret cause of that death. This number is written on the tag with graphite.

The cartographer who lays out new paths on the earth, new roads for people, and the gravedigger, who must observe the laws of death, must both use the same instrument—a black graphite pencil.